▶▶▶ ACCEL·WORLD 20

THE RIVALRY OF WHITE AND BLACK

REKI KAWAHARA

ILLUSTRATION BY
HIMA

DESIGN BY
bee-pee

"Come
at me,
Lotus!!"

NIKO

Red King, Prominence Legion Master.
Duel avatar: Scarlet Rain.

"Here we go, Rain!!"

KUROYUKIHIME

Legion Master of the new Nega Nebulus.
Vice president of the Umesato Junior High
student council.
Duel avatar: Black Lotus.

GLACIER BEHEMOTH

True identity unknown.

"I-is that ... an Enemy ...?"

"Th-this requires caution ...!"

"It can't be... I mean, this is the Territories battles."

YUME YURUKI
Former member of Legion Petit Paquet. Currently belongs to Nega Nebulus. Duel avatar: Plum Flipper.

SHIHOKO NAGO
Former master of Legion Petit Paquet. Currently belongs to Nega Nebulus. Duel avatar: Chocolat Puppeter.

SATOMI MITO
Former member of Legion Petit Paquet. Currently belongs to Nega Nebulus. Duel avatar: Mint Mitten.

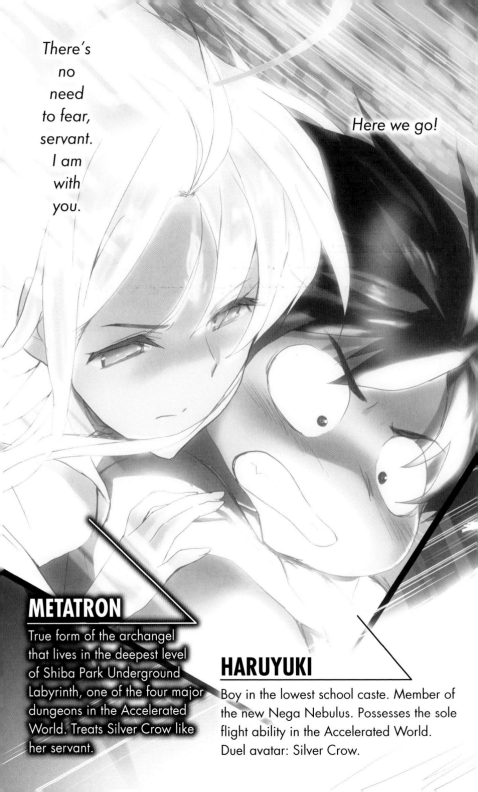

There's no need to fear, servant. I am with you.

Here we go!

METATRON

True form of the archangel that lives in the deepest level of Shiba Park Underground Labyrinth, one of the four major dungeons in the Accelerated World. Treats Silver Crow like her servant.

HARUYUKI

Boy in the lowest school caste. Member of the new Nega Nebulus. Possesses the sole flight ability in the Accelerated World. Duel avatar: Silver Crow.

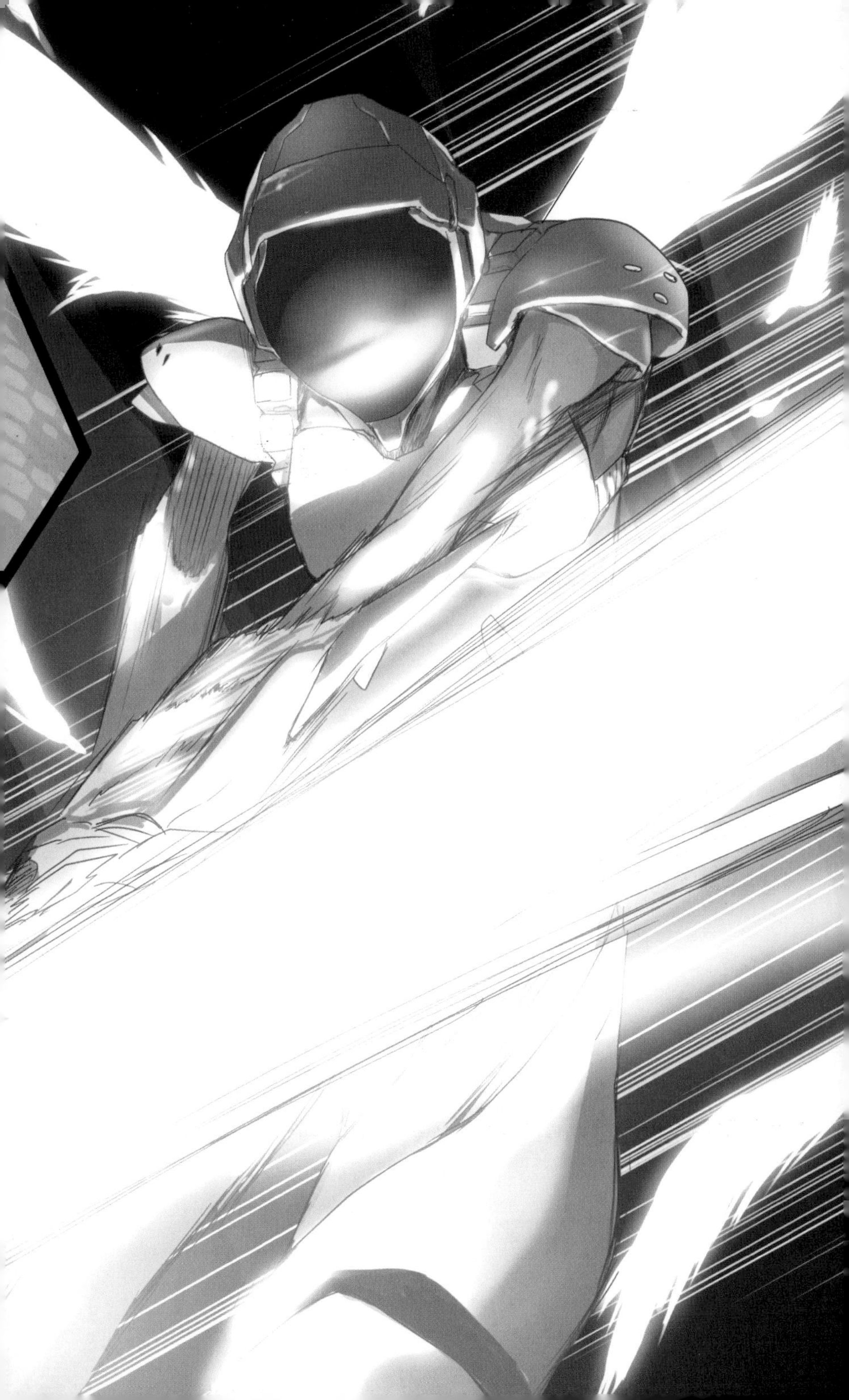

Black Legion: Nega Nebulus
Master: Black Lotus (Kuroyukihime)
Executive branch name: Four Elements
Wind: Sky Raker (Fuko Kurasaki)
Fire: Ardor Maiden (Utai Shinomiya)
Water: Aqua Current (Akira Himi)
Lime Bell (Chiyuri Kurashima)
Cyan Pile (Takumu Mayuzumi)
Silver Crow (Haruyuki Arita)

Red Legion: Prominence
Master: Scarlet Rain (Yuniko Kozuki)
Executive branch name: Triplex
No. 1: Blood Leopard (Mihaya Kakei)
No. 2: Cassis Moose
No. 3: Thistle Porcupine
Blaze Heart
Peach Parasol
Ochre Prison
Mustard Salticid

Blue Legion: Leonids
Master: Blue Knight
Executive branch name: Dualis
Cobalt Blade (Koto Takanouchi)
Manganese Blade (Yuki Takanouchi)
Frost Horn
Tourmaline Shell

Green Legion: Great Wall
Master: Green Grandé
Executive branch name: Six Armors
First seat: Graphite Edge
Second seat: Viridian Decurion
Third seat: Iron Pound
Fourth seat: Lignum Vitae
Fifth seat: Suntan Chafer
Sixth seat: ???
Ash Roller (Rin Kusakabe)
Bush Utan
Olive Grab
Jade Jailer

Yellow Legion: Crypt Cosmic Circus
Master: Yellow Radio
Lemon Pierette
Sax Loader

Purple Legion: Aurora Oval
Master: Purple Thorn
Executive branch name: ???
Aster Vine

White Legion: Oscillatory Universe
Master: White Cosmos
Executive branch name: Seven Dwarves
Ivory Tower

Other Legions

Acceleration Research Society
Black Vise
Argon Array
Dusk Taker (Seiji Nomi)
Rust Jigsaw
Sulfur Pot
Wolfram Cerberus (Armor of Catastrophe Mark II)
Petit Paquet
Master: Chocolat Puppeter (Shihoko Nago)
Mint Mitten (Satomi Mito)
Plum Flipper (Yume Yuruki)
Computation and Martial Arts Research Club
Aluminum Valkyrie (Chiaki Chigira)
Orange Raptor (Yuko Hori)
Violet Dancer (Kurumi Kuruma)
Iris Alice (Lilya Usachova)
Affiliation unknown
Magenta Scissor (Rui Odagiri)
Avocado Avoider
Trilead Tetroxide
Nickel Doll
Sand Duct
Crimson Kingbolt
Lagoon Dolphin (Ruka Asato)
Coral Merrow (Mana Itosu)
Orchid Oracle
Tin Writer

Enemies

Four Divines
Archangel Metatron (Shiba Park underground labyrinth)
Goddess Nyx (Yoyogi Park underground labyrinth)
???
???
Four Gods of the Four Gates
East gate: Seiryu
West gate: Byakko
South gate: Suzaku
North gate: Genbu
Eight Gods of the Shrine of the Eight Divines
???

▶▶▶ACCEL·WORLD 20

THE RIVALRY OF WHITE AND BLACK

Reki Kawahara
Illustrations: HIMA
Design: bee-pee

YEN ON

NEW YORK

■ Kuroyukihime = Umesato Junior High School student council vice president. Trim and clever girl who has it all. Her background is shrouded in mystery. Her in-school avatar is a spangle butterfly she programmed herself. Her duel avatar is the Black King, Black Lotus (level nine).

■ Haruyuki = Haruyuki Arita. Eighth grader at Umesato Junior High School. Bullied, on the pudgy side. He's good at games, but shy. His in-school avatar is a pink pig. His duel avatar is Silver Crow (level five).

■ Chiyuri = Chiyuri Kurashima. Haruyuki's childhood friend. Meddling, energetic girl. Her in-school avatar is a silver cat. Her duel avatar is Lime Bell (level four).

■ Takumu = Takumu Mayuzumi. A boy Haruyuki and Chiyuri have known since childhood. Good at kendo. His duel avatar is Cyan Pile (level five).

■ Fuko = Fuko Kurasaki. Burst Linker belonging to the old Nega Nebulus. One of the Four Elements. Rules wind. Lived as a recluse due to certain circumstances but was persuaded by Kuroyukihime and Haruyuki to come back to the battlefront. Taught Haruyuki about the Incarnate System. Her duel avatar is Sky Raker (level eight).

■ Uiui = Utai Shinomiya. Burst Linker belonging to the old Nega Nebulus. One of the Four Elements. Rules fire. Fourth grader in the elementary division of Matsunogi Academy. Not only can she use the advanced curse removal command "Purify," she is also skilled at long-range attacks. Her duel avatar is Ardor Maiden (level seven).

■ Current = Formally known as Aqua Current. Real name: Akira Himi. Burst Linker belonging to the old Nega Nebulus. One of the Four Elements. Rules water. Known as "The One," the bouncer who undertakes the protection of new Burst Linkers.

■ Graphite Edge = Real name: unknown. Burst Linker belonging to the old Nega Nebulus. One of the Four Elements. Their identity is still wrapped in mystery.

■ Neurolinker = A portable Internet terminal that connects with the brain via a wireless quantum connection and enhances all five senses with images, sounds, and other stimuli.

■ Brain Burst = Neurolinker application sent to Haruyuki by Kuroyukihime.

■ Duel avatar = Player's virtual self, operated when fighting in Brain Burst.

■ Legion = Groups composed of many duel avatars with the objective of expanding occupied areas and securing rights. There are seven main Legions, each led by one of the Seven Kings of Pure Color.

■ Normal Duel Field = The field where normal Brain Burst battles (one-on-one) are carried out. Although the specs do possess elements of reality, the system is essentially on the level of an old-school fighting game.

■ Unlimited Neutral Field = Field for high-level players where only duel avatars at levels four and up are allowed. The game system is of a wholly different order than that of the Normal Duel Field, and the level of freedom in this field beats out even the next-generation VRMMO.

■ Movement Control System = System in charge of avatar control. Normally, this system handles all avatar movement.

■ Image Control System = System in which the player creates a strong image in their mind to operate the avatar. The mechanism is very different from the normal Movement Control System, and very few players can use it. Key component of the Incarnate System.

■ Incarnate System = Technique allowing players to interfere with the Brain Burst program's Image Control System to bring about a reality outside of the game's framework. Also referred to as "overwriting" game phenomena.

■ Acceleration Research Society = Mysterious Burst Linker group. They do not think of Brain Burst as a simple fighting game and are planning something. Black Vise and Rust Jigsaw are members.

■ Armor of Catastrophe = An Enhanced Armament also called "Chrome Disaster." Equipped with this, an avatar can use powerful abilities such as Drain, which absorbs the HP of the enemy avatar, and Divination, which calculates enemy attacks in advance to evade them. However, the spirit of the wearer is polluted by Chrome Disaster, which comes to rule the wearer completely.

■ Star Caster = The longsword carried by Chrome Disaster. Although it now has a sinister form, it was originally a famous and solemn sword that shone like a star, just as the name suggests.

■ ISS kit = Abbreviation for "IS mode study kit." ("IS mode" is "Incarnate System mode.") The kit allows any duel avatar who uses it to make use of the Incarnate System. While using it, a red "eye" is attached to some part of the avatar, and a black aura overlay — the staple of Incarnate attacks

■ Seven Arcs = The seven strongest Enhanced Armaments in the Accelerated World. They are the greatsword Impulse, the staff Tempest, the large shield Strife, the Luminary (form unknown), the straight sword Infinity, the full-body armor Destiny, and the Fluctuating Light (form unknown).

■ Mental-Scar Shell = The emotional scars that are the foundation of a duel avatar (mental scars created from trauma in early childhood)—this is the shell enveloping them. Children with exceptionally hard and thick "shells" are said to produce metal-color duel avatars.

■ Artificial metal color = Refers to a metal-color avatar that is not generated naturally from the subject's mental scars, but rather produced artificially by a third party through the thickening of the Mental-Scar Shell.

■ Unlimited EK = Abbreviation for Unlimited Enemy Kill. The subject avatar is killed by a powerful Enemy in the Unlimited Neutral Field, and each time they regenerate (after a fixed period of time), they are killed again by that Enemy, falling into an infinite hell.

▶▶▶*ACCEL·WORLD*

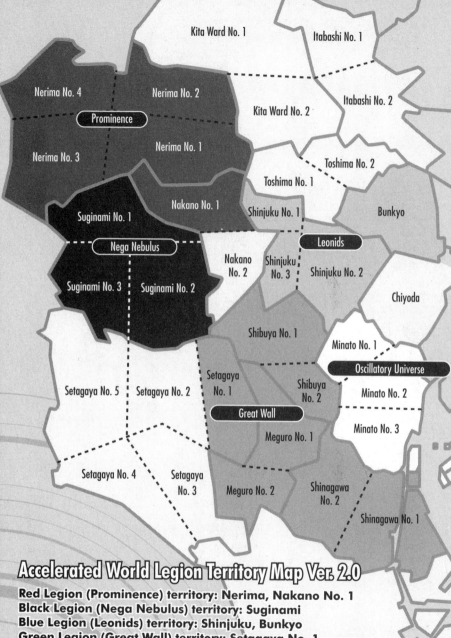

Accelerated World Legion Territory Map Ver. 2.0

Red Legion (Prominence) territory: Nerima, Nakano No. 1
Black Legion (Nega Nebulus) territory: Suginami
Blue Legion (Leonids) territory: Shinjuku, Bunkyo
Green Legion (Great Wall) territory: Setagaya No. 1,
Shibuya, Meguro, Shinagawa
White Legion (Oscillatory Universe) territory: Minato

Vacant areas: Itabashi, Kita Ward, Nakano No. 2, Chiyoda,
Setagaya Nos. 2/3/4/5

1

Haruyuki's daily school commute was a 1.6-kilometer walk, so it wasn't much of a challenge for him to walk a kilometer or two on any other occasion. It was exactly one kilometer to Nakano Central Park, so the walk wouldn't burn through too much of his energy—or so he'd thought.

"Hey, Haru. You're looking kinda pale," Chiyuri Kurashima said as she walked to his left. She stretched out a hand to his forehead. "You're not getting heatstroke, are you?"

"I-I'm okay." Haruyuki hurriedly shook his head. "Totally fine."

From his right, Kuroyukihime offered him a thermos. "Mm. I'm pretty sure you're not getting enough water. Drink this."

"N-no, I'm really okay," Haruyuki politely refused before glancing around and adding under his breath, "I mean, walking around *like this*, of *course* I'm gonna be pale…"

It wasn't just Chiyuri and Kuroyukihime to either side. Ahead of him, members of Nega Nebulus's Four Elements—Fuko Kurasaki, Utai Shinomiya, and Akira Himi—were walking alongside each other, while to the rear, Ash Roller, aka Rin Kusakabe, was sticking close to him, and even farther back, the Petit Paquet group—Shihoko Nago, Satomi Mito, and Yume Yuruki—were giggling and chatting.

All of which was to say, Haruyuki was completely penned in by the armed convoy of the Nega Nebulus girl squad, which had grown explosively as of late. When he cast his eyes about for his close friend and other rare male of the group, he found Takumu Mayuzumi in conversation with Magenta Scissor (aka Rui Odagiri) at the very tail of the group.

That looked like its own minefield, but still, Haruyuki wasn't going to let himself get beaten down by the unbearableness of it all. He'd no doubt get an earful from every direction if he described the feeling as "lying on a bed of needles," but the real issue for him was the looks he was getting from passersby and the secretly raised eyebrows at someone like him walking along in the middle of a group of beautiful girls.

No, no, no. It's all in your head, he told himself as he once again scanned his surroundings. *You're just self-conscious. People don't pay attention to other people.*

The party was walking along a municipal road that stretched out east to west along the JR Chuo Line overhead rails. Washed out and pale in the bright sunlight, the redbrick sidewalk had been widened in the 2030s and was more than enough to accommodate them all, and from the trees that rose up on either side of the generous road, cicadas were belting out their summer song. Beneath the trees, students of all ages smiled as they walked to and fro on their way home from school.

Their joyful smiles could be attributed to the fact that the rainy season was finally over and summer vacation was starting the following day. But Haruyuki couldn't bring himself to look directly at their faces no matter how he tried, and so he cast his gaze downward, launching the map app on his virtual desktop.

Nakano Central Park was a mixed-use facility to the northwest of Nakano Station. It was bigger than the shopping mall on the lower floors of Haruyuki's condo, with a wide variety of tenants, so it was bustling even on the weekend. The majority of schools in the city had their closing ceremonies today—Saturday, July 20,

2047—so the park would be incredibly crowded with students and families.

As a general rule, Haruyuki didn't do well in crowds, but today at least he was grateful for them—and that was because the full rosters of the Black Legion, Nega Nebulus, and the Red Legion, Prominence, were gathering in the park that day. The black side had a total of twelve people, including Rin, who was temporarily joining their number; the red side was expected to exceed thirty people. No matter how big the facility, a group that large would stand out if the place was deserted, inevitably leading to all of them being cracked in the real.

The Legion Master of Prominence, the second Red King, Scarlet Rain, aka Yuniko Kozuki, and the deputy Blood Leopard, aka Pard, aka Mihaya Kakei, were already out in the real to the majority of the black members, so in the worst case, there shouldn't be anything like a PK clash. But even so, there was more than a little resistance to them exposing their real selves to an opposing Burst Linker group.

Haruyuki understood this. The values of high rankers like Kuroyukihime, Fuko, Niko, and Pard were remarkably different from those of other young people their age, most likely because of the unfathomably long hours they'd spent in the Accelerated World. While they didn't judge people based on appearances, they were especially harsh on the field of psychological warfare. This tendency was widespread among nonveteran Burst Linkers as well, and about the only one who sneered at Haruyuki to his face, calling him a "pig," had been Dusk Taker/Seiji Nomi when he fell to the dark side. And with his careless eating habits, it was Haruyuki's own fault that he was so round and pudgy, so at the very least, he figured he was mentally prepared to endure open stares or laughter and come out with only a few hit points of damage.

*I thought I was, but here we are...*He turned his gaze back to the three-dimensional map. The two wings of Nakano Central

Park—South and East—were built so that they enclosed the entire area. There were food shops facing the park on the first and second floors of both buildings, so the members of Prominence had probably split up and were on standby in several of those restaurants.

There were fifteen of them in total, and there was no guarantee that members from the Promi side would be present in the one that Haruyuki and his friends went into. He didn't think that side would be able to guess they were Burst Linkers at first glance, but things would get pretty uncomfortable for both sides once the meeting ended if people next to each other gave the Burst Link command at the specified time.

Here, Haruyuki belatedly realized he had a question. "Um, Kuroyukihime?" he asked the older girl. "That reminds me. Why are we all going out of our way to go to Central Park for a meeting with Red? Usually two people are the starters, and then everyone else dives as part of the Gallery. So aren't the starters the only ones who need to go to Central Park? Isn't it the same if all the other participants are somewhere in Nakano One?"

"Mm. Well, that is true." Kuroyukihime nodded and then glanced at the group walking ahead of them. "But I would feel bad sending Fuko alone to Central Park as our starter. And since this battle is limited to members of both Legions in the Gallery using the park's local net, we do actually need to gather at the location in the real."

"Um. But…" Although mostly convinced, Haruyuki kept at it. "The duelers have the right to forcibly remove any of the Gallery, so couldn't they just clear out any outsiders after the duel starts?"

"Now look, Haruyuki. That would basically be the same as declaring to the world that Black and Red are planning something," she said. She threw him a wry smile, but it soon grew brooding. "Until the Territories with Oscillatory start at four, we absolutely cannot let them get wind of the merger between Nega Nebulus and Prominence. If the White King learns of it, she very well might suspect we'll attack Minato Ward Area Three today.

If our attack is leaked beforehand, they'll naturally focus the full might of the Seven Dwarves in Minato Three. In the worst case, Cosmos herself might show up. I have faith in your abilities, but if that happened…"

"You can't, Sacchi." Ahead of them, Fuko Kurasaki whirled around and cut their legion leader off. While signs of the usual soft and gentle Raker Smile lingered, her silent rebuke was understood by those in the know to be quite firm. "'Even if the White King might show up'—that's all the more reason that you can't go to Minato area. Whatever happens with Nega Nebulus, so long as *you*, at least—so long as the Black King—are in good health, we can come back. However many times it takes. But…"

Next to Fuko, Utai Shinomiya picked up the thread in her text chat. UI> IF SOMETHING HAPPENED TO YOU, SA, WE WOULD DEFINITELY NOT BE ABLE TO GET BACK UP AGAIN THIS TIME. NEGA NEBULUS IS A LEGION MADE UP OF PEOPLE WHO LOVE YOU AND COME TOGETHER FOR YOUR SAKE. THAT HAS NEVER CHANGED.

Even Akira Himi, who was normally extremely short-spoken, chimed in, touching the red frames of her glasses. "Fu's exactly right. Today's Territories are definitely not the final battle with the White Legion and the Acceleration Research Society. It's the first in a prolonged series of battles. It's a fight we can't afford to lose, but if we do, we'll pick ourselves back up. However many times it takes."

"……"

Kuroyukihime said nothing in response to her generals, a serious yet pained look on her face.

At some point the members to the rear had also stopped talking, and the entire party had stopped moving.

Fuko was the first to open her mouth, the smile on her face somewhat dry. "In the old days, this would be when Graph said something ridiculous to cheer us all up."

UI> HE'S SO ANNOYING WHEN HE'S AROUND, BUT SOMETHING'S MISSING WHEN HE'S NOT. THAT'S GRAPH FOR YOU.

"If we're not careful," Akira said with a completely straight face, "he'll sense with some mysterious power that we're talking about him and appear before us even though we really didn't ask for him. Let's watch our tongues."

The strain finally left Kuroyukihime's face, and she let out a small sigh. "I suppose. It's true that I'm in quite the fighting mood today. Perhaps I hadn't realized how deeply provoking it was to see Cosmos at the school festival last month."

"That's right, Kuroyukihime. Please have faith in us today and wait in Suginami for a report!" In his heart, Haruyuki silently congratulated himself for having the wherewithal to say the right thing at the right time for once.

"Aaah, totally like you, Haru!" Chiyuri retorted mercilessly. "Even at a time like this, you can't say 'have faith in *me.*'"

Kuroyukihime and the Elements shared a laugh, followed by the Petit Paquet crew and even Takumu in the rear of the group. The moment the laughter started to die down, a hand stretched out from behind Haruyuki.

"Uh. Um." Rin Kusakabe hesitantly looked for a chance to speak, poufy hair tied in two small bundles at the back of her head.

Somewhat surprised, Kuroyukihime blinked a few times until a smile stretched across her face. "Kusakabe—ah, Rin. Today, you're a member of Nega Nebulus. You don't have to raise your hand every time you want to speak."

"O-okay. Um. I was listening. And I had this thought. Now." Rin looked serious as she spoke in her usual halting way. "If. The White King had really. Wanted to provoke Kuroyukihime when. She came to the Umesato school festival…That would mean. Her goal was to draw Kuroyukihime into a fight with the. White Legion. Right?"

"Mm." Kuroyukihime exchanged glances with Fuko, Akira, and Utai before nodding slowly. "Yes…that's what it would mean. If she hadn't shown up then and acknowledged that she was the one behind the ISS kits and also the leader of the Acceleration Research Society, we wouldn't have been able to get Grandé and Knight to cooperate in carrying out the attack on Minato area."

"And right before she turned into a butterfly and flew away," Haruyuki started, as he dug back into his memory of that day nearly three weeks earlier, "she said she was looking forward to the time when you would stand before the White King of your own will…" He felt like the cries of the cicadas and even the heat of the summer sun faded away as he simply remembered how the White King—Transient Eternity, White Cosmos—looked when she charged into the Black Legion meeting in a simple dummy avatar in the middle of the school festival.

She'd been ready to fight both Kuroyukihime and Niko with that dummy avatar, even though it would have had essentially no battle power. Even though she knew that according to the level-nine sudden-death rule, if she lost there, she would lose all her points and be forever banished from the Accelerated World. He shuddered at the memory.

A small hand grabbed tightly onto the hem of his shirt as Rin started to speak again. "I trade with my brother in the. Accelerated World, so my memories of duels are. Usually vague…But weirdly. I remember. That one very well. Even though the White King didn't look. Hostile or angry at all, I was. Afraid of her. It was like she could. Read every single one of my. Thoughts. I'm sure it's impossible. But there's no chance…she figured out that we're. Attacking Minato area in the Territories today?"

Kuroyukihime and the Four Elements pursed their lips once more.

The White King had marched into the school festival alone and confirmed their suspicion that she was the leader of the Acceleration Research Society. She'd obviously had a purpose in doing so, and if that purpose was to make Nega Nebulus attack Oscillatory Universe, then Haruyuki couldn't deny that it was possible she was expecting an attack on the location of the White headquarters, Minato Area No. 3.

If she was, the defense team for the area would be a formidable lineup of Oscillatory's most elite members. According to the information file Kuroyukihime had prepared, the White executive branch, the Seven Dwarves, were naturally part of this elite, but even the rank-and-file members looked to be fierce warriors. Haruyuki had no intention of admitting defeat before they even fought, but it was a fact that their chances of victory would drop off against such a defensive line.

The late-July sun burning down on them, the party fell into an oppressive silence in the middle of the sidewalk.

"This sure isn't like you," came a voice from the rear abruptly, and Haruyuki lifted his face.

The speaker was a girl in a short-sleeved sailor uniform with asymmetrical bangs, the Burst Linker who had been the cause of many of Haruyuki's fiercest fights. She was also Nega Nebulus's newest member, having only just joined the Legion that very day: Magenta Scissor/Rui Odagiri.

A faint smile bleeding onto her beautiful, shadowed face, Rui made her husky voice heard once more. "The Nega Nebulus I know isn't the kind of Legion to get freaked before a fight. You're always saying once you accelerate, the only thing you can do is fight with all you got and all that. You're not actually trying to tell me you can scrap the whole thing if you haven't accelerated yet?"

"Of course not. If we pulled back here, I can't imagine what the Red King would say," Kuroyukihime replied, also smiling, and took a deep breath before straightening up and announcing, "Even if, hypothetically, Oscillatory is anticipating the Territories attack, they can't have foreseen that it would be today. Systemwise, the areas separating Suginami and Minato—Shibuya One and Two—are green territory, and the White King couldn't possibly guess that they'll be transferred immediately before the Territories with no contest. Not to mention that it's beyond the realm of imagination that Nega Nebulus and Prominence would merge to not only double our battle force, but triple or quadruple it. If we can do even one thing they don't see coming, we will have a chance at victory."

The former members of Petit Paquet nodded as one, and the other members joined them.

"Master," Takumu began from beside Rui, "I was a member of Blue Legion, Leonids, until nine months ago, and I took part in the Territories then, too. The Blue Legion won by a long shot in terms of numbers, but even against them, Nega Nebulus always had one thing that put them on top: the element of surprise. This Legion has the strength to turn the tables in any situation, no matter how difficult. And that's a strength that's impossible to see coming."

Here, for some reason, he glanced at Haruyuki, and then he turned his gaze back on Kuroyukihime. "Even if Oscillatory Universe has figured out every detail of our strategy, even if they've prepared every possible countermeasure, Nega Nebulus won't go down so easily. Not a chance."

"Oh-ho-ho!" Chiyuri chirped. "You've really started talking Negabu style, too, huh, Taku!"

Takumu pushed up the bridge of his glasses as though embarrassed, so the entire party burst into laughter once again.

"It's just as Takumu says." Kuroyukihime nodded firmly and brought the impromptu roadside meeting to a close. "Even supposing Oscillatory concentrates all their battle power in Minato Three, that doesn't mean we're doomed to fail. And even if we *are* defeated, that does not spell the end of everything. I am utterly and thoroughly vexed that I cannot take part myself, but I will wait and have faith in your victory. Now let's head off toward our first mission. Everyone, disconnect from the global net!"

At this, Haruyuki finally noticed that they were nearly at the border between Suginami and Nakano. If they kept walking with global connections on, every member of Nega Nebulus would appear on the matching list for Nakano Area No. 1, and any Burst Linker who happened to check the list would wonder what was going on.

He hurriedly reached up and cut the global connection on his Neurolinker. The 3-D map he had open switched to offline mode, and the real-time traffic information disappeared. Swiping the map away, he looked up at the pure, blue summer sky. The anxious desire to flee had faded from his heart at some point, and in its place he felt prebattle nerves and a hint of excitement rise up.

Five minutes later, they were at Nakano Central Park, which was even busier than he'd expected. A number of cafés and fast-food joints stood on the north side of the mall that faced Shikinomori Park, but every one of them was jam-packed with young people and families. Some even had lines stretching out the door.

Given that it was currently 1:50 PM and the meeting with Prominence started at two, they didn't exactly have the luxury of wandering around looking for a restaurant that could seat them all. Panicking, Haruyuki went into crisis mode, but for some reason, Kuroyukihime and the others were as relaxed as ever.

"Uh. Um, Kuroyukihime? Everywhere's jammed with people," Haruyuki started, his voice somewhat shrill.

"Don't get flustered, Haruyuki." Kuroyukihime grinned. "I expected it would be busy today."

"S-so then, did you make a reservation?" he asked anxiously.

Rather than replying directly, she snapped her fingers. "Supply troops, you're up!"

"Roger!" the Petit Paquet group—Shihoko, Satomi, and Yume—barked in immediate response. Haruyuki looked closely and saw they were carrying bags and baskets.

Looking resolute, Shihoko saluted and pointed toward the park spreading out to the north of the mall. "We have already found a suitable location, Commander!"

"Good! Then we move!" the commander shouted in response.

Haruyuki chased after them, wondering what exactly this little performance was all about.

Shihoko walked ahead to lead the entire party to the base of a broad-leaved tree rising up in the center of the park. Around the trunk was a plaque informing them that it was a beech tree. The large canopy cast plenty of shade across the green lawn, and a pleasant breeze brushed over Haruyuki's skin once he stepped into the large shadow.

Satomi pulled a large tarp out of a bag and flapped it out over the grass. Instantly, Shihoko and Yume were fixing the corners with small pegs before encouraging the rest of the Legion onto it with a unified "Please sit!"

Chiyuri took off her sneakers and then stepped onto the tarp, followed by the rest of the girls' squad. They sat down in a circle, and Haruyuki and Takumu added themselves to one corner.

Once seated, Haruyuki's attention was immediately drawn to the two baskets set down in the center of the circle. If they were playing picnic, then he would assume the baskets had tasty treats inside, and he would further assume that these had been handmade by Shihoko and her friends, members of their school's cooking club. He further concluded that they would be receiving them shortly.

Following this train of thought, Haruyuki was unconsciously inching closer to the baskets when he was suddenly yanked back by the collar. "Hrnk!" Groaning, he turned to find the angelic Raker Smile.

"Not yet, Corvus. That's for *after* the meeting."

"Hy-hyaah." Bobbing his head up and down, he looked at the bottom right of his virtual desktop and saw that it was 1:58 PM.

Right about now, the Red Legion Burst Linkers would also be waiting somewhere nearby. Haruyuki surveyed their surroundings. There were several other groups of people their age picnicking in the area, each of which looked quite suspicious to him.

"Come now! If you keep whirling around like that, they'll figure out who we are, Haruyuki," Kuroyukihime scolded.

"S-s-s-s-sorry." Haruyuki shrank into himself and then followed Takumu's example by sitting formally on his knees on the tarp. He straightened up, clenched his stomach, and took a deep breath.

"All right, then. I'll check the matching list first," Fuko offered calmly. She then called the Burst Link command and quickly closed her eyes. "Right now, every Burst Linker on the list is a part of the mission today."

"That sounds about right," Kuroyukihime remarked. "If you were looking to duel in Nakano, you'd head for Area Two around Broadway. And while Central Park *is* equipped with a local net, it's a completely family-oriented facility, so most Burst Linkers stay away. Which is exactly why we chose this location."

"And in the event that there *is* someone in the way, we can pick a duel and neatly beat them back from the local net, hmm? ♥" Fuko spoiled Kuroyukihime's technical explanation with a smile, and then composed herself in a manner befitting a deputy before lightly bringing her hands together. "Now, then. Thirty seconds left. Everyone except Rin, connect to the Central Park local information net. Sorry to leave you out, Rin."

"No, it's. The only way this. Time." Rin shook her head vigorously at the apology from her usually strict parent. "I'm in GW. If I show up, it will put everyone in Promi on guard."

"We'll soon let you know how it goes," Fuko said, winking. "Just hang on for one point eight seconds."

"Okay." Rin nodded, and the rest of the party moved as one onto their virtual desktops.

Haruyuki selected the target net from the list of networks that popped up and connected. The Central Park logo was displayed in his field of view, and windows opened up showing assorted coupons and the seating availability at the various shops, but he quickly got rid of these.

The digital numbers in the bottom right of his view were steadily marching toward two PM. He'd been in this situation any number of times before—and this time, he wasn't even going to actually duel. Still, he was overcome with a nervousness he'd never felt before. He clenched both hands into tight fists.

Haruyuki had gotten the Brain Burst program from Kuroyukihime and become a member of Nega Nebulus last fall. Although a great many things had happened in the nine months since then, the power structure of the Accelerated World, divided and controlled by the six Great Legions, was basically unchanged.

However, the world was about to change significantly, starting with the meeting today. It wasn't just that Nega Nebulus and Prominence were going to merge and become a major Legion with territory straddling Nerima, Nakano, and Suginami. If they could succeed in stripping Oscillatory Universe of its right to block the matching list in the Territories later in the day and have the Leonids' Coba-Manga sisters confirm the presence of Acceleration Research Society members in Minato area, the Accelerated World would be plunged into war, setting the White Legion against an allied force of the five Great Legions. The difference in numbers was overwhelming, but their opponent was *the* White King, and to get to her, they had to face the terrifying battle power of the Armor of Catastrophe, Mark II. The war would be a hard one.

His heart's desires were to rescue his friend Wolfram Cerberus, now that the Acceleration Research Society had forced him to join with the Armor, and to get back the thruster from the Red King's Enhanced Armament Invincible, currently the vessel for the Armor.

If he could achieve these two goals, the plot of Kuroyukihime's tormentor the White King and her Acceleration Research Society would necessarily fall apart. This would be their highest-level, most difficult mission so far, but if he just had faith in his other half, Silver Crow, the duel avatar he'd worked hard to train; his Legion comrades, the players he'd built such strong bonds with; and his own self, whom he'd come to hate just a little less lately…If he just gave it everything he had, they would definitely…absolutely…

At 1:59:59 PM, Fuko called the acceleration command. A second later, the flaming words A REGISTERED DUEL IS BEGINNING!! blazed up before his eyes and carried Haruyuki's consciousness off to an instance of a world.

2

Burst Linkers inevitably felt a sense of joyous luck or ominous foreboding the moment they saw the duel stage with its diverse characteristics, attributes, and idiosyncrasies. For instance, the Purgatory stage, with metal insects wriggling around organically twisted buildings; the Primeval Forest stage, its pools of purple poison welling up in forests of withered trees; and the ultimate dark type, Hell stage, which Haruyuki had never seen himself, were all ominous; while conversely, the Sacred Ground stage, with its countless crystals floating in a snowy white field; the Moonlight stage, where a full moon hung in the night sky; and the Heian stage, in which madder-red *torii* gates rose up in the midst of red and yellow autumn leaves dancing through the air, were thought by pretty much everyone to be fortunate stages.

Praying that the setting for the all-important general meeting with Prominence would please be a lucky stage, Haruyuki slowly opened his eyes.

A strangely yellowish-green sky and damp, gray earth filled his field of view. The brilliantly leafy green beeches of the real world had been transformed into massive lopsided and twisting trees with trunks as white as bone, while the buildings of Central Park that he could see on the south and east sides were half-rotted, reddish-brown rusty liquid coloring their walls.

"Gah. A Corroded Forest stage?" Haruyuki muttered.

Before he could reject the idea in his head, a chocolate-colored, chocolate-flavored young lady poked his back. "What ridiculous nonsense are you speaking here? There aren't any buildings in a Corroded Forest stage!"

"R-right..."

Choco, you're still wildly different on this side! Unable to voice his thought, Haruyuki searched the list of stage data in the back of his mind. Scenery-wise, it seemed like a natural type with wood affiliation, but this poisoned atmosphere could also mean it was a dark type.

Before Haruyuki could reach a conclusion, however, a slender F-type avatar whose entire body was wrapped in reddish-purple film-type armor muttered in a rough voice, "We got another rare stage here, huh?"

It was Magenta Scissor. She shrugged.

"Honestly." Black Lotus nodded, her onyx-colored crystal armor shining. "And it's a somewhat—no, a very annoying one, too."

"Huh? What do you mean, annoying?" Haruyuki asked his mentor, giving up on remembering the name on his own. "It looks a lot like a Corroded Forest, but at first glance, there don't seem to be any poison swamps or insects."

It wasn't Kuroyukihime who answered him, but rather Fuko, the duel's starter. "Come now, over there, Corvus." Seated in her wheelchair, the avatar in the white dress pointed off to the north.

Squinting, he saw a sinister pink mist seeping out of the school-like building on the opposite side of the road. At last he succeeded in extracting the data and slapped a fist into the palm of his other hand. "Oh! This is that one. Um...A Plague stage!"

"Correct. And it does seem like that poisonous mist is coming this way," Kuroyukihime murmured, narrowing her bluish-purple eye lenses.

Categorized as a mid-level dark type, the Plague stage was not exempt from the troublesome field gimmicks that characterized a dark stage. The poison mist before Haruyuki now was one of these, gushing up from the ground at random. If you touched it, you were "infected" with the plague. Depending on the color of the mist, you would be hit with slip damage, nullification of special attacks, visual impediments, aural impediments, or loss of balance, among other de-buffs. Not to mention that since the mist was no simple poison, but rather a pathogen, the duel avatars who came into contact with it also became a source of infection, bringing about the same symptoms in nearby avatars. In a normal duel, a player would actively try to use these to take down their opponent, but drawing this stage in the Territories was basically the worst. And it wasn't much better if you were using the stage as a meeting venue, as they were doing now.

"And I'm pretty sure a pink mist is slip damage, right, Lotus?" Fuko said. "Pard and I will be the only ones infected, since we're the duelers, but it won't be much of a meeting if the deputies keep losing health."

Kuroyukihime groaned. "I suppose we have no choice. Shall we discuss with the Prominence side and try for a new stage? That reminds me. Where are they?"

The entire party looked around. When the duelers were so far apart that they could not visually confirm each other's presence, a guide cursor indicating the enemy dueler's position was displayed in each one's field of view. Given there were no guide cursors in view for either Fuko standing before them or the other player, Pard had to be somewhere nearby at least, but there was no sign of anyone in the desolate park or the rotted buildings.

"Are the Promi peeps really logged in?" Plum Flipper, aka Yume, cocked her head and its round hat to one side quizzically.

"Whoa, whoa!" Mint Mitten, aka Satomi, jabbed her with a mittened fist. "Leopard's health gauge is displayed right there."

Just as she said, the avatar name BLOOD LEOPARD was neatly inscribed beneath the right-hand health gauge. And if Pard hadn't been there, Fuko wouldn't have been able to generate the duel stage in the first place.

But then why hadn't anyone from Prominence shown up despite the fact that it had already been over a minute since the start of the duel? Maybe the enemy forces were obstructed by... some kind of unexpected situation? Haruyuki began to wonder beneath his face mask.

"SRY. Late."

A quiet voice echoed from above, and the entire party hurriedly turned their heads to see a silhouette slipping soundlessly down the trunk of a twisted tree. The slim torso, four powerful limbs, and long tail belonged to none other than the Prominence deputy "Bloody Kitty," Blood Leopard.

"Oh. Um. How long have you been up there?" Haruyuki asked when Pard reached the ground mere seconds later, neglecting to say hello.

"Start, basically," Pard responded briefly.

"Th-then why didn't you come down right away?" Haruyuki frowned.

"Minor situation," she said, with a sigh for some reason, and raised a hand to point toward the building on the east side of the park, Central Park East.

"......"

Haruyuki and the other ten people silently turned their attention in that direction. The half-rotted East building fell back into silence. Nothing moved. And then suddenly a loud voice thundered overhead.

"Sorry for the wait, Nega Nebulus!!"

Two silhouettes—both fairly large, arms crossed tightly in front of their chests—appeared on the roof of the East building. For some reason they stood far apart. They were followed by two new figures from behind, and then another two behind them, and then, in the blink of an eye, a couple dozen silhouettes had formed a long row on the roof until finally a small duel avatar appeared with some force in its center.

This middle avatar raised a silent hand and pointed at the yellowish-green sky. As if this were a signal, the thirty-odd people took on poses from ancient *tokusatsu* masked-hero TV shows and shouted in unison, "We are Promineeeennnce!!"

Four or five sparks were launched from the rear and exploded together with a *pa-pa-pa-pum!* sound that was a little lacking in impact.

"......"

The eleven members of Nega Nebulus found themselves at a loss for words.

"SRY," Pard muttered with another sigh.

"...Leopard," Fuko said. "Are you saying the reason it took a while for them to appear was because they were...getting *that* ready?"

"Yes." The crimson cat avatar nodded apologetically. "Rain says stuff like this is decided in snap judgments right at the start."

"Ha-ha-ha! That does totally sound like something Niko would say." Haruyuki waved a hand at the Red King, "Bloody Storm" Scarlet Rain, posing smartly in the center of the duel avatars lined up neatly on the roof of the East building. "Heeey!"

After about two seconds, Niko released her pose somewhat awkwardly and kicked off the edge of the roof to jump down to the ground. While her comrades jumped one after another, she trotted over to the Nega Nebulus group and jabbed Haruyuki in the side.

They were both members of the Gallery, so naturally he took no damage, but even so, he reflexively groaned before protesting, "Wh-what are you doing?"

"Now look!" the smaller girl snapped. "Don't 'heeey' me there! Ruins the whole impression!"

"Th-then what should I say?"

"Time like this, you all gotta snap to attention and give us your poses in return!"

"Wh-what? Like, how?" Haruyuki was honestly baffled.

"Like, you'd be all 'Nega Nebulus on the scene!'" Niko suggested. "'Nega Nebulus unite!' or something."

"We absolutely will not," Kuroyukihime responded extremely curtly. Shaking her head in exasperation, she cleared her throat loudly before continuing in a slightly louder voice. "At any rate, I appreciate that you are here participating in today's meeting with all your Legion members as promised, Red King. We don't have much time, however, so I would like to get to the central issue soon."

Niko took a step back from Haruyuki, and her voice when she responded was so dignified, it made him realize all over again that whatever else, she really was a king. "Oh! And you, Black King, coming all the way to Nakano One. Sorry for the hassle. I'd like to suggest we get right to it, but…"

She cut herself off and glanced toward the north side of the park, so Haruyuki also turned his eyes in that direction and saw that the problematic pink mist was already on the verge of crossing the road and drifting into the park.

"Dang. We really drew an annoying piece of work here. Plague stage." She shook her head. "Can't let Pard and Raker get poisoned, so maybe we should restart this jam?"

Before anyone on the Nega Nebulus side could react, a fairly intimidating voice rang out from the Prominence side. "I've got a good idea, boss!"

"Yeah?"

As Niko turned around, a smallish duel avatar jumped out from the group. From the timbre of the voice, it was probably an M-type, and that was about all Haruyuki could say about him. Because he was wearing a hat with an excessively large brim, and the cloak wrapped around his body was so long that it dragged along the ground.

"Mm. This guy," Kuroyukihime muttered.

"Do you know this person, Kuroyukihime?" Haruyuki asked in a low voice.

"Probably. But let's hear him out now. Although I have a feeling he won't say anything particularly helpful."

Kuroyukihime's prediction immediately became reality.

"And what's this good idea, Dine?" Niko asked.

"Make the stage a Battle Royale!" Dine called back confidently, as if that were the smallest deal in the world. "Then I can sterilize that poison mist in a flash!"

The only ones who could currently take or deal damage or interfere with the stage were Sky Raker and Blood Leopard. But the instant the rules switched to Battle Royale mode, Haruyuki and every single person in the Gallery would become a dueler, and the likelihood of an unforeseen situation occurring would certainly increase, the most extreme possibility being that either Kuroyukihime or Niko would be retired through total point loss, according to the level-nine sudden-death rules. Naturally, Niko would reject the idea out of hand—or so Haruyuki thought.

"Hmm." The small crimson girl avatar turned her large eye lenses up at Kuroyukihime. "So we got this proposal. Whaddya wanna do, Lotus? Quitting the duel and accelerating again's a whole hassle on its own."

"Mm." Kuroyukihime also didn't immediately reject the idea, but rather turned toward Fuko. Apparently, some instantaneous telepathic communication took place there, and when she turned back to the Red King, she was nodding. "Well, I suppose. And going back to the start would mean you'd have to perform your ultracool appearance sequence again, which would be, well, you know."

"Hey! What d'you mean by that?!" Niko erupted, but soon reined her outrage in and sent Pard a signal with her eyes.

The leopard avatar deftly moved a finger down her Instruct menu, and a duel mode change confirmation window appeared before all the members of the Gallery. Haruyuki had a vaguely bad feeling about this, but given that Kuroyukihime had already agreed to the change, he couldn't exactly object. Not to mention that Takumu and Chiyuri were nonchalantly tapping the YES buttons in the windows before them, along with Chocolat and her friends, who were below Silver Crow in terms of level. So Haruyuki sent a brief prayer up to the gods of the Accelerated World that the meeting would end without incident as he pushed his own YES button.

The word "god" called to mind the thirteenth member of Nega Nebulus. She would normally have been present, but there was no way he could summon her today, unfortunately. If anyone on the red side questioned him and demanded to know her true identity, the inevitable ensuing commotion would take up the whole thirty minutes of the duel.

I feel bad for Metatron, but I'll introduce her to the red people once the meeting is over.

While he was thinking this over, all the YES buttons had apparently been pressed, since the flaming text A BATTLE ROYALE IS BEGINNING!! blazed up before his eyes, followed by the start of a ten-second countdown. The readout quickly hit zero, and the health gauge in the top left changed from Sky Raker's to Silver Crow's own. In the top right, the gauges of the other Burst Linkers were displayed vertically in a compressed format.

As soon as the duel mode switchover was complete, a figure started to run toward the northern side of the park, the Prominence avatar in the hat and cloak who had proposed the change to Battle Royale. Niko had called him Dine, and Haruyuki looked to the right again to find the avatar's official name. But there were far too many gauges there for him to be able to pick out which one was Dine's.

Dine stopped about fifteen meters from the group and shouted, "All riiiiiight!" He thrust slender arms out from beneath his cloak. Ahead of him, the poisonous pink mist writhed like a living creature. Dine had boasted that he would make the mist disappear with a single blow, but how exactly would he do that?

With forty-some pairs of eyes focused on him, Dine struck a pose like he was about to launch a special attack and froze like that for about two seconds before turning just his head to say, "Sorry. Someone charge up my special-attack gauge."

"...... "

Once again, everyone on the Nega Nebulus side was speechless. Niko let out a long sigh. "We don't have a lotta time, so I'll charge you up quick and simple!" She drew the small pistol Enhanced Armament from her left hip. *Shk!* She rotated the cylinder, froze in position, and nonchalantly pulled the trigger.

The energy bullet shot mercilessly through the long, brown cloak but seemed to only graze the avatar body hidden within it. Dine simply shook slightly at the hit. His special-attack gauge now apparently charged from the damage, he called the technique name in a loud voice: "Here we go…Antidote Mist!!"

His hands shone a vivid yellow, and a light of the same color sprayed outward. The instant it touched the pink mist, the poison began to melt away with an effect perfectly befitting his technique's name. Mere seconds later, the twenty-meter mass of poison mist was completely gone.

"And *that* is *that!*" Dine turned around, clapping his hands together dramatically.

Cheers and applause erupted from the Promi camp.

"Nice! The king of poison killers!"

"Gimme some detox, too!"

They're setting the rhythm here, Haruyuki thought as he also clapped along.

"So that *is* Stronger," Kuroyukihime murmured. "He's still in Prominence then, hmm?"

"Stronger? Is that that Dine person's nickname?" Haruyuki asked.

"Mm." She nodded. "More precisely, Stronger Name. Take a look at his health gauge."

Haruyuki obediently turned his gaze toward the column of gauges once more. Since only one had taken any damage, he was quickly able to spot what was presumably Dine's gauge. The avatar name inscribed below it was IODINE STERILIZER.

"I-Io…How do you pronounce that?"

"It's Iodine Sterilizer, Corvus," Fuko said from the other side of Kuroyukihime.

"Whoa," he said. "Sounds like two super-robot names stuck together." Unconsciously reeling slightly, he stared again at the avatar in the broad-brimmed hat. He couldn't fathom what was inside the cloak, and he didn't know the meaning of the English word "iodine" or "sterilizer," but at the very least, the name was the coolest of all the avatar names he'd seen so far. "Oh! So that's why his nickname is Stronger Name, then, huh? But why just 'Stronger'? With an incredible name like that, I think it should be the top level, 'Strongest.'"

Kuroyukihime and Fuko exchanged a look and then giggled in unison.

"If your thinking's made it that far, then you'll arrive at the answer in another second," Kuroyukihime assured him. "At any rate, it seems that the meeting is finally starting."

He turned and saw Niko heading toward them, twirling her pistol on one finger.

"That stupid poisonous mist is gone," she said. "So how 'bout we get right down to business? Lotus, you okay with deciding on the chairperson like we discussed in advance?"

"Yup. No problem," Kuroyukihime replied.

"Wohkay. So then, Pard, Cassi, Pokki, step forward." Niko snapped her fingers, and three avatars stepped forward out of the Prominence group.

One was the familiar Blood Leopard, but the other two were new faces: a superlarge M-type avatar with massive horns growing from both sides of his head, and a medium F-type avatar whose back was covered in long, fluffy fur. Even though they weren't acting the least bit aggressive, Haruyuki felt a pressure on par with that caused by the executive branch of the Green Legion, Great Wall, the Six Armors.

"Oh," he murmured. "Is that maybe Prominence's..."

"Yes. The remaining two members of the Triplex." At some

point, Takumu had come to stand to his right, and now he explained quietly, "The big one's Cassis Moose, and the small one is Thistle Porcupine. They're both high rankers with abilities on par with Leopard's."

"That's some aura they got. But our Elements are no slouches, either," Chiyuri murmured from his other side. And indeed, as they stepped forward from the Nega Nebulus side, Sky Raker, Aqua Current, and Ardor Maiden showed absolutely no fear and stood tall in front of the Triplex.

With the six members of the executives of both Legions facing each other, the entire stage snapped to attention. And rightly so—this was the intimidating Battle Royale mode. If this tension reached its ignition point, a catastrophe large enough to rend the heavens and split the earth was inescapable. Haruyuki nervously watched over the six high rankers squared off between the two Legions.

"One, two!" Niko shouted from behind the Triplex. "Rock!"

All six Burst Linkers thrust their right hands up with astounding speed before bringing them back down again. The six fists froze in midair, and the shock wave that was generated beat at the earth and caused clouds of dust to rise up.

Before the dust had settled again, Kuroyukihime yelled, "Paper! Scissors!!"

Whp! The air shook even more fiercely, and bolts of pale lightning crackled in the space between the two sets of hands. Two of the six were eliminated after two more throws, and the process was repeated three more times until only Thistle Porcupine and Ardor Maiden were left standing.

While Haruyuki wondered if it was mere coincidence that the two smallest avatars remained or if speed worked as an advantage for rock-paper-scissors in the Accelerated World, the pair threw out their last hands inhumanly fast, and after an instant of stasis, the white-and-crimson shrine maiden avatar slowly raised her scissors hand above her head.

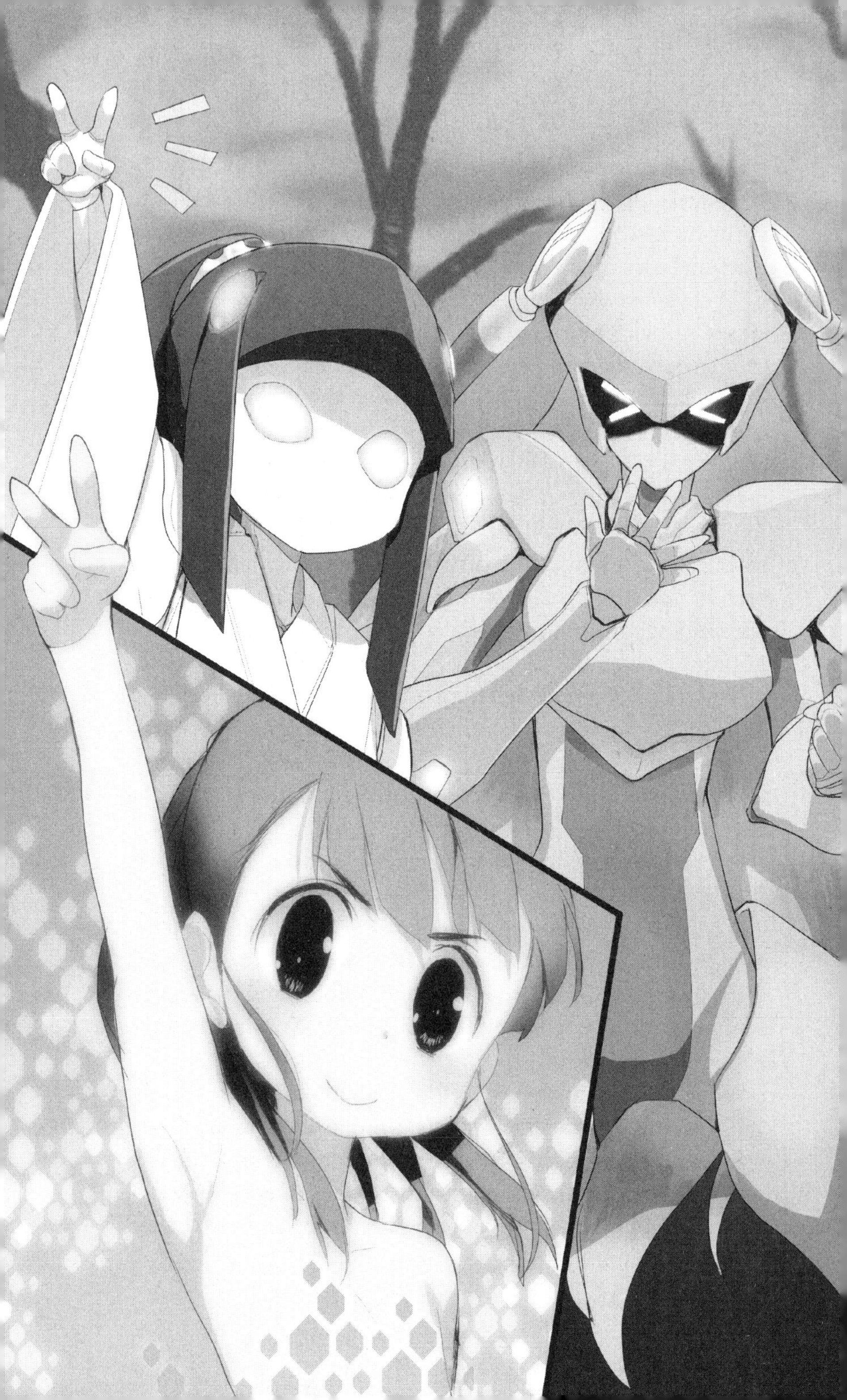

Shrugging, Cassis returned to her own camp, while Ardor Maiden stood up tall and announced in a clear voice, "Now then, I, Ardor Maiden, shall assume the role of this meeting's chair."

"No objections," Niko stated.

"Please and thank you." Kuroyukihime nodded, and the two leaders stepped back to their respective camps.

Even with the gazes of the forty or so people gathered there turned on her, Utai showed no sign of shyness as she operated her Instruct menu to make some massive object materialize. Looking closely, Haruyuki saw that it was a single white wood panel about two meters tall and one meter wide. A square peg stretched out from the bottom to push into the earth.

"Wh-what is *that*?" Haruyuki muttered.

"Notice board, extra large," Magenta Scissor leaned forward to reply. "Use it for notices and stuff just like you'd expect."

"H-huh. So they sell stuff like that in the shop?" Haruyuki said.

"But looks like Maiden's using it for a different purpose," Magenta added.

And indeed, Utai next produced an excessively thick and long brush, which was apparently automatically charged with black ink, before brandishing it like a sword and dragging it quickly across the new board. The words she spelled out across the top right were:

PROMINENCE   LEGION MERGER MEETING
NEGA NEBULUS

"Ooh…," came the excited murmuring, mainly from the Prominence side. And with the agenda written down in black and white, the merger, a relatively rare phenomenon in the Accelerated World, instantly took on a feeling of reality, and the tension at the venue increased palpably.

But Utai, the youngest of all of them, showed no signs of shrinking and instead set her brush to work once more. After dividing the space on the left side of the board into three large sections, she wrote at the tops of the sections YEA, CONDITIONAL YEA, and NAY.

Utai then put the brush down and turned around to speak, her voice carrying across the meeting space. "As you are all aware, Prominence and Nega Nebulus concluded a truce approximately six months ago, in January of this year. But this was at best an agreement not to attack the other's territory, and essentially no large-scale exchange has taken place between the Legions. More than a few members are seeing each other for the first time here at this meeting, and I believe that some among us will not immediately be able to agree to the merger of our two Legions, even for the sake of the greater mission of a united front against the White Legion. Thus, I would first like you all to consider whether you are in favor of the merger, if you have conditions, or if you are opposed."

Utai managed to get this frighteningly lengthy speech out without stumbling even once, which so deeply impressed Haruyuki that he very nearly missed what she had to say next.

"I ask that all members of Nega Nebulus in favor of the merger please raise your hands and give your names."

Everyone around him swiftly raised their hands, so Haruyuki hurriedly thrust his own into the air. When he gave his name—"I'm Silver Crow!"—after Kuroyukihime, Fuko, and Akira, there were some exclamations from the red side—"What?" "That guy?"—but Chiyuri drowned them out with her own cheerful voice. Then the three members of the Petit Paquet group—Shihoko, Satomi, and Yume—stated their names, but that's where the naming ended, so he hurriedly looked back and saw that Takumu and Rui had not raised their hands.

Before he had the time to be surprised, Utai had finished writing down the names of nine people, including her own, in the YEA column. "Now then, those of you who agree conditionally, raise your hands."

Now Takumu and Rui swiftly lifted their hands into the air and gave their names—"Cyan Pile," "Magenta Scissor."

While Utai was writing these down, Haruyuki asked quietly, "H-hey, Takumu. What's with the conditions?"

"Simple stuff," his childhood friend responded briefly. "I'll tell you later."

Takumu's reply left him no opening to pursue the question, so he was forced to turn to the front again just as Utai was lowering her pen.

"That's everyone from Nega Nebulus, then. With myself included, that's nine yeas and two conditional yeas. Next I'll ask the members of Prominence in favor of the merger to raise your hands and give your names."

The instant she was done speaking, Niko thrust her right hand into the air. "Scarlet Rain."

She was followed, thankfully, by all three members of the Triplex.

"Blood Leopard."

"Cassis Moose."

"Thistle Porcupine."

Haruyuki focused on trying to remember all the duel avatars who shouted their names one after another.

"Mustard Salticid!" A slender F-type with a vivid mustard color.

"Moss Moth." A dull-green M-type with large antennas.

"Navy Lobster." A shrimplike M-type covered in heavy dark-blue armor.

"Carnelian Alpheus." This was a similarly shrimplike M-type, but he was more stylish, and only his right hand was excessively large.

The next duel avatar was an opponent known to Haruyuki. "Peach Parasol!" A light-peach F-type carrying a large umbrella-shaped Enhanced Armament. She was one of the group of three who had come to attack Suginami in the Territories at the end of the previous month. Although he was pretty sure she was a veteran member from the days of the previous Red King, Red Rider, he guessed that she was agreeing to the merger because of that fight.

Even while his mind wandered, the hands kept going up.

"Persimmon Monk." A tall M-type in a long robe.

"Carrot Turret!" A small F-type the color of carrots, just as her name suggested.

"Aconite Archer." An M-type equipped with a crossbow the same bluish purple as his armor.

"Hypericum Cheerer. ♪" A pale-yellow F-type with small wings on her back.

"Ochre Prison…" A yellowish-brown M-type with massive claws. He had attacked Suginami with Peach.

"Malachite Hex." A dark-green F-type with a marble-like pattern on the surface of her smooth armor.

"Cantal Tank!" A midsize M-type with fibrous brown armor.

"Elinvar Governor." A slender M-type whose head was a complicated machine.

"Brick Block!" A reddish-brown M-type whose entire body was made up of square bricks.

Here a white smoke suddenly erupted from the Promi ranks, and colorful laser lights flashed, so Haruyuki gulped in surprise at what appeared to be a sneak attack. But it wasn't. From beyond the smoke, three dazzling avatars had no sooner bounded forward than they were giving their names in adorable voices.

"Freeze Tone!"

"Cream Dream!"

"Blaze Heart!"

And then in unison, """We aaare…Heliosphere!"""

Snap! The instant they settled into their respective poses, the lasers danced and flashed even more brilliantly, and Haruyuki reflexively started clapping. To his right he heard Satomi clapping too and shouting, "Amazing! Helios!"

He took a few steps over to her. "H-Helios…What's that?"

"You don't know, Corvus? They're basically the second- or third-most-popular idol group in the entire Accelerated World! Their song cards sell like hotcakes!"

"…Second or third…" Which meant there was at least one

idol group even more popular, but he decided not to follow that thread at the moment and turned his gaze forward again.

Blaze Heart, striking a pose on the right side of the group, was the fire user who had challenged them in the Territories with Peach Parasol and Ochre Prison, and at the time he'd actually thought she seemed sort of "idol-ish," but he'd had no idea that she really *was* an idol.

I'll have to grab one of their song cards. But wait. Where do they even sell song cards? As he ruminated on this new puzzle, the threesome released their poses and stepped back, and with that, the yeas had spoken.

Utai neatly jotted down every name. "Thank you very much. That's twenty-one yeas. Now I'd ask for the conditional yeas to speak."

Immediately a new voice carried across the stage. "Spruce Brevis!" A brown M-type with enormous eye lenses.

"Cinnamon Palaemon." A light-brown F-type with excessively long arms.

"Paprika Capriiiice." A small vivid-orange F-type.

"Beet Beat." A reddish-purple M-type with roundly swollen arms.

"Lavender Downer…" A light-purple F-type equipped with a costume that looked exactly like a school uniform.

"Amber Captor." A small F-type about the same size as Niko with semitransparent armor in an amber color, just as her name suggested.

"Straw Barrier." A large M-type in armor like bundles of thin, pale yellow tubes.

"Furs Stick." An M-type that resembled Straw Barrier in form and texture, but his entire body was wrapped in even thicker brown sticks.

Three duel avatars raised their hands together, looking very much like a team somehow. He sensed a faint ripple in Akira's flowing-water armor when they appeared, but he didn't get the chance to ask her why.

"Vermillion Vulcan." An M-type with dark-red armor carrying an Enhanced Armament like a large auto-cannon in both hands.

"Carmine Cannon." A tall F-type whose armor was indeed a very pure red.

"Maroon Motor." An M-type with purple-red armor and a massive cylinder on his back.

Here the hands stopped, and Utai turned around. "Thank you very much. We have eleven conditional yeas. Now, finally...those of you who are opposed to the merger, please."

Haruyuki thought there wouldn't be anyone opposed at this late stage. But one person pushed aside his long cloak and thrust his hand up high into the air. There was no mistake—it was the boy in the wide-brimmed hat who had proposed the change to Battle Royale mode and gotten rid of the Plague stage's poison mist with a single shot.

"Iodine Sterilizer!! Even if I am entirely alone, I am opposed!" The hat-wearing owner of the cool nickname Stronger Name proudly announced his dissenting opinion and then lowered his hand.

Utai scribbled his name in the NAY column. "Thank you very much, everyone. Totaling the votes from both Legions, we have thirty yeas, thirteen conditional yeas, and one nay. Which means that the majority agree to the merger, but as the chair of this meeting, I believe it would be best to discuss all objections thoroughly so that we can all come to an agreement. Is there anyone who objects to the proceedings thus far?"

"I object!" The hand that immediately snapped up was that of the lone nay voter, Iodine Sterilizer.

"Please go ahead, Iodine."

The small boy sprang forward and spoke loudly, his voice surprisingly adult. "Just as I said before, I am opposed to the merger of Promi and Negabu, and I have no intention of being turned through discussion! Or rather, if any opinions are swayed here, it will be that of the conditional yeas!"

"Well, yeah, I guess it would be," Chiyuri muttered, and a few people around her nodded, including Haruyuki.

"If you don't mind," the meeting chair replied calmly, "could you explain why you are opposed, Iodine?"

"I have every intention of doing so! Listen! The sole reason that I am opposed..." Here, Dine paused, and then for some reason he snapped a finger and pointed at Haruyuki. "...is because not only will the ceasefire not end, but we will merge, and then I will never be able to truly fight Silver Crow and at last stop his bid for the throne of Antidote King!"

Silence fell over the venue, and Haruyuki whirled his head around, as if to confirm that he was the only Burst Linker there named Silver Crow. "Wh-whaaaaat?! I-I'm not making a bid for anything like that! No one's ever called me Antidote King, not once!" he shouted, sounding a bit put out.

"Shut uuuuuup!!" Dine roared back immediately, brandishing a fist as he whirled around. "Now, I have always despised silver antibacterial goods, antiperspirants, and the like! They say the antibacterial spectrum is broad, despite its having essentially no germicidal properties—they're just selling a stylish image!"

"I-I'm telling you, I've never made a selling point of germicidal power or anything!"

"You! Are! A! Liar!!"

This kid will probably really hit it off with Ash when the Legions merge. Or hate his guts. One of the two, Haruyuki thought, half in an attempt to escape from the reality before him.

Dine snapped a finger out at him once more before making an unexpected claim. "Don't tell me you forgot your declaration when we fought before in Chiyoda Ward! 'Poison doesn't work on me,' you said! 'I'm silver!' you said!"

"Wh-what?! I—I said that?! I dunno." Haruyuki frantically rummaged through his memory.

"You did say that," Aqua Current whispered.

"Huh? H-how do you know that, Curren?"

"Well, we were on a tag team together."

TEAM FLOWER

Lavender Downer

Hypericum Cheerer

Aconite Archer

TEAM STONE

Amber Captor

Malachite Hex

Ochre Prison

TEAM IRON

Elinvar Governor

Cantal Tank

Iodine Sterilizer

TEAM PIGLET

Furs Stick

Straw Barrier

Brick Block

TEAM IDOL (HELIOSPHERE)

Cream Dream

Freeze Tone

Blaze Heart

TRIAD (TEAM ARTILLERY)

Maroon Motor

Carmine Cannon

Vermillion Vulcan

Red Legion
MEMBER LIST

Legion Master
Scarlet Rain

TRIPLEX (TEAM BEAST)

Thistle Porcupine

Cassis Mousse

Blood Leopard

Moss Moth

Spruce Brevis

Mustard Salticid

TEAM INSECT

Cinnamon Palaemon

Carnelian Alpheus

Navy Lobster

TEAM SHRIMP

TEAM FRUIT

Persimmon Monk

Peach Parasol

(Cherry Rook) (Eliminated)

TEAM VEG

Beet Beat

Carrot Turret

Paprika Caprice

Haruyuki's memory finally cleared. "Oh!"

It had been last November, back when he'd just gone up to level two. Due to a careless level-up, he'd been in a seriously tight spot, his points very nearly exhausted, so he'd hired the lone bouncer in the Accelerated World, The One, aka Aqua Current—although he hadn't known at the time that she was one of Nega Nebulus's Four Elements—and had gotten her help in tag-team matches in Chiyoda Ward so he could get his points back up into the safe zone.

The first of those fights had been a Corroded Forest stage, covered in poisonous bogs, where Haruyuki had taken on the formidable electricity user Nickel Doll. After he had dragged her into the poison bog with him, he had indeed said, "I'm silver. Poison doesn't work on me!"

"Oh…S-sorry, Dine." Haruyuki hung his head. "I *did* say that."

"So you *finally* remember!" One hand still aimed squarely at Haruyuki, the avatar in the wide-brimmed hat waved his other hand around and around. "Once I heard about this little incident, I decided that in a duel one day, I would make it perfectly clear which of us was fit to sit on the throne of the Antidote King! And yet, before I got my chance, we suddenly had a ceasefire with Negabu! And *now*, after I've waited a full six months to be free of these terrible chains, I'm faced with a Legion *merger*?! What about my disinfectant soul? What about the fire that burns so brightly within me?!"

It was a powerful speech, befitting the mega-mech name of the avatar, and Haruyuki was dumbstruck for a moment.

"Uh. Um." He raised one hand. "You can have your Antidote King throne…I never wanted it to begin with…"

"Don't! Mesu! Wizu! Me!!" Setting the question of pronunciation aside, Dine's English was at least more grammatically correct than Ash's. "In the Accelerated World! You can win nothing without a fight!! I must trounce you utterly in a fierce duel before I can stand tall and claim the title of Antidote Kiiiiiiiing!!"

"So what do you want me to do?" Haruyuki muttered.

Kuroyukihime and Fuko shook their heads in exasperation.

"Stronger hasn't changed a bit, hmm?" The girl in black sighed.

"Not a bit," the girl in white agreed. "Looks like he still hasn't let go of that fight."

"Um, Master? What do you mean, 'that fight'?" Haruyuki asked in a small voice.

Fuko rolled her wheelchair back a little. "Iodine lost his nickname after losing to a certain Burst Linker way back when."

"Huh? You mean Stronger Name?"

"Yes and no." Fuko frowned slightly. "To be precise, he became Stronger after losing that fight. His opponent at the time also said they would let him have whatever nickname he wanted."

"Uh...uh-huh..." He didn't get the whole story, but it was painfully clear that Iodine Sterilizer had always been this kind of character, and Haruyuki sighed.

The chair then offered him a life raft. "Iodine, if your objective of fighting Silver Crow is achieved, will you also agree to the merger?" asked the shrine maiden with black hair, one of the top-five cutest duel avatars as far as Haruyuki knew.

"W-well." Dine stiffened up for a moment before cocking his head at an uncertain angle. "That's more-or-less fine, I guess."

"I understand. In that case, how about we do this?" Utai turned to face Haruyuki directly. "C, I do realize this is a bother, but since the mode is Battle Royale, could you possibly fight Dine right now?"

"Wha...whaaaaat?!" he squealed, and he looked around at his comrades. But from Kuroyukihime to Chiyuri to Choco to Magenta Scissor, they were nodding in agreement without exception.

In that case, he thought, and he turned to Niko and Pard, but here, too, all he got was a shrug from the leopard avatar as if to say *SRY* and a sword hand slashing through the air from the Red King.

Meanwhile, the remaining thirty-two members of Prominence—the yeas and the conditional yeas—banded together.

"Oh! That'd be great!"

"I totally want to see the Antidote Battle!"

"I came all the way to Naka-One, after all. Gotta get a little bang for my buck!"

They were all cheering.

This *is why I didn't want to switch modes!* Haruyuki groaned inwardly, but he knew there was nowhere for him to run now. He wasn't the least bit interested in the nickname Antidote King—in fact, he'd only heard of it that day, so there was no need for him to win the duel in that regard.

The real issue was that the place was brimming with the powerful warriors on the Prominence side, beginning with the Triplex across from him. If he went easy and tried to lose, they'd see through that right away and condemn him—*You dishonor the spirit of the duel!*—and then the Legion merger would fall apart. Or at least it was certainly possible that things could go that way. In other words, if he accepted the duel, he would have to fight with everything he had, in a way that wouldn't embarrass Nega Nebulus, given that he would be its proxy in front of this large crowd.

He stood frozen to the spot, feeling the virtual cold sweat on his avatar body beneath his armor.

Kuroyukihime took a step back next to him and raised the sword of her right hand. The sharp tip was enveloped in a warm light, and then with a faint snapping sound it separated into five fingers. She gripped his hand tightly with this Incarnate hand and brought her face mask in close.

"Just have fun with it, Silver Crow. Not a single person here bears you any ill will. Iodine simply wants a real fight with you, since he considers you a rival. And you are a Burst Linker; you have accepted a challenge in the Accelerated World. In which case..."

"The only thing to do is give it all I've got, right?" he replied to his swordmaster, and the tension in his body melted gently away.

Right. The eleven members of Nega Nebulus, the thirty-three people in Prominence, they were all the same: Burst Linkers. They all truly loved the game Brain Burst, the duel, and they were all there because they wanted to protect it. Haruyuki was no different. In which case there was no reason to be afraid.

All he had to do was give the fight everything he had, just like always, and be happy if he won and annoyed if he lost—that was enough.

He squeezed Kuroyukihime's hand for a mere instant before releasing it and taking a few steps forward, away from his comrades. "I understand, Iodine!" he called. "I accept your challenge!"

"All right! That's how it's gotta be!" Dine shouted energetically, and he grabbed the brim of his hat with his right hand and the collar of his cloak with his left. *Fwp! Fwp!* These were peeled away to reveal Iodine Sterilizer's true form.

"Huh?!" Haruyuki cried out the second he saw this.

Because Dine's duel avatar was absolutely nothing like a mega mech. The torso was cylindrical, with a few indentations, and thin limbs and a tapered tube of a head were attached. The body was a rich brown, while the head and limbs were a vivid red. The coloring was that of a long-range type, but Haruyuki hadn't the first clue about what kind of attack would come. Plus, he got the feeling that the torso and head looked a lot like something he was very familiar with, but he couldn't remember exactly what that was.

I should've asked someone what iodine *and* sterilizer *mean,* he said to himself, but that was crying over spilled milk at this point. He would just have to suss out his opponent's strengths and weaknesses during the battle.

The members of both Legions retreated to the walls of the buildings around the park to get some serious distance from Haruyuki and Dine facing off against each other. Only Utai remained.

She cocked her head to one side as if realizing something. "That reminds me, Iodine. You took that blow from Rain earlier so that you could eliminate the poison cloud from the stage. Do you really want to start in that condition?"

She was exactly right. Narrowing his eyes, Haruyuki could see where the energy bullet had grazed Dine's shoulder armor.

But Stronger raised his thumb in a theatrical gesture. "It's! No! Problemo!"

"I understand. Well, then..." Utai nodded and held her right hand above her head. "In this corner, Iodine Sterilizer of Prominence. In the opposite, Silver Crow of Nega Nebulus. And now...begin the duel!!"

Fwsh! Utai brought her hand down.

Dine instantly closed the distance between them, defying Haruyuki's expectations. He was a red type, so his coming to challenge a metal color—fundamentally suited to close-range combat—to a fistfight meant that either he was excessively confident in his fighting abilities or he simply didn't think too much of Haruyuki's abilities.

Even as these thoughts flickered in a corner of his mind, Haruyuki instinctively dropped into a ready position. Picking up on the state of hostilities, the system automatically displayed a larger version of Dine's health gauge in the top right of his view. The level beside his name was six, the same as Silver Crow's. This made the idea of losing even more unpalatable.

But Dine's first attack caught him off guard nonetheless.

"Take! Diss!!" he shouted in English as he thrust out his right hand, five fingers splayed. He was too far away for his fist to actually hit Haruyuki, but then a brown mist jetted from the nozzle in the center of his palm.

Haruyuki had no way to dodge and took the mist squarely in the face. Suddenly he was blinded, and an intense odor took his breath away. Duel avatars did not require oxygen, and they could fight underwater or in outer space, but the naked body of the avatar beneath the armor had the sensation of breathing. So when that sensation was obstructed with a scent or an attack, the body reflexively stopped moving momentarily.

Recovering from his momentary stiffening, Haruyuki hurried to wipe his mirrored goggles clean and tried to leap back, but Dine had already slipped in close.

"Smash!!" He launched a middle kick together with an American-style cry and caught Haruyuki squarely in the right side. Without pausing for breath, he followed with a right overhand punch.

Haruyuki just barely slipped past this and kept moving to the right diagonally before somersaulting to put some distance between them.

As he looked back, he checked that he hadn't been hit with some kind of de-buff when he was showered in the brown mist, but he found no ongoing damage or disorder in any of his senses. His health gauge, however, was down over 5 percent from the kick.

So then what exactly was that brown liquid with the painful scent Dine was shooting? The question popped up in his head, but the answer came to him from an unexpected place.

Dine's torso, which had indeed been a rich brown at the start of the battle, had turned a semitransparent gray around the shoulders. Haruyuki could make out the hazy shape of the very slender avatar body inside. And the border between the brown and the semitransparent areas rippled with Dine's movements.

Is it a liquid?

Was the semi-transparent cylindrical body filled with *liquid*? And the level dropped when he shot it out of his hand?

"Ah...Ah!" Haruyuki finally remembered what Dine's torso reminded him of. The old-school gargle in the first-aid kit at home. The painful stench when he'd been showered in the liquid was exactly what the gargle smelled like.

"You look like...Isodi—"

"Stooooooooop!" Dine thrust out a hand to check Haruyuki, and he snapped his mouth shut. The "Antidote King" held up an index finger and waved it back and forth in an affected manner. "That is the brand name; you're not allowed to say it. If you really must, use the ingredient name: *povidonyodo.*"

"*P-povidonyodo...?*" Haruyuki stumbled over the unfamiliar term.

"In English it's *povidone-iodine.*"

"Huh...So then..." Haruyuki stared at Dine's head, which looked exactly like the cap of the gargle bottle. "Iodine...The tincture... That's the element?!"

"Yes!" Dine was triumphant.

"S-so then *sterilizer* means..." Here, Haruyuki faltered again.

"I'll do you a big favor and help you out," Dine offered smugly. "A sterilizer is basically a disinfectant. In other words!" *Da-da-dum!* He struck a cool pose before announcing with panache, "Under the name Iodine Sterilizer! I disinfect all with this fine element! I am the most powerful antidote in the Accelerated World! Ha-ha!"

*Ha-ha, okay, but still...*Dumbfounded for the nth time, Haruyuki somehow managed to rouse his battle spirit once again. He had absolutely no interest in the Antidote King title, and Dine was apparently less obsessed with the result of the duel than with the process of the fight itself. Whatever his reasons, now that Haruyuki had accepted the duel as a representative of Nega Nebulus, he had to muster 100 percent of his strength and fight.

"Uh, um...Iso—I mean, povidone-iodine gargle's been good to me in the past. But my color name is silver, so I can't be beat when it comes to natural disinfectant power! I'll have you yield the title of Antidote King right here and now!!"

The challenge that left his mouth was somewhat random, but it seemed to hit home with Iodine. The horizontal eye lenses embedded in the cap-shaped head shone with yellow light, and the brown fluid inside his body shuddered and shook.

"Well said." Dine nodded appreciatively. "It appears we'll

finally go head-to-head for real…but there's also the meeting to consider. So I'll settle this in five minutes!"

"Then three's plenty for me!" Haruyuki shouted as he leapt forward.

Dine's basic battle strategy was probably striking techniques mixed in with the blindfold of the disinfectant. It was hard to evade or defend against a liquid sprayed over a wide range, but as long as Haruyuki could just put up with the smell, the spray itself caused no damage. And if the amount of liquid in Dine's body decreased every time he jetted the disinfectant, he could use the technique only a limited number of times.

"Disinfect!" Dine shouted, and he shot iodine from his left hand.

Haruyuki held his breath and guarded his goggles with one hand as he charged into the mist.

"Hah!" He launched a left mid-kick, as if in retaliation for the earlier hit, and connected with Dine's torso.

His opponent was unsurprisingly determined and threw out a right straight punch in a counterattack, but Haruyuki could see clearly this time, so he was able to block this with ease. Dine immediately shot iodine from his right hand as well, but Haruyuki spun around and took this with his back, then moved into a backhanded blow from there. His fist hit hard along the side of Dine's cap head, and although he didn't quite make it spin round and round and fly off his body, the small, lightweight avatar did stagger back.

Now! Haruyuki charged, intending to decide this contest right then and there with a rush attack.

Still reeling, Dine shot off a front kick in desperation, but a kick with no weight behind it was nothing to fear. Haruyuki brushed this away with his left arm and closed in on his enemy.

Bomf! He felt an unpleasant shock in his arm. He'd completely guarded against Dine's kick, so at first he thought this was damage to the other avatar's leg. But that wasn't it—the strong metal armor that covered Silver Crow's left forearm was cracked and deeply dented. And the silver gleam had disappeared at some point; now it was so dull, it looked rusted...

"Wha—?!" Baffled, Haruyuki once again got some distance with a somersault. Standing up, he hurriedly checked his entire body and found that his arm wasn't the only part of him that was black now. Any part of his armor that had been exposed to Dine's disinfectant—chest, shoulders, probably back—had changed color.

"I-it's rusted?! How...?" Haruyuki was stunned.

"Well, of course," Dine replied evenly. "You were showered in my spray, after all."

"Hey!" he yelled back. "Y-you said that this was just some regular gargling fluid!"

"It is. It's just a little *concentrated*." Grinning, Dine continued, "So, Silver Crow, you're still in junior high?"

He frowned. "Why do you ask?"

"Because you don't appear to have studied iodine in school. Remember this well. Iodine, the main ingredient in my disinfectant, is a powerful corrosive to most metals. It can melt iron and silver, of course, but also even titanium and gold."

Haruyuki groaned involuntarily. Indeed, he had not yet learned that in school, and even if he had, he probably wouldn't have been able to deal with the situation on his first go. Dine's disinfectant was not a simple stinky, blinding spray, but rather a terrifying jet to exterminate metal colors. The offensive and defensive power of the blackened parts of his armor was already essentially zero. He would have to evade the spray and any blows completely while he dealt damage with his unharmed right fist and legs. And was that even possible against a fellow level six?

He unconsciously touched a hand to his hip and then yanked it away. He hadn't completely mastered *that* yet. He had plenty of other tricks up his sleeve before he was forced to turn to an immature technique. Even against an opponent who was apparently a metal color's natural enemy.

Given that he was so ill equipped to fight this enemy, the old

Haruyuki would have accepted that loss was inevitable, and there was a little of that in his head now. But now he had a conviction like a precious gem in his heart thanks to Kuroyukihime and the Four Elements, who had given him firm guidance when he dragged his feet; Takumu and Chiyuri, who never failed to cheer him on in hard times; Niko, Rin, and all his comrades; and the countless friendly rivals who'd joined him in fierce battle over and over…It was still small, and from time to time he nearly lost sight of it, but this gem was always there shining deep in his heart, and its name was courage. The courage to reveal his ugly, weak, awkward, pathetic self.

It was all right to lose. But he couldn't lose until he had squeezed out every drop of strength and wisdom in his bones and brains, until he'd layered struggle on top of effort.

He took a deep breath and readied himself once again, and perhaps sensing this change in Haruyuki, Dine suddenly grew serious and raised one hand. The spray nozzle in his palm caught Haruyuki in its sights like the barrel of a gun.

It seemed about 10 percent of the disinfectant in his torso was used up with every shot, so he had about 70 percent left. Meaning the tank would be emptied if he fired another seven times, but of course Dine already knew that. And then there was the pressing question of whether Dine's disinfectant would run out before Haruyuki's armor was completely corroded.

"It ends here!!" Haruyuki shouted, and he kicked at the ground. He closed the distance with a high-speed dash straight at his opponent.

Judging in an instant that this was not a feint, Dine thrust out his other hand as well and shot mist from both nozzles simultaneously.

Haruyuki was definitely not going to be able to evade this double cloud. Instead he abruptly decelerated as he deployed Silver Crow's greatest weapon, tucked away on his back—his silver wings. The vanishingly thin metal fins were flecked with black, perhaps because some bit of the disinfectant had penetrated his armor, but the damage was not such that they had lost their function. Bracing his feet firmly, he faced forward and released his propulsive force for a counterspray of sorts.

Pwah! The air twisted violently, and the brown mist was instantly pushed back before Haruyuki's eyes.

"Hyoya—?!" Dine let out a shriek that was maybe English, maybe Japanese, as he tried to protect his face, but he was a touch too late. The disinfectant glommed on to his eye lenses. "It buuuuurns!!" he yelped, rubbing his eyes.

Of course, Haruyuki did not let this opportunity pass. "Unh…Yaah!" Reversing the thrust of his wings, he came into a full-speed, low-level dash. He stabbed at Dine's torso with a left toe kick, digging into him. He heard the dull roar of impact and saw the semitransparent armor buckle inward over five centimeters. The intense shock finally did real damage to his enemy's health gauge.

The way Haruyuki usually fought, he would normally bring it home here with an aerial combo using the wings on his back, but it was too dangerous to fight this opponent with his wings left deployed. Hurriedly storing them on his back, he once again put some distance between them.

"As if I would let you get away!" Dine crossed both arms and then, his eyes shining bright red, cried out, "Acid Mist!!"

Special attack!! Haruyuki tried desperately to escape the range of the technique, but it was a waste of his energy. The bright-red mist that shot from Dine's hands spread across the stage with a force several tens of times greater than that of his regular spray to swallow Haruyuki completely.

From far, far away, he could hear the members of Prominence shouting.

"Hey! Whoa! Don't drag the Gallery into this!"

"Get back! Get out of the way! You'll take damage!"

But Haruyuki didn't have the mental leeway to pay the voices any mind. Before his eyes, his armor darkened as it touched the red mist, and his health gauge dropped vigorously while a burning pain danced across his nerves.

He assumed from the name that the technique scattered a powerful acid over a wide range. Even if he wanted to try to outrun it, the mist was steadily melting away even the ground, which was as a rule indestructible, leaving behind a viscous sludge that trapped his feet. The special attack was simple, but the effect was great and terrifying. His only remaining means of escape was his flight ability, but if he deployed his wings in this mist, the already injured metal fins might very well take decisive damage.

So what would the high rankers of Nega Nebulus do at a time like this?

Kuroyukihime always moved by hovering, so the viscous sludge wouldn't affect her. She would escape the acidic cloud in an instant and rain painful counterattacks down on her enemy.

Fuko's wheelchair might not be able to move because of the sludgy earth, but she had the Enhanced Armament Gale Thruster. All she would have to do is fire those boosters with their sturdy armor to break free of the mist.

Utai had no particular special means of movement, but she *did* have an incredibly powerful fire attack, befitting her nickname Shrine Maiden of the Conflagration. With one shot of her special-attack Flame Torrents, she could make anything evaporate, including this mist.

For Akira, the acid mist most likely would have no meaning. Her flowing-water armor could purify impurities, although it might take a bit of time, so she would have been able to neutralize the acidic mist without any problems.

Unfortunately, Haruyuki couldn't copy any of those strategies. In which case, what would the final member of the former Four Elements do—the Anomaly, Graphite Edge?

The dual swordsman had poured all the potential of his duel avatar into his two swords, to the point where Fuko had declared that he was more sword than person. As far as Haruyuki knew, the avatar himself had absolutely no special abilities. His armor was also thin, and it didn't seem that he would have any particular way of handling this mist, but Haruyuki absolutely could not picture a scenario in which Graphite Edge just stood there and let his health gauge drop until he eventually collapsed. He would casually, lazily come up with another way of escaping that no one else would even dream of.

Right. Graphite Edge'd probably...

A chemical reaction flashed in his mind, a mix of his own knowledge and this idea, and fireworks went off inside his head. If the sky was no good, then he had to go...

"Down!!" He lined up the fingers of his right hand and stretched them out straight before plunging them down at his feet with everything he had. Silver Crow's sword hand, sharp like an actual sword, stabbed deep into the acid-softened earth of the stage, up to his elbow.

Of course, he couldn't escape the acid mist like this, and his health gauge continued to drop steadily. However, the instant he yanked his arm back, something gushed forcefully out of the hole he left behind—a brilliant blue gas, the poison mist of the Plague stage.

The stage's terrain effects were random jets of poisonous mist from the earth below. So then, if you made a hole in the ground, you could maybe make it happen on purpose. And then maybe you could get rid of Dine's acidic mist in a few seconds with the force of that jet. This was the basic idea of Haruyuki's plan.

He was right on the mark, and the red of the acidic mist was replaced by the blue of the new poison one. His armor was rusted, so the silver's antidote effects were not activated, meaning this mist would no doubt de-buff him in some new way. If it rendered his special-attack gauge useless, his gamble would end in total failure, but what came over Haruyuki was the sensation of all sound receding. The mist most likely caused an aural obstruction... which likely wouldn't have any effect on what he was about to do.

"—!!" Letting forth a soundless battle cry, he fully deployed the wings on his back. Now that the corrosive mist had been pushed back, there was no risk of damage to his metallic fins. The poison mist was too thick for him to see the sky, but he turned his head back in the opposite direction of the ground and vibrated his wings with all his might. The viscous gray liquid holding his legs stretched out like rubber, impeding his takeoff, but only for an instant. The adhesive power of the half-melted ground was no match for the thrust of the silver wings Haruyuki had so carefully cultivated, and his avatar shot up into the sky.

He cut through the concentration of poison mist and ascended with ever-greater speed. He couldn't hear the wind in his ears or the voices of the Gallery below because of the obstruction to his hearing. In a silent world, he raced up toward a yellowish-green sky.

Once he was over a hundred meters up, he spread his wings and abruptly decelerated, shifting into hovering mode as he looked downward. On the east side of the park, the crimson acid mist that had shot from Dine's hands started to mix with the blue poisonous mist that had jetted up from the ground in complex patterns, giving shape to a chaotic situation.

The silhouette whirling his head around on the edge of the doubly poisoned area had to be Iodine himself. Apparently, he didn't take damage from the acid mist he produced, but because he could no longer hear after touching the blue mist, he hadn't noticed Haruyuki shooting up into the sky.

In contrast with Dine's robust health gauge, still at 70 percent, Haruyuki's was at 30. This was his last chance to turn this fight around.

"Here...we...gooooooo!!" He could barely hear his own voice, but he shouted with all he had anyway as he plummeted like a shooting star. The tip of his right leg, extended like a lance, compressed the air, making it glow red. Even his blocked ears could faintly pick up the high-pitched sound.

On the ground, Dine finally noticed it, too. He turned his head up. But a millisecond later, Haruyuki's fully powered dive kick stabbed into the body of the "Antidote King."

He wasn't aiming for the head, nor for the arms equipped with spray nozzles, but rather for the lower half of his body, where the armor had been dented by his earlier toe kick.

Haruyuki could hardly hear anything due to the intensity of the impact racing through his body. Silver Crow's sharp toes brilliantly cut through Dine's sturdy but damaged semitransparent armor, and the force of the collision sent the small avatar soaring high into the sky.

Having managed to land on his feet, Haruyuki immediately started running to the rear in order to escape the ever-expanding poison mist area as he looked up at Dine in the air.

Dine was spinning around, likely screaming, while the remaining disinfectant spilled dramatically from the large hole in his body and fell as a brown rain. Haruyuki sped up to avoid the droplets, and once he passed under Dine, he turned and waited for his opponent in the place where he expected him to land.

After the direct hit from Haruyuki's drop kick, Iodine's health gauge had dropped to 50 percent, and he hadn't even touched the ground again before Haruyuki started in with his special attack Aerial Combo.

"Aaaaaaah!!" With a force that used up the remainder of his special-attack gauge, Haruyuki propelled himself with a short-distance thrust to assault the other avatar with a flurry of punches and kicks, showy techniques he normally didn't get to use in succession like this. Every last drop of disinfectant had spilled out of the hole in Dine's torso while he was ragdolling through the air, so Haruyuki had no need to worry about getting hit with the spray attack again. He charged Dine with all his pent-up frustration multiplied fivefold.

Naturally, Iodine wasn't simply allowing things to continue in this fashion; he tried to counterattack with sharp punches that showed he was accustomed to close combat, but because Haruyuki was floating in midair, he couldn't land a hit. Haruyuki

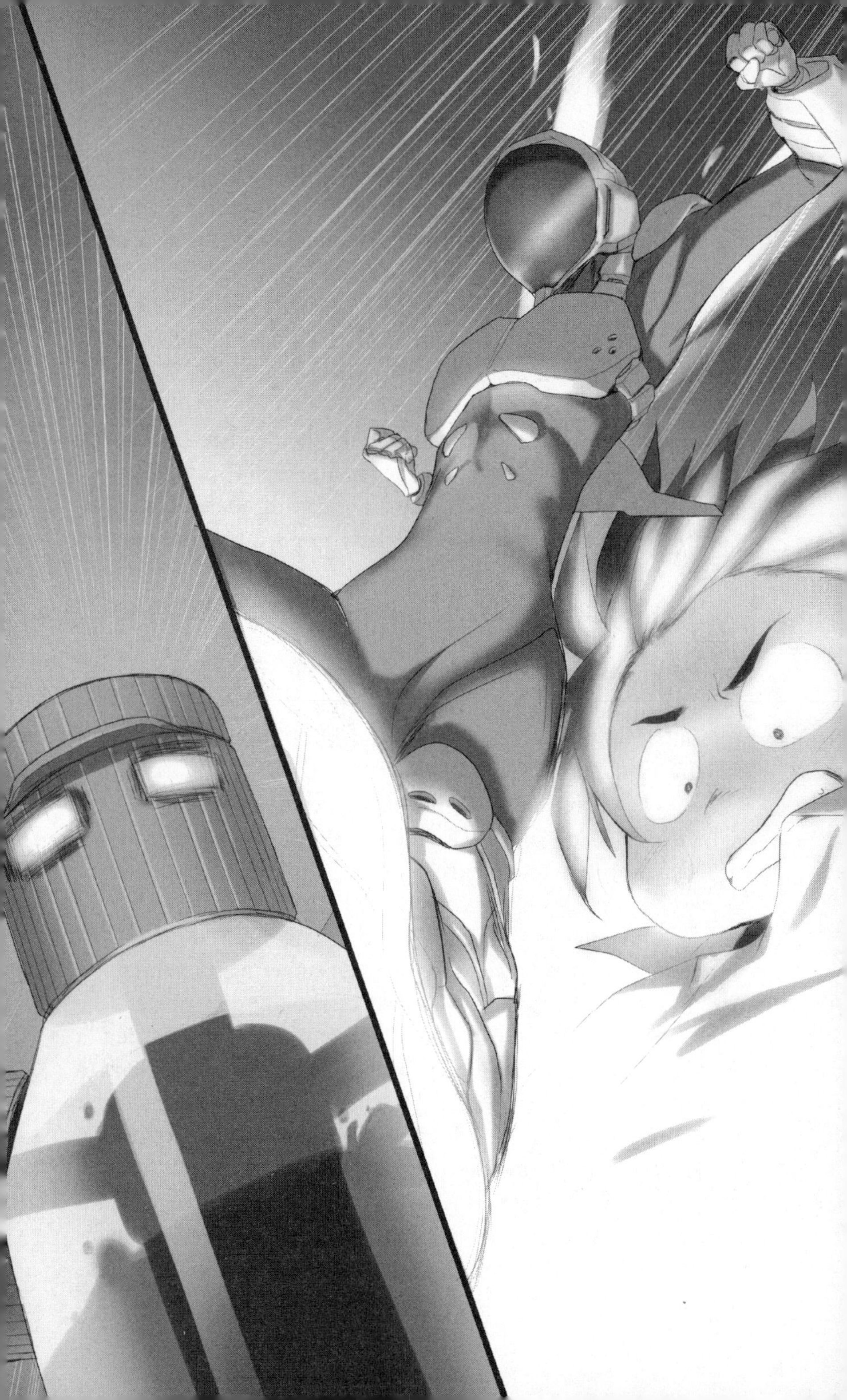

perhaps should have been on guard against the special attack Dine could use regardless of how much disinfectant he had left, but he had no intention of giving his opponent the luxury of an opening to shout the technique name.

Around the time when the other avatar's health gauge was down to 20 percent, the auditory block vanished, and he heard Dine groaning above the din of his machine gun–like blows.

"I—I won't be done in so easily!"

"Save it! This is my win!!" Haruyuki shouted back and began punching even faster to eat up the remainder of Dine's gauge.

"That's enough!!" A cool voice cut crisply through all the noise of the fight, and Haruyuki reflexively stopped his attack with a backward leap.

Dine dropped heavily to the ground, then quickly looked to the center of the park.

Raising one hand straight up into the air from the base of a large withered tree was Ardor Maiden, the referee for their match. The small shrine maiden brought her hand down. "That shall be the end of the fight. Both of you, please stop your attacks."

"O-okay." Haruyuki lowered his readied hands.

Dine also stood up slowly and then shook his head as if in disbelief. "Aah, you totally turned that around in an incredible way. Never dreamed you'd escape my Acid Mist like that."

"Uh. Th-thanks…" Haruyuki dipped his head in an unconscious bow, then looked to the rear, remembering something.

Although Dine's Acid Mist had essentially disappeared, the blue poison mist was still swirling around on the east side of the park. It would soon be picked up by the wind and start to move, and if anyone touched it, they wouldn't be able to hear anything anymore. The cloud would be quite an annoyance in the sense that it would obstruct the meeting.

Haruyuki was the one who had made the hole, so he felt a responsibility to dispose of it, but even his wings couldn't blow away a mass on that scale. As he panicked about what to do, Dine stepped up beside him.

"Don't worry. I'll take care of it with my special attack, since you were kind enough to charge my gauge for me there." He casually pushed his hands out. "Antidote Mist!"

Yellow liquid jetted from the nozzles in his hands and touched the blue poisonous mist. The area of contact glittered brightly as Dine's special attack purified the enormous cloud of poison in mere seconds.

"Nice fight!!"

"That was a great duel!!"

"Next time, you gotta fight me, too!!"

Cheers erupted from all sides, and Haruyuki hurriedly turned around to see the members of Prominence and Nega Nebulus standing chummily alongside one another on the second floor of the Central Park East building, which stretched out from east to west.

Iodine immediately raised both hands and responded to the cheers, so Haruyuki nervously followed suit as he asked the question that just now nagged at him. "Um, Iodine, so…what happens with the title of Antidote King?"

Dine glanced up to check both their health gauges and then shrugged dramatically. "No way around it, your gauge has more left in it. It's unfortunate, but I'll have to leave the title with you until our next duel." Then he abruptly raised his voice to twice as loud and announced, "Silver Crow! As of today, you are the Accelerated World's Antidote Kiiiing!!"

Whaaaa—?! Haruyuki screamed inwardly as Dine grabbed his hand and held it up high in the air. He hurriedly tried to yank it back down, but it was already too late. Waves of applause poured down from the East building, and all Haruyuki could do was bring a stiff smile to his face.

Once the impromptu duel was over, and the members of both Legions had assembled in the center of the park once more, they had fifteen minutes left on the clock.

The first to speak was Iodine Sterilizer himself. He turned

toward the chair, Utai, and smoothly declared, "Oh, I change my vote from nay to yea."

Even Utai froze for a moment before responding with a short "Understood." She sent the brush racing across the white wooden board, putting two lines through Dine's name in the Nay column and moving it to the Yea column before turning neatly on her heel. "So we have thirty-one yeas and thirteen conditional yeas. I would now like to hear the opinions of the conditional yeas... Could someone stand as your representative?"

"All right. I will," Haruyuki heard someone from the Prominence side say. He couldn't tell who the speaker was from the voice alone.

He stared curiously and saw an M-type avatar stand up hard enough to make the ground shake. He was easily the largest of any of the thirty-three members of Prominence. His fiery scarlet armor was thick, but didn't appear to be cumbersome, while the Gatling gun Enhanced Armament mounted on each arm looked quite powerful. Haruyuki was overwhelmed by the large avatar's obvious strength.

"That's the head of Prominence's Triad, V-Three, aka Vermillion Vulcan," Akira murmured in his ear.

"Tr-Triad?" he parroted. "There's more than just the Triplex?"

"They're the only members of the first Prominence executive branch who stayed in the Legion after the change of kings," she explained.

"So then they're close friends...of Red Rider?" He gulped hard, and almost as if sensing Haruyuki's gaze, Vermillion Vulcan turned his sharp eye lenses on him. Fortunately, "V3" soon shifted his gaze to look down at Utai before speaking in a dignified voice.

"I stand as the representative for the Prominence conditional yeas," he said, his voice grave. "Allow me to explain."

"Please go ahead, Vermillion." Utai ceded the floor.

"Well, then. To get straight to the point, the questions that concern us are who will be the new Legion Master and whether the Legion name will live on after the monthlong period of merger preparation."

"In other words, do you mean who will have the right to the Judgment Blow?" Utai asked, and when Vermillion nodded wordlessly, tension in the venue rose.

Haruyuki had reviewed how the system handled a Legion merger in Brain Burst just in case. When two Legion Masters with adjacent territory made a formal agreement and the merger was concluded in the system, a merger preparation period of thirty days began. During that time, it was possible to change the new Legion's name and the new Legion Master, and the two former Legion Masters both held the right to Judgment Blow. In other words, for thirty days, Kuroyukihime and Niko would both be able to Judge all members, which was a kind of fairness in its own way. But the instant the preparation period ended, the right to Judge would belong to the new Legion master alone, and the members of the Legion that person—most likely either Kuroyukihime or Niko—had not belonged to would be left with significant dissatisfaction and unease.

Vermillion Vulcan looked around before speaking again. "Of course, given that we have agreed to the merger, albeit with conditions, we don't suspect that this merger proposal is a trap or something similar. Hypothetically, if the Black King is the new Legion Master after the end of the preparation period, we don't expect that she will blindly Judge the members of the old Prominence. However…we never want to lose the master to whom we swore our loyalty ever again. We don't want to create the possibility that such a thing could happen, even in the worst case."

His words were calm and rational…and therefore dug deeply into Haruyuki's heart. The Black King standing in front of him now had been the one who took the head of the first Red King, Red Rider, the former master of the Triad's Vermillion Vulcan, and banished him for all time from the Accelerated World.

Vermillion hadn't called her out by name, but there had to be some among Prominence's veteran members who didn't trust Kuroyukihime—or perhaps even held a grudge against her.

Blaze Heart, Peach Parasol, and Ochre Prison, who had attacked Suginami in the Territories at the end of the previous month, were among those who didn't trust her. Through the intense battle with Haruyuki, Utai, and Akira and the trading of blows, they'd been able to communicate something to each other—and maybe that was why the three of them had agreed to the merger with no conditions, but he was sure they were still anxious about it.

Furthermore, in the middle of the fight with the ISS kit main body at Tokyo Midtown Tower, Kuroyukihime had apparently had a chance meeting with Red Rider's residual memory. She had accepted a message from him there and given it to Niko: "Thanks, it's up to you now." Hearing this, Niko had pressed her face to Pard's chest and sobbed like a small child. As he witnessed this, Haruyuki had felt that the succession of kingship from Red Rider to Scarlet Rain was completed, and this also facilitated Prominence's reconciliation with Kuroyukihime.

But at best that had been a moment shared among only the three of them. He couldn't imagine that Niko had told the Legion members the details, so it was no wonder that the veteran members still had reservations.

When he thought about it like that, it was practically a miracle that Iodine Sterilizer was the only one who had voiced any opposition to the merger (and the reason for that had had nothing to do with Red Rider). Even the conditional yeas had stopped at eleven people, with the other twenty-one announcing their unconditional agreement. Most likely, Niko and Pard had used every bit of persuasive power they had to win their comrades over.

If that was the case, then Haruyuki and his friends had to do whatever it took to win over Vermillion Vulcan and the other ten. But no matter how desperately he wanted to speak and persuade them, his feelings simply swirled formlessly inside him, never coalescing into words. There was no way Kuroyukihime would Judge the former Prominence members, especially Niko, after the Legion merger. It was easy to say that, but Vermillion and the others were probably looking for something more than words. Something they could believe in, a promise that would make everything all right.

Haruyuki was clenching his hands tightly as he stood rooted to the ground when a firm voice came from directly behind him.

"Please allow me to respond to Vermillion and the others." Takumu stepped forward without waiting for the chair's response and stopped about two meters away from the group. He turned his avatar, which was nearly as large as Vermillion's, directly toward the group of conditional yeas.

"Go ahead, Pile," Utai urged.

Takumu nodded slightly. "First of all, I'll state my own condition for agreement. I will agree to the merger only if all Prominence members agree to accept me as a member of the new Legion once you all hear what I'm about to say. If even one person refuses, then I will leave the Legion."

"Wh..." *What are you saying, Taku?!* Haruyuki very nearly shouted the real name of his best friend. But a hand reached out from behind and grabbed firmly onto his shoulder.

"Crow, hear him out," Magenta Scissor whispered in his ear. Her voice was quiet but very tense, and Haruyuki could only nod in response.

In the motionless Plague stage, the air itself stagnant, the only sound was Takumu's voice. "Nine months ago, when I belonged to Leonids, I used a backdoor program—a cheat tool given to me by my parent—and hid myself from the matching list while I attempted to hunt the Black King, Black Lotus."

It appeared there were some who hadn't known about the incident; a low murmuring rose up on the Prominence side. But Takumu stood tall and continued to speak clearly.

"Once this was revealed after Silver Crow defeated me, my parent was Judged by the Blue King and left the Accelerated World, but due to the mercy of Silver Crow and the Black King, I transferred to Nega Nebulus and have continued on as a Burst Linker, as you can see...And that was not my only crime. When I was caught in a real attack by a PK group, although it was to protect myself, I equipped an ISS kit and brought them all to total point loss with that power. I still have not atoned for these crimes. If there is even one person who thinks I should not be allowed to join the new Legion, I will gladly withdraw. That's my condition for agreement."

"......"

No one spoke for a while. The first to move was Magenta Scissor, another conditional yea. She put some strength into the hand that still rested on Haruyuki's shoulder and pushed forward, stepping away from the group to stand alongside Takumu.

"Will you let me say a few words, too?" she asked.

Utai nodded after a moment. "Please. Go ahead."

The tall avatar slowly bowed at the waist and then made her husky voice carry. "I'm sure some people know, but...I, Magenta Scissor, was the one who spread the ISS kits in southwestern Tokyo, centered in Setagaya. I gave Cyan Pile the ISS kit he used, and I sliced open the armor of many, including Mint Mitten and Plum Flipper, and forcibly parasitized them with the kits. If Cyan Pile's gonna make you question his crimes, then naturally, I gotta do the same."

Once again, excited chatter broke out on the Prominence side, louder than before.

This merger was being made so they could fight the Acceleration Research Society. The Society had stolen Niko's Enhanced Armament and created the ISS kits, and naturally, the members of Prominence had to be aware of this. Although Magenta had done what she had because of her own beliefs, the end result was that she had acted as a member of the Acceleration Research Society. It wouldn't be any wonder if the reaction she received was one of rejection.

But Haruyuki would never accept a scenario in which Takumu and Magenta had to leave Nega Nebulus in order to make the merger happen. He resolved to throw himself down on his hands and knees or do whatever he had to if there was even one person who raised their voice to say they should leave, and he waited for what would happen next with bated breath.

"Why would you tell us that? You didn't have to." The voice, severe like steel, was that of Vermillion Vulcan.

"That's..." Takumu tried to answer somehow, but then closed his mouth and hung his head slightly.

Vermillion's voice came again a few seconds later, and this time, it contained the hint of a smile. "You are absurdly serious, Cyan Pile, just like they say." The auto-cannon user, likely more of a veteran than either Niko or Pard, shrugged lightly. "Whatever crimes you and Magenta Scissor might have committed, if the people involved have forgiven you and welcomed you as comrades, then there's no need for us to say anything. After all, we're about to merge with the Legion led by the Black King, and she drove our former Red King to total point loss. So when you look at it that way, there's no point in reproaching you for such modest mistakes."

As he took in the silent Takumu, Vermillion's eyes shone sharply all of a sudden. His voice was powerful once more, shaking earth and air.

"However, the condition we put forward is still not fulfilled. In the event that the Black King becomes the new Legion Master, she could hurt our king once again to achieve her supreme goal of reaching level ten. We want you to show us proof of some kind that this will absolutely never happen."

Takumu now responded to the difficult problem Vermillion posed. He used his Instruct menu to materialize a silver card item, and this he held out to the other avatar. "This card is charged with all the Burst Points I got in the sudden-death duel with the PK group Supernova Remnant, along with the points

Magenta Scissor collected using the ISS kit. There are enough points for a Burst Linker who just hit level eight to go up to level nine."

The Red members erupted into whispers and murmurs louder than anything so far, and even Kuroyukihime, Fuko, and the others let out faint cries.

Although there were more than a few level eighters in the Accelerated World, there were a mere seven level niners. That was exactly why they were called kings, and everyone knew that the path to this place was endlessly long. Given the current ongoing peaceful stagnation of the mutual nonaggression pact among the major Legions, in practical terms, level nine was nearly impossible to reach. And yet the card before them was charged with enough points to topple the power balance of the Accelerated World; it shone so strongly even in the weak sunlight of the Plague stage that it was almost ominous.

Card still held out to Vermillion, Takumu opened his mouth again. "Those Remnant guys attacked a ton of Burst Linkers in the real world and built up this stock of dirty points through threats and violence. I definitely didn't want to use them, but I couldn't think of a safe way to get rid of them. So I decided to have Master—Black Lotus—hold on to them, but she told me that at some point, she was sure I would find the correct way to use them. So I should hang on to them until then. And now I've finally found that way."

Takumu took a few slow steps forward to stop in front of Vermillion.

"If Black Lotus or any of the members of the current Nega Nebulus betray you, please use these points and Judge their crime. They're dirty points, but…I think it would be acceptable to use them for righteous vengeance. And I'd ask…I want to be the first one you Judge."

"Of course, second would be me."

An almost grim determination bled into the calm voices of

both Cyan Pile and Magenta Scissor, and Vermillion didn't open his mouth right away. Takumu and Magenta's proposal couldn't guarantee the safety of the Red King with utter certainty. But although it would never happen, if Kuroyukihime decided to betray Niko and take her head, in that moment she would have to think little of Takumu and Magenta's lives.

Eventually, the auto-cannon user turned, armor clanging, and looked at Niko behind him, who had her arms crossed.

The Red King nodded without a word, then spoke in a voice that made her kingly majesty felt. "You hold on to that. And if you think the time to use it has come, use it."

But Vermillion shook his head ponderously. "No. If we were to seek vengeance for our king…there's someone more suitable than me." He took the silver card from Takumu's hand and walked over to the deputy standing at Niko's side, Blood Leopard.

"Leopard. Keep this safe." Vermillion spoke as though he was ceding a privilege to her and asking if she was prepared to accept it.

But Pard nodded evenly and took it with zero fuss. Spinning it around with the fingers of her right hand, she opened her Instruct menu with her left and tossed it into storage. "K."

Hearing this simple reply, Vermillion turned back toward Takumu. "Cyan Pile, Magenta Scissor, and the Black King, Black Lotus…you have indeed shown us your intentions. We shall deem our condition fulfilled with this. I and the other ten members change our conditional yea and leave the matter of the provisional Master and Legion name to the two kings."

Takumu also stood up tall. "Similarly, our condition has been fulfilled. I also change my vote to yea."

"I'm on board, too," Magenta added.

All three nodded at each other slightly and then turned on their heels and returned to their respective camps.

Standing at the white wooden board, Utai lifted the massive brush and quickly crossed out the names of the thirteen people in the SMALL CAPS CONDITIONAL YEA column before rewriting them all in the YEA column.

"With that, all forty-four people gathered here are now in agreement!" Utai sounded proud somehow, and the sound of applause rose up out of nowhere to instantly melt together and fill the stage.

Haruyuki earnestly clapped his own hands together while he glanced over at Takumu standing a ways off. There was no expression on the face mask with its narrow slits, but even so, it looked to him like the face of his childhood friend was shining with relief and satisfaction. Magenta Scissor, on the other side of Takumu, looked the same, and he wondered when exactly the two of them had met to set this up.

As Haruyuki's thoughts slid in this direction, Kuroyukihime began to hover soundlessly, and Niko took large strides forward from the Prominence side. They stopped in front of the wooden board and opened their Instruct menus at the same time.

"...Finally..." The word slipped unconsciously from Haruyuki's lips.

Fuko, beside him in her wheelchair, picked up his thought. "Finally the time has come, hmm?"

Akira nodded on his other side without a word, and the three members of Petit Paquet locked their hands together in front of their chests. As for Chiyuri to his left, even now she moved on her own time in her own way.

"I wonder if they'll make it in time." She gave voice to an entirely practical concern. "Only three minutes left."

So Haruyuki unconsciously grabbed her hand. "It'll be fine. Niko and Kuroyukihime just have to press the button, that's all."

"I *know*," Chiyuri replied, annoyed, but she still squeezed his hand warmly.

Haruyuki held his breath and watched over the two kings. Soon...in a few mere seconds, the two Legions would vanish and a new great Legion would be born.

In the LEGION tab that only Masters had, Niko and Kuroyuki-hime nimbly flicked around the screen, but their hands soon stopped. Their gazes clashed for a mere three seconds before they suddenly started to yell.

"Here we go, Rain!!"

"Come at me, Lotus!!"

Huh?! This can't be the start of a king-versus-king battle?! Haru-yuki nearly fainted, but after an instant of silence, the two raised their voices and shouted as one.

""Rock!!""

Niko's small fist and Kuroyukihime's Incarnate-generated one swung down at top speed, and the compressed air became a sudden gust that reached even Haruyuki.

""Paper!! Scissors!!""

The two fists shot out with even greater force, and a shock wave, the aftermath of some kind of explosive-type special attack, shook the entirety of the stage. The energy generated was far greater than from the rock-paper-scissors competition of the six candidates for meeting chair, causing the members of both Legions to reel backward. Haruyuki braced himself to ride out the shock wave, determined to see the results of this contest.

Niko had thrown paper.

Kuroyukihime had thrown scissors.

The two kings remained motionless for about three seconds, and then the Red King slowly roused herself and raised her still-open hand in submission.

"Aah, I lose. Which means..." Niko turned back to the forty-plus Burst Linkers watching with bated breath, her small avatar radiating dignified authority as she announced, "For the month-long prep period, it's gonna be Black here doing the Legion

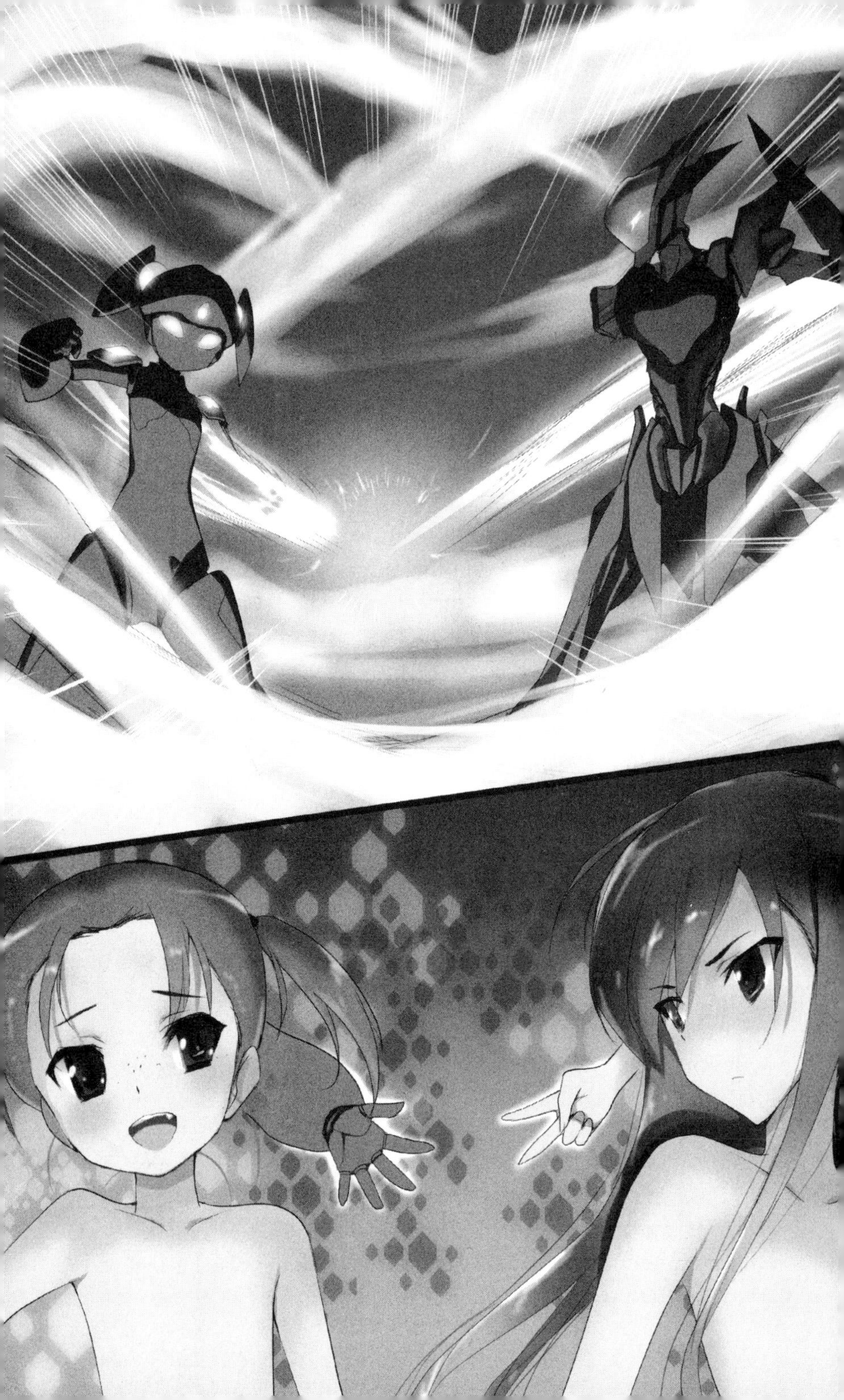

Master thing! And we'll inherit Nega Nebulus as the provisional Legion name! The official new master and Legion name'll be discussed again in a month! Anyone got any complaints about this decision?!"

Haruyuki looked over at the members of Prominence, his heart in his mouth. Naturally, the ten on the Nega Nebulus side had no objections, but for the thirty-two on the Prominence side, even if it was just a provisional master for a single month—and even if it was the Red King's decision—he thought it would still be a pretty tough thing to accept.

"No objections!!" the head of the Triad, Vermillion Vulcan, shouted loud and clear. The other members nodded one after another at the authoritative words of the one who had first voiced concerns about the Black King becoming Legion Master.

"So then, once again..." With a flourish that was suddenly lacking in dignity, Niko tapped away at her Instruct menu, and Kuroyukihime similarly moved her right hand. In front of each of them, a clear window of shining gold appeared, looking like no ordinary thing.

The two kings nodded at each other and raised their hands high. Moving so fast that he could hear the sound of the air ripping, they hit the centers of the two windows.

At the same time that both windows disappeared, a sublime sound he'd never heard before rang through the stage, and a brilliantly dazzling golden light enveloped the duel avatars gathered there. Haruyuki saw the system message YOUR LEGIONS HAVE BEEN COMBINED!! before it was enveloped in flames and disappeared. At last, the merger between Prominence and Nega Nebulus was done.

Haruyuki hung his head low, slammed with all kinds of feelings he couldn't quite name, and saw the shadow of someone walking up to him. He hurried to lift his head and found Iodine Sterilizer there, wearing his hat and cloak once again. He couldn't see the other avatar's face mask, hidden as it was by the wide brim, and he braced himself, wondering what on earth he was planning to say.

"Looking forward to fighting together, Antidote King." The voice was curt, but also embarrassed somehow, as Dine stuck a hand out.

"Right. Let's fight again one of these days. I'm looking forward to it." Haruyuki shook the hand of his new friendly rival and reassuring friend.

When he returned to the real world's Nakano Central Park and lifted his eyelids, the first thing that leapt into Haruyuki's field of view was Kuroyukihime sitting across from him. She was looking at her open hand with a complicated expression on her face.

"K-Kuroyukihime," he started. "Is something the matter with your hand?"

She smiled as she shook her head. "No, nothing. I just feel as though that little Niko went and lost the final rock-paper-scissors to me on purpose...Anyway, isn't there someone you have to report to right away?"

"Huh?" Blinking in confusion, Haruyuki looked to his right for some reason, and there was the face of Rin Kusakabe sitting on her knees, leaning forward to the very close range of approximately five centimeters. "Whoa! ...S-sorry for the wait, Rin." He threw his head back reflexively.

"Wh-what happened, Arita?" Rin brought her face in ever closer. Her extremely thin voice was filled with an anxiety that threatened to spill over any second, and Haruyuki hurriedly put a smile on his face.

"It's okay. The Legion merger went off without a hitch...Well, I also got a weird title— Whoa?!" He wasn't able to finish because of the arms that were suddenly flung around his neck.

Rin threw herself at him, large tears brimming in her eyes as she murmured, "Thank goodness!" and squeezed tightly.

"Hey, hey, heeeeey! Slow down! Too close there!!" Chiyuri grabbed Rin's collar and tried to peel her off, but her arms showed no signs of loosening.

"N-no! Um." Haruyuki flapped both hands and hurriedly

started talking to the small ear immediately to the left of his face. "W-we still have a ways to go! I mean, we gotta go through the whole entry procedures for Ash, Utan, and Olive!"

The statement led him to imagine what would happen if he accelerated like this and met Ash Roller, and Haruyuki grew even paler.

3

Koto and Yuki Takanouchi were identical twins.

Normally, family can tell even identical twins apart by tiny differences—the location of a mole, the timbre of a voice, the tilt of one's eyes. But neither Yuki nor Koto had a single mole, and they had exactly the same voice and gaze. Thus, ever since they were babies, not even their own mother could tell who was who at first glance.

And then their mother introduced a simple way of figuring it out: She gave the Koto, the elder sister, a red newborn Neurolinker, and Yuki, the younger sister, a white one, and used those colors to distinguish them. Neurolinkers were equipped with a function to authenticate brain waves, and as with fingerprints, no two sets were exactly the same, not even for identical twins. For all intents and purposes, it appeared that these Neurolinkers definitively identified the girls, and the problem was seen as solved.

However, when they started preschool, their new Neurolinkers could not distinguish between them. Perhaps this was because of some issue with the machines; perhaps it was because their brain waves had come to be almost the same through shared experiences growing up. Either way, the fact that they were the only ones who realized this only complicated the issue.

At first, it was just as a bit of a mischief that Koto and Yuki traded their devices. Their mother and father were easily deceived, which they found quite funny, and the pair started trading Neurolinkers frequently, with the one wearing red spending the day as Koto and the one with white as Yuki. They were always together, which made the switching of various child protection functions of the Neurolinker that much easier. Examples of these functions included an alert that would appear in their view if their name was called, or holotags with their names on it that would appear above their head.

At some point, this risky but fun "game" had become a daily practice, and it continued for the entirety of their three years of preschool. They finally decided to stop switching the night before they started elementary school. They would be in different classes there, and no matter how much support the Neurolinker could provide, they thought sharing their memories would be too difficult to pull off. But when they decided to return the red and white Neurolinkers to their rightful owners, the girls realized a fact more frightening than anything else.

Was I Koto to start with? Or was I Yuki? Because they'd been playing at switching for three years at that point, they couldn't say with certainty anymore which name really belonged to whom. Koto and Yuki were still only five years old, and the terror of this realization was equivalent to the annihilation of their senses of self. They desperately wanted to run to their parents crying and begging for help, but they had no hope at all that their mother and father would be able to tell who was who after failing to notice the switch they'd been pulling for three whole years.

With no other choice, the twins decided to close their eyes and each choose a Neurolinker; the one who took the red would live as Koto and the white would be Yuki. They also wanted to add a visually identifying element, and so they decided that Koto would wear her hair in pigtails while Yuki put hers in a ponytail, and that this would never change.

Once they started elementary school, there were no issues on the surface, but in the depths of their hearts, there was always an indescribable anxiety. This idea, the terror that perhaps each girl was not who she thought she was, never completely disappeared, and instead grew up to become an impenetrable barrier. This wall not only rejected other people but also threatened to crush their senses of self little by little. And then, one day, an encounter with a game program changed their lives forever.

Brain Burst 2039. This program, which read a player's "mental trauma" and produced a "duel avatar" from it, gave Koto and Yuki a decisive way of identifying themselves. Their duel avatars did of course look very much alike, but the horns on their heads, the colors of their armor, and, above all else, their names, were different. Koto's avatar was Cobalt Blade. Yuki's was Manganese Blade. These utterly unique names absolutely could not be traded, even if, hypothetically, Koto was really Yuki and Yuki was really Koto.

Having gained this means of "defining" themselves at long last, the pair ended up distinguishing themselves as Burst Linkers in the Blue King's Legion, the Leonids.

On the western edge of Shirokanedai in Minato, Tokyo—i.e., Minato Area No. 3—there was a massive park, or rather a forest: the Institute for Nature Study. During the Edo period, it had been a villa of the Takamatsu clan; later it was designated an imperial asset under the name of the Shirokane Reserve; and later still, about a hundred years earlier, after the end of the Pacific War, it had been opened to the general public as a park. Although it was considered an annex, the institute that managed it, the National Museum of Nature and Science, was in far-off Ueno Park in Taito; the Tokyo Metropolitan Teien Art Museum, which stood on the southwest side of the site, had more presence there.

The Teien Art Museum was originally a Japanese art deco–style manor known as the residence of Prince Yasuhiko Asaka, and the building itself had been designated an important national cultural asset. Of course, because it was an art museum, anyone was permitted to go inside (for a fee), and the building now also housed a café.

Which brings us to Saturday, July 20, 3:30 PM. The twin sisters Koto and Yuki Takanouchi were seated across from each other at a table by the window of the Teien Art Museum café and staring intently at the plate of chiffon cakes that had only just been brought to them.

Koto had ordered the lemon and mint, and Yuki the marbled matcha. Both actually looked delicious, but they weren't immediately inclined to dig into either. With a drink (Koto had mixed berry soda, Yuki iced milk) each order fetched the super dreadnought price of 1,400 yen. Adding in the museum entrance fee, that was 1,950 yen per person. If they didn't very carefully examine the cakes in front of them and expend every effort in appreciating their beauty, they'd never get their money's worth.

"Hey, Koto? Maybe we can invoice Negabu for this as a necessary expense," Yuki suggested glibly.

Koto shrugged. "Probably no way. And *you* were the one who said we should come into the café because it's too hot out. We were going to wait on standby on a bench in the park."

"But, I mean, I'm no good in the heat. And that's not a park. It's a forest. A *forest*. There's flies and snakes and bears! I just know it!"

Grinning painfully at this, Koto glanced outside. The café had a modern interior with white as the keynote, but a green lawn spread out on the other side of the large glass window, and beyond that a dense, deep forest. It had been left to grow naturally since it had been planted as a firewall in the 1700s during the Edo period, so the history of this forest was that of the imperial palace itself—or rather, Fukiage Omiya Palace's gardens. There might very well have been raccoon dogs or some other semimythical animals living in it. "If there *are* bears in there, I want to see one. Well, thanks to this price, there aren't any other kids in here at least. We'll tighten our belts tomorrow."

"Wohkay. So trade once we eat half." Yuki's appetite meter had apparently dipped into the red zone.

Koto picked up her fork at the same time as her sister and gently pushed it into the edge of the pale-yellow chiffon cake. Then, out of the corner of her eye, she saw the automatic café door open, and Koto glanced in that direction.

A slightly younger boy walked in. Navy blazer, ivory pants, slightly long hair in a bowl cut, he was attractive in a very Japanese way. Perhaps he had run there—he pressed a handkerchief to his forehead to dry the sweat as he spoke to the waitress, and she showed him to a table a little ways off from Koto and Yuki.

Even as she brought the chiffon cake to her mouth, Koto kept taking peeks at him. It wasn't, of course, because he looked like her type or anything like that. She was instead considering the possibility that he was there to interfere with their mission—in other words, he might have been an enemy Burst Linker.

There were around a thousand Burst Linkers in the city of Tokyo, of which perhaps seven hundred were junior high students. In contrast, including both private and public schools, the total number of junior high school students was approximately two hundred thousand. A rough calculation showed that one in every 285 was a Burst Linker. So normally, there was no need to be concerned about the chances that another young person in the same café would happen to be one.

But the bowl-cut boy slightly hidden behind Yuki definitely had something of that air about him. Although he seemed completely different on the surface, he had something in common somehow with the real-life Ardor Maiden, whom they'd met in a family restaurant in Nakano area three days earlier.

"It really is delicious, though, hmm?" Koto murmured as she deftly operated her virtual desktop, still cut off from the global net, and set up an ad hoc connection with her sister's Neurolinker. For safety's sake, she actually would have preferred to direct, but she had to avoid doing anything suspicious. She sent a camera feed from her own Neurolinker and started to talk in neurospeak. *"Yuki, don't turn around. Look at the video. Have you ever seen the boy behind you?"*

The normally flighty Yuki was a Burst Linker at heart, so the look on her face didn't change in the slightest as she munched away on her cake. *"Nope. He's cute, huh? But…mm hmm. He doesn't seem like an ordinary boy."*

"Is he maybe one of Oscillatory's?"

"Dunno." Yuki shrugged mentally. *"But if he is, then that means the whole mission today's been blown."*

Koto signaled her agreement with her eyes. The twins were not, in fact, the main actors that day; that would be the Black Legion. When the Territories started in twenty minutes, Nega Nebulus would launch a surprise attack on Minato Area No. 3, thought to be the headquarters of the White Legion. If Black won there, White would lose control of the area, and its right to block the matching list would be stripped away. Then, finally, it would be the twins' turn. They would check the list immediately after the Territories ended, and if any of the confirmed members of the Acceleration Research Society—at present, the Burst Linkers Black Vise, Rust Jigsaw, and Sulfur Pot—were on it, that would be proof that Oscillatory Universe was itself the Society's parent body.

To be honest, Koto (and most likely Yuki, too) still half disbelieved this—well, she was about 40 percent belief and 60 percent doubt. She *wanted* to trust Silver Crow and Ardor Maiden after they'd gone so far as to expose themselves in the real in order to ask the twins to take on this role of checking the matching list. But when they told her that the White King, White Cosmos, also known as Transient Eternity, was secretly the leader of the Acceleration Research Society, that *she* was the one wreaking havoc and sowing the seeds of war…Koto couldn't help but be bewildered before feeling anything along the lines of understanding.

She couldn't imagine what motive the White King had or what advantage it would give her to create things like the Armor of Catastrophe and the ISS kits. At the very least, there was no evidence that Oscillatory had profited at all from the subsequent chaos these had brought about. In fact, it had to have hit the

Legion fairly hard when Tokyo Midtown Tower, an important landmark in white territory, was occupied by the Legend-class Enemy Archangel Metatron. So what did the White King get out of all of this? Or was the Black Legion just mistaken? The answer would be clear in twenty minutes. Or it was supposed to be, but if the bowl-cut boy behind Yuki was an Oscillatory assassin, Yuki was right—they would have to assume that Nega Nebulus's greater mission had failed before it even started.

"*So then, what should we do?*" Koto asked.

Yuki brought a forkful of matcha chiffon cake to her mouth as she replied, "*If the kid's here to get in our way, he'll probably challenge us before we can check the matching list. I can't imagine we've been cracked in the real, but...*"

"*If we were cracked in the real, there's also the risk of PK. But that's unlikely. I mean, he's exposed in the real here, too.*"

"*Well anyway, we're probably just overthinking this,*" Yuki finished.

Koto looked at the boy once again. He had an indigo Neurolinker equipped on his neck that was a slightly more saturated tone than the ones the twins wore. It was customary for Burst Linkers to match their Neurolinker color with their duel avatar color, so was he a blue type? Of course, the probability that he was even a Burst Linker at all was statistically only one in 285, but the hunch she'd felt when she saw him come into the café was increasingly turning to conviction rather than fading away.

Right. In addition to resembling Ardor Maiden, the boy also resembled their own parent. A calm that was beyond his years, and a fathomless depth behind that.

She kept thinking and moving her fork until her lemon cake was exactly halved. She traded for the remaining half of Yuki's matcha cake, cut off a piece of the light-green cake, and brought it to her mouth. The moist cake melted like a light snowfall, and for an instant, her tongue was enveloped in the rich flavor of matcha, which quickly faded to leave a refreshing bitterness.

Top quality. No surprise at this price. She nodded to herself as she sent a thought to her sister's Neurolinker. *"We have no choice but to let him be. If he is from Oscillatory, his name won't appear on the matching list yet, so we can't challenge him. And we don't even know his avatar name. But there's one more problem. Should we warn Nega Nebulus about the possibility of an information leak? If their strategy's been found out, Oscillatory will put their greatest firepower in Area Three and ambush them. And if that happens, they can fight as hard as they want, but they'll never win."*

At best, Koto and Yuki were supposed to be neutral observers. It was precisely because they were third parties siding with neither White nor Black that their testimony would be credible, and she wasn't sure if transmitting information to Nega Nebulus was the right thing to do in the end.

"Huh?" Yuki neatly cut off this circle in Koto's mind. *"We should probably tell them. We've barely spoken to anyone from Oscillatory in the Accelerated World, but we've met Negabu's Corvus and Maiden in the real, y'know?"*

"...Your thinking is too simple."

Although they had been two peas in a pod in kindergarten, to the point where even their own parents couldn't tell them apart, at some point their personalities had grown quite different. If Koto had chosen to be "Yuki," would her personality have turned out like that?

"But, mm, maybe that's exactly it." Koto nodded slightly. *"And if Nega Nebulus loses, we'll have spent two thousand yen each here for nothing. Okay. I'll mail Silver Crow..."* She was about to launch the mail app on her virtual desktop, but then she stopped her hand in the middle of the act.

The bowl-cut boy sitting three tables away returned the cup of tea or coffee he was drinking to its saucer and brought his right hand to his Neurolinker. The only time you needed to use a finger to operate your Neurolinker was to turn the power on or off—or do the same to a global connection. In this situation, it was probably the latter. And she was betting he was turning the connection on, not off. She stopped watching him with her naked eyes and zoomed in on his mouth with the camera feed she was also sending to Yuki. If he was a veteran Burst Linker, he would have mastered the technique of "shouting" acceleration commands at a volume that only he could hear, but he couldn't not move his mouth at all. They'd be able to guess the type of command from the slight movement of his lips.

"*Yuki!*" By the time Koto sent the sharp thought, her twin sister was already touching her own Neurolinker and pressing the global connect button.

There was no mistake; the bowl-cut boy had mouthed the Brain Burst acceleration command. And it wasn't the basic Burst Link, but rather the spell to dive into the true Accelerated World that only those who had reached level four could use. If they went after him, Koto and Yuki would definitely be cracked in the real. But it would be the same for him. Rather than avoid that risk, they needed to go after this chance to find out who this boy was.

Reaching this decision simultaneously, the twins shared their thinking with an instant of eye contact and then gave the same command a second after the boy did. ""Unlimited Burst!""

On this first visit in some time to the true Accelerated World—the Unlimited Neutral Field—the stage was a Wasteland, dry wind whistling through the spaces between massive reddish-brown rocks. Coming down to stand on the gravelly earth in the form of her duel avatar Cobalt Blade, Koto quickly looked around as she placed a hand on the hilt of the sword hanging off her left hip.

There were no human-made buildings in a Wasteland stage, but the placement of the rocks was based on the locations of real-world buildings. The Teien Art Museum where the twins were had transformed into a group of strangely shaped rocks, like long, thin pillars, and the view from them was not the greatest. On top of that, off to the south, there was a group of plants that looked like large cacti, likely the forest of the Institute for Nature Study.

Even so, she managed to confirm there were no Burst Linkers within her field of view, and she let out a weak sigh. "So he's already moved." Koto's speech here was more curt than her polite real-world speech.

"Looks that way," a voice responded from immediately behind her. "It's only natural. A single second in the real is nearly seventeen minutes here."

"......"

Turning wordlessly, she looked at Yuki's duel avatar, Manganese Blade.

Koto's speech was quite noticeably different between the real world and the Accelerated World, but the change in Yuki was on the level of a second personality. Even though it happened every time, as the older sister, she did worry a little. But they couldn't exactly maintain their usual gentle tone on this side. The menacing threat of the Blue King's closest aides, Dualis, would melt away like cotton candy in hot water if they did.

She cleared her throat and switched mental gears. "But given the stage, might still be footprints. Let's check it out."

"Right." Yuki nodded, making her ponytail-shaped horn shake, and then stared at the ground as she started to walk. Soon enough, she was pointing at a spot up ahead. "Good thinking, Sis. Faint, but footprints right there."

"Which direction?" Koto asked.

Yuki pointed not at the forest of cacti but at the rock formation on the opposite side. Without a word, Koto turned her gaze in that direction.

"So the two of you *are* Burst Linkers, too," a voice called out to them from inside the stand of rocks, and Koto and Yuki reflexively leapt back, grabbing at the hilts of their swords at exactly the same time.

Their shared special attack, Rangeless Scission, gave them a powerful ability—to extend the ranges of their blades farther and farther the longer they held this defensive posture. But they wouldn't be able to activate the move, since their special-attack gauges were completely empty at the moment, and their normal attack could never reach inside the stand of rocks over ten meters away. Even so, if the owner of that voice came at them, they would cut him down first. That much they knew for certain.

"Who's there?!" Koto barked.

Of course, Yuki followed suit: "Show yourself!"

"I understand," the voice readily replied before continuing in a slightly apologetic tone, "I'll come out now, but I'm sorry, could you please have mercy and spare me the preemptive strike? I have a meeting here, so it would be rather rude of me to die now."

At this entirely straightforward request—or rather, wish—Koto unconsciously met her sister's eyes. Yuki's eye lenses flashed, and Koto's tone was a little more relaxed as she replied, "Then come out with your hands where we can see them. If you so much as twitch, we'll cut you down."

"I accept your terms." And then a flash of blue bright enough to rouse the dead appeared from behind a reddish-brown pillar.

Cobalt Blade and Manganese Blade both had armor that was also fairly blue, but this was a step above theirs in both hue and saturation. If Koto were to compare it to something, maybe it was like the deep, serene blue of the sky right before you hit outer space. And the duel avatar's design was a Japanese-style samurai type, much like Koto's and Yuki's. But he had essentially none of their thick armor, and the blade that hung at his left hip was a straight sword. He was the very picture of a young samurai in ceremonial dress, or perhaps a Heian-era noble granted permission to wear a sword.

"Your name," Koto demanded.

The young samurai avatar bowed conscientiously. "I am called Trilead Tetroxide."

"Try-leed...?" She'd never heard that avatar name before, and the English spelling didn't immediately come to mind. She turned her gaze briefly toward Yuki, but her sister also had a faintly puzzled look on her face. Since they certainly couldn't ask their opponent the meaning of his name, she made a mental note to look it up later in her dictionary app and cleared her throat before pressing him further. "You said you knew we were Burst Linkers. Did Oscillatory Universe send you to get in our way?!"

If this Trilliad or whatever he was called was an assassin from the White Legion, she couldn't imagine that he would meekly admit it. But neither Koto nor Yuki was particularly fond of beating around the bush. The situation was already reaching critical mass anyway.

But Trilead's almond eye lenses flashed, and he shook his head. "Me, a White Legion…? No, not at all!"

"Then what're you doing in Minato Three?!"

Before Trilead could respond to Koto's interrogation, Yuki gently elbowed her and whispered in her ear, "Sis, he already told us. Something about meeting someone."

"Mm. I-indeed." She cleared her throat loudly and then changed her question. "You said you're meeting someone. Isn't that someone from Oscillatory?!"

And then it hit her—if she had scored a bull's-eye with this question, then it was a trap targeting the twins. Trilead had deliberately caused them to notice him when he dived into the Unlimited Neutral Field and made them follow him to this place, where an Oscillatory Universe attack squad would assault them. And Oscillatory didn't mess around. In the worst case, their attackers could be aiming for consecutive kills or unlimited EK until Koto and Yuki lost all their points.

Without waiting for her opponent to respond, Koto put her hand on the hilt of her sword once more. Next to her, Yuki made the exact same gesture. This time, they intended to unsheathe their blades.

Trilead gripped the sheath of his straight sword in reaction to their obvious intent to fight, and instantly, the girls were frozen in place. The design of the straight sword was quite staid for a sword-type Enhanced Armament, but an intense energy pushed at them from it, on par with that of a Legend-class Enemy or even a king-level Burst Linker.

"Hng!"

"Ghh!"

The twins gritted their teeth in unison and braced themselves. They leaned forward and tightened their holds on their beloved swords.

Meanwhile, Trilead put his hand not on the hilt of his straight sword, but toward them, fingers spread out. "Please stay calm," the young samurai said, perplexed but somehow calm as well. "I do not know your situation, but I do not belong to Oscillatory Universe."

Shaking off her paralysis, Koto took a deep breath and shouted back, "Then who exactly is this someone you're trying to rendezvous with?!"

"That's…" Trilead lowered his face the slightest bit and fumbled for words.

Not missing this opportunity when his eyes were off them, Koto and Yuki drew their blades in a single breath and snapped them up at the ready in front of their chests.

Trilead yanked his head up and finally touched his hand to the hilt of his straight sword.

A fight would inevitably explode into being if any of them so much as blinked. The dry wind of the Wasteland stage blew between the twin sisters and abruptly fell silent.

"Stooooooooopppp!!"

Koto and Yuki reflexively looked up at the sky and took a step back at the loud voice emanating from directly above them. A dark silhouette was plunging toward them like a bird of prey against the backdrop of the slightly hazy blue sky.

A surprise attack? Koto automatically moved into an attack position—until a bright silver light caught her eyes. The sunlight reflecting off the wings of the intruder…

It wasn't an Enemy. It was a flying avatar. Silver wings.

"Cobalt, that's…!" Yuki cried.

"Manga, don't attack!" Koto responded.

Booooom! The silver avatar landed on the ground between the twins and Trilead. Still in a crouch, he threw his hands out.

"Twins! Wait gradually!"

Mmm? Koto raised an eyebrow, and in that moment, another figure descended to stand next to the silver bird with a light *krnch.*

The obsidian avatar had no wings. Most likely, she had been carried by the bird, but then separated from him right before the landing and fallen down after him. She pulled her sword legs free of the ten centimeters or so they'd sunk into the ground and floated up, shrugging lightly.

"Your Japanese just now was a bit strange, you know," she commented.

"Huh?" The first on the ground released his theatrical pose and scratched his head as he stood up. "Was it?"

"*Gradually* means steadily or slowly," she said. "In this case, wouldn't it be 'wait a minute'?"

"Oh, r-right. Okay, I'll do it again—"

"No need for that!"

As she listened to this little comedy routine, Koto wondered if they'd actually prepared it in advance or something. Her battle lust vanished like the mist, and she sighed heavily before speaking to the silver flying-type avatar. "What are *you* doing here, Silver Crow? And the Black King…Black Lotus."

Koto and Yuki severed some narrower rock pillars to a height of fifty centimeters to create impromptu seats, the Black King sliced a thicker post into a table, and then the five of them sat down in a circle in a corner of the Wasteland stage at their makeshift dining set.

While the two members of Nega Nebulus were readying the tea they'd pulled out of storage, Koto ran her fingers across the stone table in front of her. The surface reflected the light of the sun like glass, perfectly level; there was nothing to catch her finger. It was proof of the extreme sword edge and the skill of the master. In comparison, the chairs that Koto and Yuki had cut were rough, albeit only slightly.

Once four steaming cups had been set down on the table and the Black King and Silver Crow had lowered themselves onto their own seats, Koto opened her mouth. "Before we get to the matter at hand, I have a question for the Black King."

"Mm? That's fine. As long as it's something I can answer," the jet-black avatar said as she brought her cup deftly upward with the sword tip of her right hand.

Koto took a deep breath. "Do you have any kind of martial arts experience in the real world?" This question violated slightly the basic etiquette of not asking about a Burst Linker in the real, but the Black King only blinked her bluish-purple eye lenses.

"No," she replied. "Not in the slightest."

This was the answer she'd been half expecting, but even so, Koto—and Yuki, sitting to her right—couldn't help but let out a deep groan.

"…So then this cross-section…," Koto moaned.

"I feel the same way." Trilead Tetroxide nodded deeply. "Truly incredible technique, as one would expect from the famed Black King."

Looking their way, that same Black King let slip the aura of a wry smile. "Don't flatter me so. This is just the fixed ability of this duel avatar; it has nothing to do with my skill. At any rate, we haven't made our introductions yet." Sitting a little straighter, the Black King looked directly at Trilead and spoke with the requisite amount of majesty. "I am the head of Nega Nebulus, Black Lotus. I truly appreciate your accepting the sudden request to meet."

The young indigo samurai also snapped to attention and bowed. "I am called Trilead Tetroxide. I was very pleased to be asked to join you, Black King. I've heard a great deal about you from my master."

"It can't have been anything good," the swordmaster retorted.

Koto raised an eyebrow, unable to pick up the thread of the conversation.

Silver Crow on her left brought his face in close. "Coba, Lead's master used to belong to Nega Nebulus."

"Oh?" she murmured. "Who?"

"Um. This guy Graphite Edge…"

""Wh-wh-whaaaaaat?!"" Koto and Yuki screeched simultaneously.

There wasn't a high ranker in the Accelerated World who didn't know the name Graphite Edge, the Anomaly, one of the former Nega Nebulus's Four Elements. The sisters' most bitter enemy was "Strong Arm" Sky Raker—they still had not forgotten the humiliation from when she hung them by wire from the top of the government building—but Graphite Edge was very firmly ranked at number two on that enemy list. Forget winning or losing—Koto had no memory of him ever giving her a proper fight. She and Yuki could hunt him down and try to strike at him, but he countered their attacks neatly with the overwhelming defensive capabilities of his twin swords. He always treated them like children—"You've still got a long way to go, Cobama!"—and then three years earlier, when they still had not managed to make him fight them for real even once, the Red King lost all his points, Nega Nebulus collapsed, and Graphite Edge disappeared from the duel world.

The idea that the Anomaly himself had taken on a student and trained him until he could paralyze Koto and Yuki with mere information pressure…

Somehow recovering from the shock, Koto pushed herself back down onto her stone stool and took several deep, calming breaths before turning to the puzzled young samurai avatar and lowering her head. "Trilead Tetroxide, my apologies. We believed you were a White Legion assassin. But if you are the Anomaly's student, then that possibility is nil. Once again, I apologize."

"No, I was in the wrong for speaking to you carelessly." Trilead shook his head. "It was only natural you would be on guard."

Silver Crow watched as the sisters and the samurai bowed to one another, and then he abruptly cocked his head. "Now that you mention it…why are you in the Unlimited Neutral Field,

Coba and Manga? Were you hunting Enemies while you were waiting?"

"You were the one who specified the Institute for Nature Study as the place to be on standby in order to check the matching list, Silver Crow," Koto responded in a sharp voice. "We encountered Trilead there, assumed he was an assassin, and pursued him."

"Huh?" Crow scratched his helmet. "But this isn't the institute forest, it's the Teien Art Museum next door, right?"

"The forest is hot, and there are flies and bees and bears!" she snapped. "We too have the right to cool ourselves in the café!"

"Ohh, I get it." He nodded understandingly. "And I told Lead to meet us in the Teien Art Museum, so that's where the near miss happened, huh?"

"All of which means," Koto started, and then shouted with Yuki, ""All of this is *your* fault!! Why would you put us on standby in the same place?!""

"I-it's not the same, though," he protested. "I split it up into the park and the museum, right? I mean, it's super-close to the leave point at Meguro Station, but it seemed like there wouldn't be junior high or high school students around, so I figured it was perfect…and basically, you're the ones who left the forest and went to the museum."

"Then you should have had *us* in the museum and *Trilead* in the forest!!" Koto yelled.

"B-b-but it costs money to enter the museum. And if you go into the café, you have to pay for tea, too…Wait. But. Huh?" Cocking his head to the opposite side now, Silver Crow turned back to the young samurai seated on the other side of the Black King. "Hang on a sec. Lead, are you maybe in the Teien Art Museum café in the real?!"

"Oh! Yes, in fact." Trilead nodded firmly.

"Wh-wh-why?!" Silver Crow yelped. "I said the Unlimited Neutral Field, right?! You could've dived off somewhere else and then come to the museum."

"That's…" The young samurai faltered and lowered his eyes, but then quickly snapped to attention again. "I came to meet you today in order to be allowed entry to the Legion. However…" He looked at Silver Crow and the Black King in turn before continuing. "I came not only for that. I wished to lend my strength to the Territories battle today, however meager it might be. To do that, I must be on standby in the target area in the real world, so I entered the Museum with the intention of looking around during that time. When my guard—I mean my companion—was not looking, I moved to the café and dived to this side. That's when I had the near miss with Cobalt Blade and Manganese Blade, so the responsibility for needlessly putting the two of you on the defensive lies with me."

"……"

The other Burst Linkers at the table fell silent.

So Trilead Tetroxide was meeting with the Black King and Silver Crow here to join the Legion, apparently. She could understand that. It made sense that the student of the Element Graphite Edge would become a member of Nega Nebulus. But taking part in the Territories right after joining…And this was no mere wresting of ground, but a battle against one of the six Great Legions, Oscillatory Universe. It wouldn't be an easy fight.

It was one thing if they managed to prove the Black Legion's suspicion that the White King was the one pulling the strings behind the scenes at the Acceleration Research Society. But if they didn't, the Black King would be severely censured at the meeting of the Seven Kings of Pure Color, and in the worst case, she could even end up with a bounty on her head again that extended to all her Legion members. Trilead seemed to have come from a good upbringing. Would he be able to withstand that kind of carnage?

The wheels in Koto's head turned round and round, but then she remembered the moment when Trilead had moved a hand toward his sword before, and a faint chill ran up her spine. That incredibly intense pressure, as though she were facing off against a king. If he had that kind of aura, he'd probably be able to dispatch with one hand behind his back the herd of Mid-Level challengers who came after him for the bounty. But had he gained this kind of power simply by receiving instruction from Graphite Edge?

"N-no, but Lead, the Territories today aren't just any regular fight," Silver Crow started, waving both hands back and forth in front of him, as if tracing Koto's own thoughts, and she shut him up with an elbow to the side before turning her gaze on the young samurai avatar, who was as relaxed and open as ever.

"Trilead Tetroxide," she said. "Apologies for the rude question, but mind telling me your level? Me and Manga are seven."

"Oh, I'm level six," Trilead replied immediately.

"One lower." Koto nodded thoughtfully. "So why do you emit a sword aura that can make *us* shrink?"

"You've trained a lot under the Anomaly, then?" Yuki added.

The young samurai shrank back almost apologetically at these compliments from Leonids' Dualis and shook his head slightly. "No. If you sensed any pressure, its source was not me personally."

"Meaning?" Koto and Yuki cocked their heads at the same time.

Trilead reached a hand down to his hip and released the Enhanced Armament mount there. *Kushunk.* He placed the straight sword on the stone table.

As soon as she focused on it, Koto felt the earlier pressure come over her again. In terms of size, it didn't compare with the twins' initial katana, much less the greatsword Impulse that the Blue King wore. The workmanship of the hilt and scabbard was simple, but the smoothed and polished steel felt decadent somehow, faithfully communicating the fact that this was no ordinary Enhanced Armament.

"The name of this sword is The Infinity," Trilead said.

"......!!"

Koto threw her head back reflexively and very nearly tumbled off her impromptu seat. Yuki had exactly the same reaction, and the twins both waved their hands wildly in the air before they somehow managed to regain their balance. Once her wild breathing had calmed, she asked the sword's owner, "The definite article and a proper noun…Is this a Seven Star Enhanced Armament?"

"Yes, it's one of the so-called Seven Arcs," Silver Crow said. "The word *epsilon* was inscribed on the dais."

"H-hang on. Crow, why do *you* know that— No, wait." Abruptly, Koto remembered something. It had been at the meeting of the Seven Kings convened the previous month to confirm Silver Crow's purification from the Armor of Catastrophe. They'd been waiting for the inspector Quad Eyes Analyst aka Argon Array when Crow looked at the sisters' swords and remarked that he'd seen a similar sword before in the Unlimited Neutral Field. "You…Then at the meeting you already knew about this treasure?" She glared at him out of the corner of her eye.

"Y-yes, actually." Crow scratched the top of his helmet. "Oh, it's great you and Manga finally get to see the real thing, too!"

"That's beside the point! Where did you see it?!" she demanded.

"Huh? Uh, heh-heh," he chuckled. "That's a secret."

"Don't play dumb, Crow!" Now that it had come to this, Koto wouldn't be satisfied unless she gave him a good poke in the forehead, so she stretched out a hand. Crow put up a desperate defense, but her low-stakes attack was relentless.

"O-oh, please don't get mad! I'll explain!" Trilead leaned forward to intercede, so she had no choice but to pull back.

In retaliation, Koto downed all her tea and let out a loud sigh as she waited for the young man to continue.

"The place where I came into possession of this sword"— Trilead dropped his eyes to The Infinity on the table, his voice slightly tense—"and where Crow saw the sword's dais was the deepest level of the main building of the Castle."

A few seconds passed.

"The…," Koto groaned.

"The Castle?!" Yuki shrieked.

Although it was in the center of the Unlimited Neutral Field, it was the biggest and final mystery of the Accelerated World,

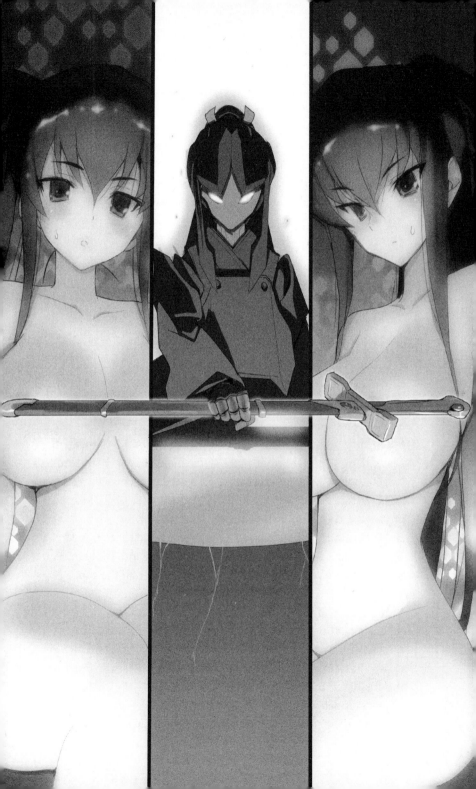

protected by the super-class Enemies the Four Gods and unapproachable no matter how many people you had in your party. *This* was the Castle—the Imperial Palace of the Accelerated World. The previous Nega Nebulus had been destroyed because it had dared to challenge the Four Gods and suffered serious losses. And yet Trilead Tetroxide and Silver Crow had managed to penetrate this absolutely impenetrable last dungeon. Was that what they were saying?

"Y-you couldn't have...defeated the Four Gods and opened the four gates?" Koto asked ever so timidly.

After exchanging a quick glance with Trilead, Crow shook his head firmly. "No. It would be absolutely impossible for us to defeat any one of the Gods."

His voice contained a chilling fear now, as if the previous feigned innocence had been a dream, and Koto held her breath again. Crow looked to the Black King and, perhaps getting permission through eye contact, continued.

"Last month, we went on a mission to rescue Ardor Maiden. She'd been sealed at the Castle's south gate for a long time—she'd fallen into an unlimited EK. The plan was for K—I mean the Black King to get the south gate's guardian, the God Suzaku, to target her, while me and Master...I mean Sky Raker charged the altar in front in a two-stage booster. Ardor Maiden would appear at just the right time, and I'd catch her and bring her back out. But the instant I grabbed hold of her, Suzaku started to target us. I couldn't turn, so we had no choice but to charge into the gate. And it was open just a little bit, so we slipped in through the gap."

"The gate was open?" Yuki muttered, dumbfounded. "Even though the Four Gods hadn't been defeated?"

"Each of the Castle's four gates has a seal on the inside that matches its respective guardian beast," Trilead told her. "It's set up so that defeating the guardians destroys the seals. But from the inside of the gate, it is possible to destroy the seals with a physical attack."

"...What...?" It was all Koto could do to get that single word out.

As a veteran Burst Linker, she had assumed that she well understood the presence of the Castle and its importance. But now she was painfully aware that she had never once thought of the fortress rising up in the center of the Unlimited Neutral Field as a tangible target for attack. But the members of the Black Legion were different. Of course, there was the fact that their executive members were sealed away at the four gates. But rather than simply saying "It's the Castle" and giving up, they'd investigated and then investigated the investigations, hammered out a strategy, and finally slipped past the guard of the Gods to succeed in the great enterprise of entering the Castle, a feat no one from the six Great Legions had ever managed.

Honestly, who are *these people?* Koto groaned to herself, not in the voice of Cobalt Blade but that of her own flesh-and-blood self, before pulling herself back together and giving voice to a new question.

"But in that case, when Crow and Maiden approached the south gate, someone had to have already destroyed the seal disc from the inside...Isn't that what you're saying? Otherwise the gate wouldn't have opened, yes?"

"Yes." Trilead nodded before stunning the sisters again. "I was the one who cut the seal. However, I wasn't working in concert with Crow's mission. I did this out of the vague hope that someone might come in through the gate someday."

"Come *in*...through that gate?" This wording deeply puzzled Koto. It almost sounded as if Trilead Tetroxide could normally dive freely inside the Castle—he couldn't have been locked up there or anything, right?

She was about to question him further, but before she could open her mouth, Trilead shook his head.

"Please excuse me. I still can't answer your question yet, Cobalt Blade. If there were one thing I *could* say...It's because Crow opened the Suzaku gate and came flying inside that day that I am able to come outside like this after being in a certain sort of confinement in the Castle for a long period."

"Th-that's—I mean, same here," Crow put in immediately. "If you hadn't smashed the Suzaku seal for us, Lead, the gate wouldn't have opened and we would've been stuck in an unlimited EK."

"No," Trilead counterprotested. "Breaking through Suzaku itself has to have been any number of times more difficult than destroying the seal."

"Not many more times." The silver avatar shook his head. "The soldier Enemies in the Castle are superstrong, and they keep popping up forever."

The Black King abruptly giggled. "Just as I'd heard, you make a good combo."

"Huh?" Silver Crow turned to his king. "H-heard? From who?"

"Maiden and Raker, of course. Trilead, please keep being a good friend to Crow."

"Gah! What are you saying, K—?!"

You two make a nice combo, too. Koto forced herself to keep this thought to herself and sorted through the information in the back of her mind. As long as Trilead Tetroxide himself wouldn't talk about his mysteries, she couldn't pursue it any further. But the bits of information that he *had* supplied were so astonishing they made the core of her mind go numb.

At present, ownership of only three of the Seven Arcs was known: The alpha, Impulse, was owned by the Blue King; the beta, Tempest, by the Purple King; and the gamma, Strife, by the Green King. These had been discovered in the deepest levels of the so-called four Great Dungeons in the Unlimited Neutral Field. But only the empty dais of the delta, the Luminary, had been found in the underground labyrinth at Shiba Park; no one knew who had taken the Arc. And legend remained that the zeta, the full-body armor Destiny, had been polluted by dark Incarnate at the dawn of the Accelerated World and transformed into the Armor of Catastrophe, Chrome Disaster.

Silver Crow, who sat now beside Koto drinking tea, had been the sixth Chrome Disaster, but he broke the curse and sealed the

Armor away in some corner of the Accelerated World. Or at least, that's what he had announced at the meeting of the Seven Kings the previous month. Which meant that he had to know the whereabouts of the Enhanced Armament that had once been the zeta, but just as with Trilead's secrets, she knew he would never tell her, even if she asked nicely. And Koto wasn't the least bit interested in knowing where that fearsome armor slept, anyway.

In short, the only Arcs whose names and locations were not known were the epsilon and the eta, and every high ranker had spent long years chasing after them. And now, in the place where she sat quietly having tea, it was finally clear that the fifth Arc, The Infinity, had been inside the Castle and Trilead Tetroxide had obtained it. Which implied that the zeta had also been in the Castle, enshrined alongside the epsilon, which in turn meant that the first Chrome Disaster had gotten into the Castle through some means other than defeating the Four Gods to get the armor. So then the seventh—the final Arc—also had to be inside the Castle. And perhaps no one could touch it yet?

"Silver Crow," Koto started, ready to check if her assumptions were correct. However, she faltered the instant those mirrored goggles turned toward her. She felt awkward casually asking about the seventh Arc, the greatest secret in the Accelerated World. She turned instead to Black Lotus across from Crow. "Black King. Why would you reveal such critical information to the executives of a hostile Legion? The seal structure of the four gates is information of greater value than the strategy for the gimmicks in the four Great Dungeons."

"The executives of a hostile Legion?" The Black King turned a gaze so gentle on the twins that Koto almost disbelieved it possible for her to have driven the Red Rider to total point loss with a single blow before going on to attack the other kings. "Well, Leonids do attack Suginami area every so often even now, so I suppose in terms of position, that *is* what you would be. But in that case, I'll just ask: Why did you accept Crow's dangerous and troublesome request? I would have thought it only natural to refuse something like moving all the way to Minato Three in the real world to check the matching list."

"…Well…" Koto was surprisingly at a loss for words.

"I'll tell you right now," Yuki replied, somewhat thornily. "We didn't give our word without due consideration of the past and the future. It was only after we crossed swords with Silver Crow and then came face-to-face in the real, after we carefully tested how serious he was. And the Acceleration Research Society is our problem, too. If the White Legion is suspected to be the real group behind them, we have to lend a hand at least. Even if the request comes from an *enemy* Legion."

Black Lotus remained lazily amiable. In fact, when she opened her mouth again, she even seemed to be smiling slightly. "When I received the report on this matter from Crow, I was more surprised that you had met them in the real than I was that you'd accepted our request. At any rate, if you've fought in the Accelerated World and eaten a parfait in the real world, then you're no longer an enemy, are you?"

"So if we're not enemies, then what are we?!" Koto demanded, childishness flaring up without her meaning it to.

"Friends, of course," the Black King replied neatly.

"Fr—" Normally, she would've grabbed the hilt of her sword the instant she heard the word and yelled about not underestimating her. But she had almost never heard the word *friend* in the Accelerated World, and for some reason it pierced her heart now.

In the family restaurant in Nakano, they had sat down not as armored warriors Cobalt Blade and Manganese Blade but as ninth graders Koto and Yuki Takanouchi with the flesh-and-blood Silver Crow/Haruyuki Arita and Ardor Maiden/Utai Shinomiya and talked over strawberry parfaits. She hadn't been tense or nervous at all then. Just the opposite, in fact. After she and Yuki got home, she had even thought it would be nice to do something like that again, although she'd never felt like that toward her comrades in the Blue Legion before, much less members of a hostile Legion.

Struck by the Black King's words, her mental defenses crumbled, if only for an instant, and Koto turned her gaze toward Silver Crow. "Are we…your f-friends?" she muttered, only to kick herself a moment later for asking such a dumb question.

"Huh? Um…Oh!" The silver duel avatar also stammered, sounding bewildered, but eventually he nodded firmly. "Yes. I think we're friends."

Koto and Yuki couldn't remember having had anyone they could attach the priceless tag *friend* to in the real world since finishing elementary school. The reason for that was probably the fear that had penetrated deep into their hearts that they might not be the real them. Since they had set their individual hairstyles, there was no longer that immediate confusion about who was who, but the faint unease that welled up each time a classmate called "Koto" or "Yuki" hadn't gone anywhere. The pressure of this left them unable to open up to anyone, and children were sensitive to such things. The twins were more and more often left out of the group, and they put on a show of strength, acting as if it didn't matter so long as they had each other. This mental-scar "shell" didn't completely disappear after they received their unique names as Burst Linkers, and they hadn't been able to blend into their classes at school over the last three years. At some point, they'd gotten used to it, and just when they'd thought it would keep going like that after they went on to high school, they were hit with this declaration of friendship from Silver Crow.

"""……"""

Speechless for a full five seconds, Koto and Yuki cleared their throats at the same time, apparently on purpose.

"W-well, if you say that, we might do that for you," Yuki started. "That…The whole f-friend thing."

"B-but don't get carried away," Koto warned with a sigh. "We're at best all Burst Linkers. When we find the names on the list, we'll charge in without hesitation."

Silver Crow bobbed his head up and down at top speed, and the Black King let slip a faint smile for the nth time.

"Hee-hee. I'm simply glad we've reached a consensus. Now I

can answer your previous question. I disclosed the information about the Castle to you, Dualis, because you are Crow's friends."

"Th-that's it?" Koto asked, stunned.

Black Lotus shrugged. "Do I need anything else?"

"……"

Koto was struck dumb, wavering between exasperation at this recklessness and admiration at the impressiveness of a king.

"Hee. Hee-hee…Ha-ha-ha-ha…" Trilead Tetroxide abruptly burst into laughter. The young, sky-blue samurai laughed for a while, sounding like a cool breeze blowing through, before composing himself and bowing. "P-please excuse me. I apologize. I was simply thinking the way the Black King speaks, she truly is Crow's parent."

"Oh-ho!" Black Lotus nodded. "That's a glad thing, then."

"Huh?" Silver Crow cocked his head. "Y-you think so?"

Instantly, the light in the Black King's eyes grew sharp, and she raised the sword tip of her right hand as she pressed her child for details. "And what does *that* mean, Crow?"

"N-no, it doesn't mean anything!" He waved his hands in front of his face.

"So that wasn't how you *really* feel just now?!" she snapped. "Do you hate people thinking I'm your parent?!"

"N-n-n-n-no, I'm telling you that's not it! I just couldn't say anything as cool as you!"

Trilead started giggling again, and as she watched, Koto felt something rise up from her own throat. Unable to withstand it, she let it out and was surprised to discover that it was loud laughter.

"Ha-ha-ha! Ha-ha-ha-ha-ha!" As she doubled over, she glanced to her side and found Yuki laughing the same way, in the same position.

When exactly was *the last time we laughed like this?* she wondered as the bright laughter of the twins echoed through the Wasteland stage.

Koto and Yuki left the two members of the Black Legion at the stone table with Trilead Tetroxide to conduct their Legion entry procedures, and then headed for the JR Meguro Station nearby (transformed into a sandcastle) to return to the real world through the portal.

Letting out a sigh, Koto cut the global connection on her Neurolinker and opened her eyes just as the bowl-cut boy was raising his face a millisecond after the twins.

So it wasn't just Silver Crow and Ardor Maiden now; they'd been cracked in the real with Trilead Tetroxide, too. But strangely, no feelings of alarm welled up in her. She didn't particularly want to go so far as to exchange real names, but she did wish him luck in the Territories with her eyes.

The boy bowed deeply and stood. It was still seventeen minutes before four o'clock, and since the actual battle probably wouldn't start exactly at four, he was probably planning to move to another location in the building and dive into the Territories stage from there.

After watching Trilead leave the café, Koto wet her throat with her still-cold mixed berry soda and turned her gaze on her twin sister.

Yuki stuck out her tongue playfully. "Friends, he said."

Koto was stuck for a minute on how to react as the older sister. "So then we have to do something friend-like. Once this issue's taken care of, let's have parfaits together again."

"I was just thinking the same thing!"

The sisters exchanged a giggle, and then looked up together at the summer sky as it started to take on a faint golden color.

4

After waking up inside the automatic EV bus heading from the Nakano area to Shibuya, Haruyuki unconsciously let out a long sigh as he sank deeper into his seat.

Instantly, Kuroyukihime jabbed him lightly in the side. "Too soon to relax, Haruyuki. The main event's about to start."

"H-hyah. I know." He looked up at the AR map displayed on the ceiling of the bus. Their current position was near Nakano-sakaue Station on the Tokyo Metro Marunouchi line. The West Tokyo Loop Bus was the perfect line for their current mission, going as it did from Nakano south into Shibuya to pass through Minato before heading north up to Shinjuku and cutting across Toshima to return to Nakano. If they kept going south down Yamate-dori Street, they would cross Honan Street in a few minutes and enter Shibuya Area No. 1.

"It's finally starting," he muttered.

"Mm." Kuroyukihime nodded deeply. "It's such a terrible, terrible shame I can't take part in the Territories."

"It's all right. Please wait without worry like you're sailing on a large warship!" Haruyuki slammed a fist against his chest, but all he got in response was the familiar wry smile.

"That's a rather iffy analogy. The warship of the Edo shogunate only *looked* wonderful; it was actually useless."

"Th-then the ironclads of the American Civil War?"

"Why are you dragging out ships from ancient history?" She raised a skeptical eyebrow. "Well, fine. I will relax about the main event as though I'm on a nuclear-powered aircraft carrier. I'm actually more concerned about the procedures that come before that, however."

Haruyuki was forced to nod his thorough agreement. The main mission that day was the attack on Minato Area No. 3—Oscillatory Universe's headquarters—but they had to jump through a number of complicated hoops before they could carry that mission out.

Currently, a total of sixteen members of the Legion born from the merger with Prominence—provisionally known as the third Nega Nebulus—were riding the EV bus. Specifically, there were the twelve from the previous Nega Nebulus: Haruyuki, Kuroyukihime, Fuko, Akira, Utai, Takumu, Chiyuri, Shihoko, Satomi, Yume, Rui, and special guest Rin. From the former Prominence, there were Niko, Pard, and the remaining members of the Triplex, whom they had seen in the real only now, for a total of four. The only other passengers were three older ladies at the front, so there was no chance of a Burst Linker from another Legion in the mix.

Bush Utan and Olive Grab, who had completed the transfer procedure in Nakano, were moving to Minato by train, so it was just the sixteen of them entering Shibuya Area No. 1 (still the territory of the Green Legion, Great Wall at present), together with the bus itself. And at ten seconds before four PM, the Great Wall side would renounce its rights to the area. If Nega Nebulus immediately registered an attack on the vacant area the instant the minute hand hit four, Shibuya Area No. 1 would be ceded to them in a no-show.

After that, when the bus entered Shibuya Area No. 2, Great Wall would abdicate its control over Area No. 2 in the same way, ceding rights with zero bloodshed. Once Nega Nebulus had come this far, it would finally be ready to attack the territory that bordered Shibuya Area No. 2: Minato Area No. 3—the head-quarters of Oscillatory Universe. The bus carrying the attack squad would turn left off of Yamate-dori onto Komazawa-dori, cut across Shibuya Area No. 2, and enter Minato Area No. 3. If Nega Nebulus registered the attack immediately before it did, the instant the bus was straddling the boundary, the conditions for invoking the Territories would be met, so the attacking team captain would watch for the right moment to accelerate and challenge the White Legion to a fight.

If they couldn't pull off this complicated sequence without a single mistake, the day's mission would be a failure before it had even begun. And level niners Kuroyukihime and Niko couldn't exactly take part in the Territories, so they would be away from the attacking team, shifted to the defense of Suginami. The plan was for them to change buses at Honan Street, the boundary between Nakano and Shibuya, and return to Suginami, so they would be able to sit next to each other like this for only another five minutes or so.

Haruyuki found it discouraging to be parted from the swordmaster in whom he placed his absolute confidence, but Kuroyukihime had to be feeling more anxious about the success or failure of the mission. In which case he had to keep his own concerns to himself.

"It's okay. Leave it to me!" Haruyuki slapped his chest. "I've got all the transfer procedures right here in my head!"

However, the moment he said this, Niko popped her face up in between the headrests ahead of them.

"Now listen, Haruyuki," she said, sounding exasperated. "The only ones actually fiddling with the menu are Raker as attack team leader and whoever from GW, y'know? You're just gonna be sitting there."

"Th-that's true, but...it's, like, about feelings..."

"I'm actually more worried about whether GW'll abandon the territory at the right time like they promised," Niko mused. "They're not gonna be all, *Aaactually, this is a* total *waste—let's give the whole thing uuuup* right before, right?"

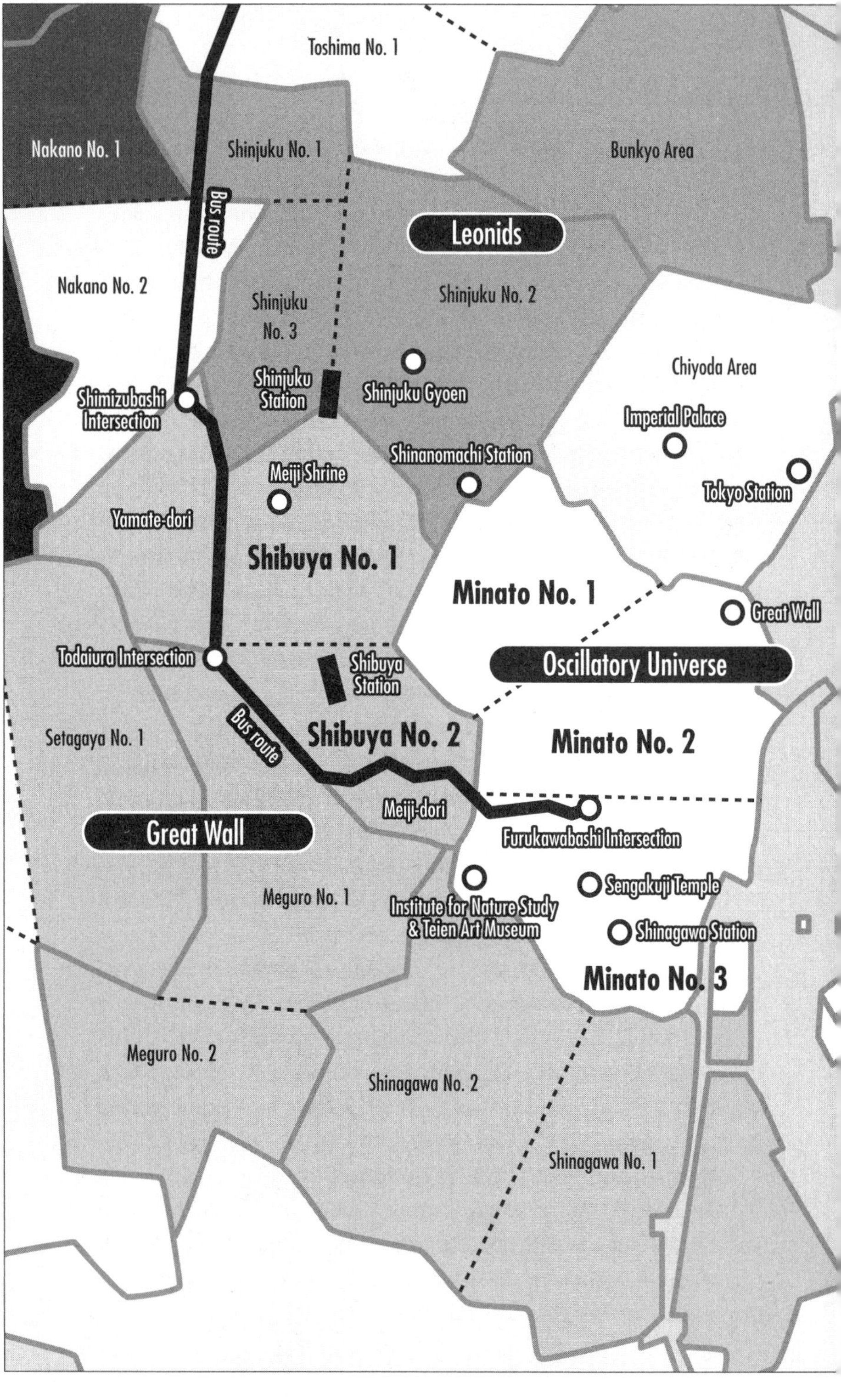
Toshima No. 1
Nakano No. 1
Shinjuku No. 1
Bunkyo Area
Bus route
Leonids
Nakano No. 2
Shinjuku No. 3
Shinjuku No. 2
Chiyoda Area
Shinjuku Station
Shinjuku Gyoen
Shimizubashi Intersection
Imperial Palace
Shinanomachi Station
Meiji Shrine
Tokyo Station
Yamate-dori
Shibuya No. 1
Minato No. 1
Great Wall
Todaiura Intersection
Shibuya Station
Oscillatory Universe
Bus route
Setagaya No. 1
Shibuya No. 2
Minato No. 2
Meiji-dori
Great Wall
Furukawabashi Intersection
Sengakuji Temple
Meguro No. 1
Institute for Nature Study & Teien Art Museum
Shinagawa Station
Minato No. 3
Meguro No. 2
Shinagawa No. 2
Shinagawa No. 1

"We've got no choice but to trust them," Kuroyukihime stated. "At any rate, the leader on their side is apparently the first seat of the Six Armors, so I think it will be all right."

Haruyuki unconsciously brought his face close to Kuroyukihime's ear and murmured, "Th-that's Graphite Edge, isn't it?"

"Mm, indeed."

"I—I hope it works out."

While Trilead Tetroxide, whom he had met in the Unlimited Neutral Field mere minutes earlier, was the very picture of politeness, the physical embodiment of the idea of irreproachable conduct, Haruyuki would describe his parent Graphite Edge as oblivious to the needs of others.

But Kuroyukihime shrugged lightly. "Well, he was the one who paid the bill here. He won't scrap his promise after all that."

And this was exactly the case. Graphite Edge had paid the land price for Shibuya Areas No. 1 and 2 in Burst Points. He hadn't told them how much it had cost, but there was no doubt that it had been a massive number of points.

Now that Haruyuki was thinking about it, Takumu and Magenta Scissor had also paid the deposit that served as proof of trust at the merger meeting with Prominence, so he felt as if he had gotten himself into serious debt to all kinds of people. He had to at least be more active than anyone in the Territories and pay back even a little of that debt.

"Hey!" From the seat ahead of him, Niko stretched a hand through the gap between the headrests and jabbed him in the forehead.

"Ow! ...Wh-what?"

"When you get that look on your face, you're basically just spinning your wheels," she snapped. "So I worry. Listen. Don't think about showing off. You just fight like you fight and that'll be enough."

After she had so clearly read his thoughts, there was nothing he could do but nod vaguely. "R-right...I'll fight my own way."

But now a hand stretched over from his right and yanked on his earlobe.

"Ow! …What is it, Kuroyukihime?"

"Mm. Nothing. Niko went and stole my thunder, so I was just sulking."

"Th-that's…" Haruyuki tried to argue against the absurd attack, but in some terrible twist, a hand reached out from the seat behind him and tugged on the hair on the top of his head. "Ow! …What are you doing, Master?" He turned around with teary eyes.

A bright smile on her face, Fuko had an even more absurd reason than Kuroyukihime. "I just felt like this was getting a bit rom-commy, so I put a forced end to it. ♪ Anyway, the next stop is Shimizubashi, Sacchi."

"Ah. Already there, hmm?" Kuroyukihime glanced up at the map on the ceiling, twisted her body to look at Fuko, and said with a serious look on her face, "I'm counting on you."

Her statement was brief, but that was exactly why it made him feel the strength of the bond between the girls and their trust in each other.

"Leave it to me, Sacchi," Fuko replied confidently.

They bumped fists lightly, and then Kuroyukihime met Haruyuki's eyes once more with a wordless smile.

Haruyuki grinned from ear to ear as the bus began to decelerate and pulled into the left lane. The moment it stopped, Niko and Kuroyukihime stood up, and without looking back, the pair stepped from the back door onto the sidewalk, and the bus pulled out again, motor rumbling.

Haruyuki glanced at the now-empty seat to his side before turning his eyes forward again. The time was 3:50 PM. In just ten minutes, it would at last be time for the Territories of the third week of July. The main fight wasn't supposed to start right away, but his hands were damp with sweat anyway. There was no need to get all worked up, though. He had plenty of powerful comrades surrounding him. He just had to believe in them and fight in his own way, and the path forward would open up.

Niko. I'm definitely getting your Enhanced Armament back.

Kuroyukihime. I'm absolutely going to expose the conspiracy of the White King who's tortured you so.

Haruyuki clenched his hands into tight fists.

✳ ✳ ✳

When they got off the bus, Kuroyukihime turned on her Neurolinker's Friend Tag function, something she generally kept turned off. A part of the Person Tag function, it displayed in AR a holotag of name and/or icon above the heads of registered friends. It was useful when you were in danger of being separated in a crowd or when you were meeting someone, but if the tags were on all the time, you were likely to develop a habit of looking at the tag rather than the other person's face, so she normally avoided it.

But now she somehow wanted to see her friends' tags. As the function was activated, several squares with rounded edges popped up over the bus pulling away from them. She had it set to display icons alone, so the squares were filled with multicolored symbols. The white hat with a ribbon inside a sky-blue circle was Fuko. The owl with orange eyes was Utai. The simple water droplet was Akira. The yellow-green cat was Chiyuri. The blue glasses were Takumu. And the pink pig was Haruyuki Arita.

She'd set the designs to the ones her friends used themselves in SNS apps and the like. Haruyuki didn't really like the pink pig school-net avatar from back when they first met, but he still hadn't changed it—in fact, he had even made it his SNS icon. But Kuroyukihime truly loved his pig avatar, so she was happy he kept using it.

The ad hoc connections with the Neurolinkers of her friends were cut one after another as the distance between them grew, until at last the pink pig also disappeared. The bus they rode on quickly melted into the traffic, but she still stared after it soundlessly.

"Don't look so down. It's not like you're never gonna see them again."

Kuroyukihime felt a jab in her back right around her third vertebra, and she jumped. "Eeah! I am not down or anything like it! I was simply watching the bus!"

Niko, a tag with red cherries displayed above her head, grinned as she retorted, "You can be gloomy or sad or whatever you want, but unless we hustle over to the bus stop there, we're gonna miss the bus back to Suginami."

"Mmph. I—I know." She started walking briskly toward the pedestrian crossing at the Shimizubashi intersection.

"But, like, this sucks, huh?" Niko muttered grumpily from her side. "We prepped all this stuff for today, but we can't even be a part of the main event, the big battle."

"We decided that at the Legion meeting, so there's nothing else we can do."

"I *knoooooow* that, but I'm super worried about Pard and them. No point-transfer in the Territories, so I figured it'd be only natural that the sudden-death rule wouldn't apply, either, y'know."

"That's, well…I think so, too, but…" Kuroyukihime nodded as the light turned green and they crossed the road.

The reason the two Legion Masters, the most powerful members of the Legion, were not able to take part in the attack on Minato Area No. 3 and were instead left to defend their own territory was the nonzero possibility that the White King herself might be among the Oscillatory Universe defense team. Kings—that is, level niners—were bound by the sudden-death rule, which meant that in just one fight, all their Burst Points would be transferred and the loser would be pushed to a forced uninstall. But given that no record of two kings ever fighting each other in the Territories existed, Niko was probably right; it was very likely that the sudden-death rule wouldn't be applied in the Territories when no points were transferred to start with.

"But if we *are* on the attacking team and Cosmos *is* among the enemy, Raker and Leopard and the others won't be able to fight freely. They would never leave our side, after all," Kuroyukihime stated.

"Well, maybe, yah." Niko nodded, albeit while pouting. "But for all your worrying here, you guys went and fought that mock Territories with the GW team the other day, with Grandé in the mix, yeah? System-wise, that was a regular Battle Royale, so if you and G had gone up against each other, one of you woulda ended up with a sudden death. Can't believe Raker and Crow were okay with that."

"Well…Mm. But the return of Shibuya area was on the line. And Grandé and I also decided we absolutely would not fight each other directly."

"Still, all you had was each other's word. And…I mean, you never even thought about it? The possibility that the whole thing was a trap right from the start, and Grandé was coming for your head?"

"Hmm." Kuroyukihime pondered this as they finished crossing the road. They turned right, and the bus stop soon came into view ahead of them. According to the wait time displayed in AR, the next bus for Suginami would arrive in two minutes and forty seconds.

They stopped next to the bus stop sign, and she replied to Niko's question. "Grandé is the most mysterious of all the kings, but at the same time, he's also the least duplicitous…I've come to think that lately. His only objective is the continued existence of the Accelerated World—of Brain Burst 2039. He agreed to the mutual nonaggression pact among the seven Great Legions because it worked for this larger objective, and he personally has offset the shortage in points supply by hunting a large number of Enemies himself. Given all of this, Grandé no doubt feels that the Acceleration Research Society's conspiracy must be stopped. As long as we're fighting the Society, he'll likely cooperate with us."

"Hmm." Arms crossed, Niko got a kingly look on her face. "But that cooperation is a double-edged sword—wait, shield. Right now, he's inclined to protect you—well, I guess it's us now—but he'll flip the instant he determines we're any kind of threat to the Accelerated World."

"I suppose so. I did actually retire one king, and I've made it public knowledge that I aim to clear Brain Burst, so…" Kuroyuki-hime took a deep breath and looked up at the late-July sky. "But that's the one thing I will not back down from, even if it ends up making an enemy of Grandé. What will happen when I reach level ten, meet the developer, break down the four gates of the Castle, and touch the final Arc? I basically live to answer that question."

Niko threw her head back reflexively as if to say something in return, but then slowly let out a sigh and nodded sharply several times. "Yeah…I know. I won't tell you to give it up or anything. And I wanna see the inside of the Castle at some point, too."

"Honestly. I've never even made it in there once, and Crow just waltzes in there to play whenever he feels like it. I can't accept it."

"Ha-ha-ha! It ain't as easy as waltzing, though," Niko said, laughing.

Meanwhile, Kuroyukihime opened her virtual desktop to turn off the Friend Tag function on her Neurolinker. But immediately before she pressed the OK button, she noticed a bright color moving in the corner of her eye, and she furrowed her brow as she looked in that direction.

A square icon with rounded edges was approaching from the north on Yamate-dori—that is, from Nakano area. And it wasn't at walking speed. Someone Kuroyukihime had registered on SNS as a friend was riding a bus driving in the lane on the opposite side. But that seemed impossible. Essentially all of Kuroyukihime's friends were members of Nega Nebulus, and they had only just driven off toward Minato in the bus she and Niko had recently alighted from.

So then who on earth…?

She narrowed her eyes at the icon. The symbol was a thick hardcover book against a light purple background.

"Th-this mark…" She opened her eyes wide. "M-Megumi?"

There was just one non-Legion friend on her list. Umesato Junior High student council treasurer Megumi Wakamiya.

"Hey, what's up? That someone you know?"

Unable to even reply to Niko's question, she continued to stare wordlessly at the approaching EV bus and the icon above it.

A coincidence. It had to be.

Megumi would, of course, also go to places like Shinjuku and Shibuya to hang out, and she took the bus instead of the train sometimes, too. But the bus she was on was traveling along the exact same route as the bus the members of Nega Nebulus—the attack team for today's Territories—were on, and she was only one bus behind them on top of that. It was almost as though she was chasing after them.

And Megumi might not be a Burst Linker, but that wasn't to say she had absolutely no connection with the Accelerated World.

It had happened three months earlier, when they visited Henoko Beach in Okinawa on a school trip. Kuroyukihime had had an unexpected reunion with a Burst Linker acquaintance who once belonged to the Purple Legion, Aurora Oval, and she ended up helping him and his students to fight the "magiimaji-mun" (large monster).

The monster turned out to be a tamed Legend-class Enemy, and it had tormented Kuroyukihime and her new comrades in linked attacks with Sulfur Pot, a member of the Acceleration Research Society, riding on its back. But an unfamiliar duel avatar had charged in to save Kuroyukihime and her allies, using the miraculous massive technique of changing the stage attributes, and then departed again just as quickly. There was no mistake—that avatar had been Megumi.

Kuroyukihime still wasn't sure even now what had happened. After the incident, she had made some excuse to direct with Megumi's Neurolinker and scanned every nook and cranny of

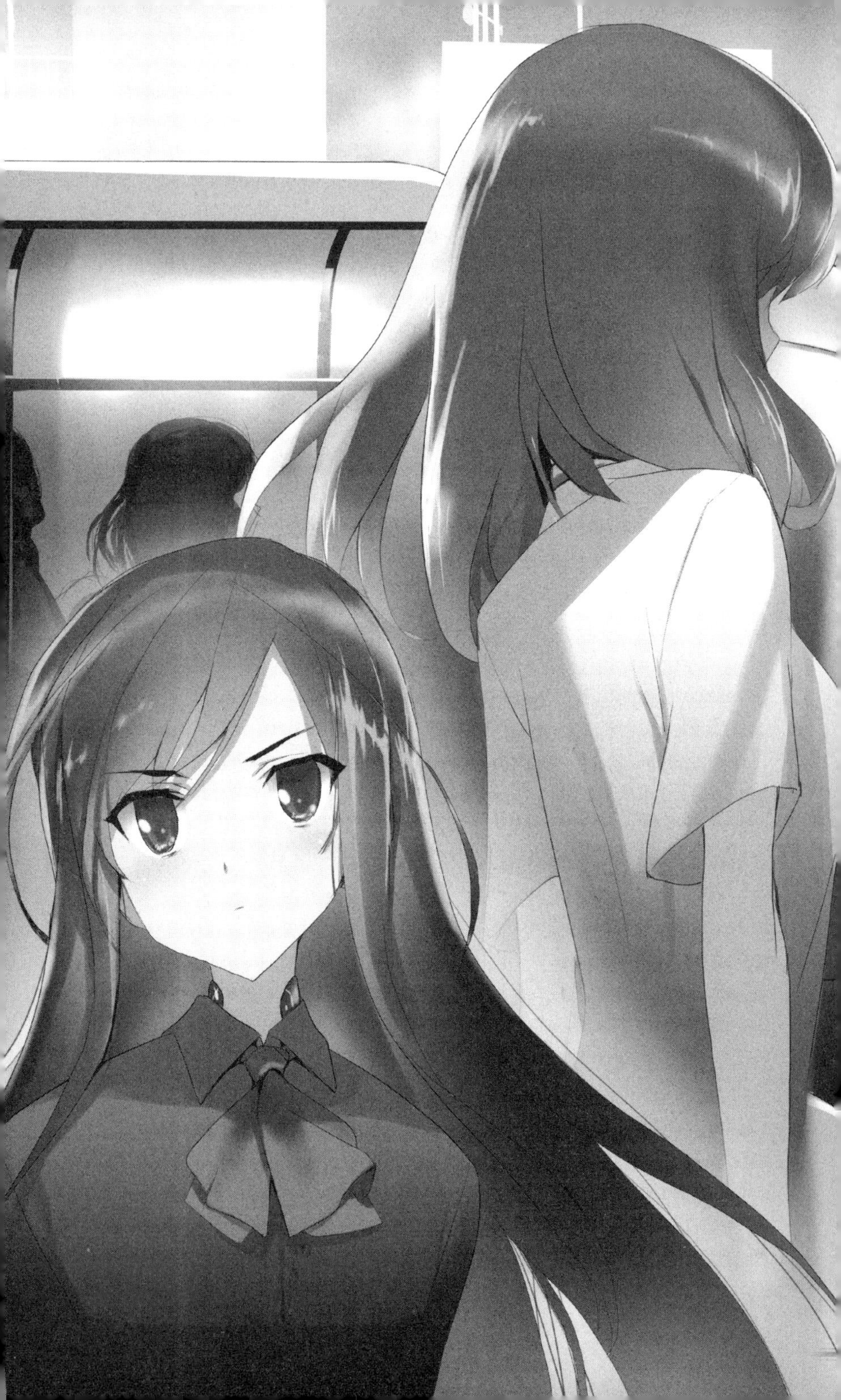

her local memory, but she hadn't been able to find the BB program. Thus, she had come to think that what happened on that southern island had been a one-off miracle.

Megumi…Why now, why here…? As she called out like this in her heart, Kuroyukihime moved her hand, still hanging in midair, to her Neurolinker's vision enhancement.

Video from the built-in camera was overlaid onto her field of view. She double-tapped the bus with a finger and enlarged the image. She zoomed in as far as she could on the window on the right side of the bus as it approached on the opposite side of the street.

The book icon pointed downward, and beneath it a person with short, fluffy hair came into view. This was without a doubt Megumi. Her head hung slightly, and there was no expression on her face in profile. But Kuroyukihime felt as if something small glinted and shone in the corner of her eye.

"Sorry, Niko!" Kuroyukihime called in a strained voice. "I can't go back to Suginami!"

"Huh?! Wh-what's happening?!"

"I'll explain later! Anyway, good luck with the Suginami defense!" She had no sooner shouted the words than she was running toward the crosswalk they had only just crossed.

The bus carrying Megumi had already passed them and was racing off to the south, not having been caught at the light, so she'd never catch up if she started running after it. But if she could at least get on the next bus or catch a taxi going in the same direction, and if she was lucky, she might be able to make it for the moment the Territories started.

She dashed into the intersection just as the pedestrian light started to flash ahead of her, and then heard footfalls chasing after her from behind. Still running, she looked back and shouted in the same strained voice, "Niko, you go to Suginami—"

"Now look! I can't just walk away from a sitch like this! Kuroyuki, you're my *Legion Master* now!"

These words stabbed deep into Kuroyukihime's heart. That was exactly right. Although she suspected that Niko had lost the game of rock-paper-scissors on purpose, Kuroyukihime had taken on the position of Legion Master of the newly formed third Nega Nebulus, albeit provisionally. If their positions were reversed, she wouldn't let Niko go off alone, either.

Once they were on the other side of the street, Kuroyukihime apologized to Niko once again. "Excuse me." She inhaled deeply to calm her breathing as she looked to the south. The bus Megumi was on had already gotten quite a ways away, and just as when she'd watched Fuko and the others disappear, the ad hoc connection was cut and the Friend Tag also disappeared.

"So something up with that bus?"

When she turned around, Niko was looking up at her with a serious face.

"Yes. My friend is on it," Kuroyukihime explained briefly. "She's not a Burst Linker now, but she might have been at one point. I can't think it's mere coincidence."

"So you mean"—Niko paused to process this—"a Burst Linker who lost all her points and had all her memories disappeared?"

"It's possible." Kuroyukihime bit her lip. "I might just be worrying too much. But..."

Niko tapped her arm. "I don't think y'are. I mean, like...we've maybe heard some stories where total point loss Burst Linkers come back to life, yeah?"

"......!!"

Kuroyukihime gasped sharply. Niko was right. Until only recently she would have thought the phenomenon utterly impossible, but she had come across two cases in the last month that had turned this common sense on its head.

The first was the residual mind of Red Rider that lived in the ISS kit main body. And the second was the residual mind of the Twilight Marauder, Dusk Taker, which survived in the right shoulder of Wolfram Cerberus. Both seemed to be memory copies that existed with no relationship to the actual flesh-and-blood person, so the situation with Megumi was obviously different. But on the other hand, there were commonalities.

The one controlling the memory reproductions of Red Rider and Dusk Taker was the Acceleration Research Society. And three months ago in Okinawa, the Society had created the reason for the fight that had brought back Megumi's memories and powers as a Burst Linker—albeit for a mere instant. And they were also the opponent her Legion was going to fight in Minato Area No. 3 that day.

"If she's being used in some way by the Society...then I really must go," Kuroyukihime declared, and Niko didn't try to argue with her.

"Then I'm coming, too."

"B-but if Cosmos is among the enemy..."

"We're gonna have to fight her one of these days. And I said this before, but there's no way I can let you go by yourself, as a Legion member." Grinning recklessly, Niko glanced over at the western sky and added, "Plus, you don't gotta worry about Suginami. We got thirty ex-Promi kids over in Nerima, so they'll be all wham-bam defending Suginami, too, trust me. They're hella strong."

"...Yes, I trust them." Something welled up in her throat abruptly, but Kuroyukihime somehow managed to swallow it back down.

Nega Nebulus was no longer the small-scale Legion that had to work hard to defend just one area. Although it had been just Kuroyukihime and Haruyuki when the Legion was reborn, Takumu had joined them, soon followed by Chiyuri, and then Fuko, Utai, and Akira. And now, today, Ash Roller, Bush Utan, Olive Grab, and Trilead Tetroxide had become new members, and if you included the Archangel Metatron, who was not in the register system-wise, they were a total of fifty people with six areas—a Great Legion.

That day...the day when she found out that White Cosmos had manipulated her into taking the head of Red Rider and she had turned a knife on her actual older sister, she thought she had lost everything. Even after she was chased out of her family home in Minato Ward and started school in distant Suginami Ward, she had stubbornly refused to connect her Neurolinker globally and kept herself locked away in a small black shell.

But one day, after a year and a half, she had met a small pink pig avatar on the squash court of the in-school local net, and he broke her shell. He broke his own shell, too, and gained the form of a silver bird, flapping his beautiful wings to cut a path forward for both of them.

If that path led to this place on this day, well, then she couldn't pull back now. Even if there was the possibility of total point loss, if she couldn't be together with him in this fight, then there was no meaning in her having accepted the position of Legion Master.

Apologies, Fuko. Sorry, Haruyuki. Let me break my promise just this once. And, Megumi. If the Acceleration Research Society is making you suffer, then as your friend, I will *save you.*

Kuroyukihime called out to these precious people in her heart and then whirled around.

A third bus was approaching from the north. Next to her, Niko slapped her fist into her hand. "Awwwwright! I'm on fire now! Yep, attacking's where it's at in the Territories!"

"For once, I'm strangely in agreement."

The two kings grinned at each other before breaking into a run for the bus stop.

***

"Burst Link." Fuko Kurasaki murmured the acceleration command at minimum volume from the back seat.

Haruyuki stiffened up and stared at the digital clock in the lower right of his field of view: 3:59:57 PM, fifty-eight seconds, fifty-nine…four PM.

"Okay. The transfer of control for Shibuya Number One went off without a hitch," Fuko whispered, returning from the instantaneous acceleration, and hearing this, Haruyuki wasn't the only one who let out a sigh of relief. Graphite Edge was indeed keeping his promise, apparently.

"What a relief." Chiyuri had moved to the seat next to him once Kuroyukihime vacated it, and now she leaned back in it. "GE's a fishy character, so I was like twenty-five percent not sure."

"Isn't that nickname kind of confusing with the G for the Green King?" Haruyuki replied.

His childhood friend pursed her lips in a pout. "So then what about Phite? Or maybe Edgy?"

"No, no. The regular Graph is fine."

"It's just *too* regular. I mean, that guy's calling Ui 'Denden' and Akira 'Kareent' and all these weird names, so we have to fight back, y'know?"

"You talk like that and you'll end up with a weird name, too, you know," he warned her.

"Heh-heh! Just what I was hoping for."

The bus kept running south along Yamate-dori. Soon they would cross another border at the Tokyo University intersection and enter Shibuya Area No. 2. When they did, Fuko and Graph would carry out the same operation once more, and the ceding of Area No. 2 would also be complete. Once the bus turned left on Komazawa-dori, passed the north side of JR Ebisu Station onto Meiji-dori, and then crossed another boundary around the French embassy, they would finally enter Minato Area No. 3. Trilead Tetroxide and the CobaManga sisters were no doubt anxiously waiting for *the* moment at the Teien Art Museum in Minato.

The clock had passed four PM, and it was already Territories time, but the attacking side was free to decide on any time before five PM to start any actual battles. Haruyuki did a quick calculation from the average speed of the bus that day and figured they would probably end up starting around four thirty or so.

In other words, they needed Lead and CobaManga to be on standby at the museum for a while still, and Haruyuki knew only too well how long those thirty minutes would be, so he felt terrible, like a Grave Sin stage, but there was nothing he could do about it. He would have at least liked to send them a mail with the expected start time, but his Neurolinker was currently not connected globally. When he'd entered the Unlimited Neutral Field to meet with Lead earlier, he'd connected globally for just an instant, with the expectation that someone would challenge him, but he wasn't sure if it was okay to try the same thing again—which made him realize something with a gasp.

Haruyuki turned himself around in his seat and peered through the headrest to ask Fuko in a quiet voice, "Um, Master? System-wise, Shibuya One's already Nega Nebulus territory, right?"

"Yes, that's right." She nodded. "Although if another Legion registers an attack during the Territories and we lose, they'll take it from us."

"Th-they will? So that's a possibility, too, huh…? What about a team to protect Shibuya One?" he asked.

"As of the present moment, I'm the only one registered," Fuko replied with a grin. "But if you'd like to take my place, Corvus, you can anytime."

"N-no, I'm fine, thanks." He paused, confused. "But if you're registered for the defense, doesn't that mean you won't be on the team to attack Minato Three?"

Which is ridiculous, because without Kuroyukihime and Niko, Sky Raker's the most powerful person on the team!

Fuko grinned once more. "It's all right. When we register the attacking team, I'll be taken off the defending team. Basically, it'll be fine as long as the territory is adjacent only for the moment of the start of the attack."

Next to Fuko, Utai quickly tapped at her holokeyboard. UI> BY THE WAY, I'LL BE IN CHARGE OF THE DEFENSE OF SHIBUYA NO. 2, BUT I'LL ALSO BE TAKING PART IN THE ATTACK IN THE SAME WAY, SO PLEASE DON'T WORRY!

"R-right…" Relieved, he felt the tension run out of his shoulders.

Chiyuri also turned around in the seat next to him. "But, Sis, then that means there won't be any defenders once we hit four thirty, right? What if the surrounding Legions realize that in the last thirty minutes? Won't they take the Shibuya areas by default?"

"Of course, there is that possibility. But..." Fuko fiddled with her virtual desktop and made visible a holomap centered on Shibuya. The three members of Petit Paquet and Rin across the aisle also leaned forward to peer at this with great interest. "As you see here, the only ones with territory adjacent to the Shibuya area are the Leonids, who control Shinjuku to the north; Great Wall, who rule Meguro to the south; and Oscillatory Universe, who rule Minato to the east. CobaManga should have already passed this by the Blue King as Leonids, and since we paid GW for the territory, we can assume there's no risk of *them* attacking. Which means the only possibility is Oscillatory. If they realize Shibuya One and Two have become Negabu territory and assemble an emergency attack team, that would actually be a lucky thing. After all..."

"Then their defense of Minato Three would be that much weaker, right, Professor Fuko?" Satomi of the Petit Paquet group said, snapping a hand into the air. A student of mixed martial arts in the real world and Shihoko's personal martial arts master, she'd challenged Fuko to a match after she transferred into Nega Nebulus and had been squarely defeated by the latter's phantasmagoric palm strikes and lightning-speed kick techniques. Ever since, Satomi had been head over heels in adoration for the older girl, as had her friends Shihoko and Yume, and they therefore now called her Professor Fuko.

Perhaps groomed for this by Haruyuki and Rin calling her Master, Fuko nodded evenly and continued. "That's exactly it, Sato. But when Oscillatory figures out that the control rights for the Shibuya areas were transferred for an attack on Minato Area Number Three...we actually need to be ready for the defense to be firmed up. And in that sense, it's better for us if we can move quickly through Shibuya One and Two and Minato Three in the real."

"But the Yamanote Line, the underground Oedo Line, and the Chiyoda Line don't pass so neatly through all three areas, riiiight?" This was from another of the Petit Paquet group, Yume. She pushed up the bridge of her glasses neatly. "We *did* consider the idea of arranging for a twenty-person microbus to race along the same course as this bus, though." Her proposal was delivered with equal parts confidence and uncertainty.

Fuko couldn't help but smile ruefully. "Now listen, Yume. I can't drive such a large vehicle with my license."

"But just the fact that you have a license and a car is amazing!" Satomi said. "Please take us somewhere one of these days!"

Shihoko tugged on the collar of her friend's blouse with an impatient look. "C'mon, you can't just go *asking* the professor like that!"

"What? You were just saying you wanted to go to the puppet house in Yokohama, Choco!"

"That's a totally different thing!"

Akira popped her head forward. "Area boundary's coming up."

Haruyuki hurriedly looked up at the map on the ceiling and saw that they had two hundred meters or so left until the Tokyo University intersection, the boundary between Shibuya Areas No. 1 and 2. Shihoko and her friends hurriedly returned to their seats, while Haruyuki and Chiyuri turned back around.

The time was 4:08 PM. The plan was for Fuko to contact Graphite Edge by mail when the bus was crossing the area border. To that end, Fuko had apparently asked Graph for his mail address when they'd had the surprise encounter with him in the Castle, but after they returned to the real world, she'd said something somewhat strange. Something about how there were no hits when she did a WHOIS search on the domain of the address he'd indicated and yet the mail got to him, which was impossible in terms of the structure of the global net.

Haruyuki wanted to ask again about this and so many other things, but he couldn't bother Fuko now. He waited quietly as the bus passed through the large intersection and entered Shibuya

Area No. 2, the Department of Education campus at Tohto University on their right.

Fuko accelerated once again and quickly returned. The party held their breath until they heard the calm voice of their attack team leader.

"Okay, the handover of Shibuya Two is complete without incident. Now all of Shibuya is provisionally the territory of Nega Nebulus."

Just as he had with Area No. 1, Haruyuki let out a deep sigh and bumped fists lightly with Chiyuri, who was sitting next to him.

If this had been a normal Territories win, he would be shouting for joy right about now, but this was nothing more than groundwork in preparation for the real fight. And although it was the result of their victory in the mock Territories six days earlier, it would look to the world as though Great Wall had ceded them the territory. Looking out at the utterly unfamiliar cityscape streaming by, he didn't really feel that their territory had grown.

Regardless, however, the transfer procedure that had worried Kuroyukihime was now finished. Haruyuki felt a sense of relief (although Fuko was the one who'd actually pushed the buttons on her Instruct menu), but at the same time, a new nervousness rose up inside him. Kuroyukihime and Niko would be back in Suginami by now. They might have already been challenged by an attacking Legion and be fighting at that very moment to defend their territory.

Staring out the window again, Haruyuki sent his thoughts toward his swordmaster. *Kuroyukihime, it's finally time. We're going to win no matter how strong our opponent is. So please wait just a little longer.*

Once the bus crossed the Keio Inogashira Line, it passed onto the old Yamate-dori, slipped under overhead expressway no. 3, and approached the southern edge of the Shibuya area. Three more kilometers until the border with Minato Area No. 3. Anticipated arrival time in seven minutes.

They'd done everything they could up to this point: reinforced

the Nega Nebulus battle lineup, negotiated the return of terri-
tory from Great Wall, merged with Prominence, asked Cobalt
Blade and Manganese Blade to act as witnesses, brought Trilead
Tetroxide out of the Castle, and invited him to join the Legion.
And Haruyuki had enhanced his own self, Silver Crow.

Whether or not all these efforts would bear fruit would
become clear in seven minutes. They couldn't accept defeat, but
the general principle of the Accelerated World was that there
were no absolutes. Now that they'd come to this point, all they
could do was give the fight everything they had. Muster up
every bit of strength inside them—well, except for the Incarnate
System—and break through the enormous wall in front of them.

"It's okay. I know you can do it, Haru," Chiyuri said as if she
had read his mind, and proceeded to squeeze his hand lightly.
He looked over to see the familiar smile of the friend he'd known
since birth, and yet it still made him suck in a tight breath. "Once
it all starts, don't think about stuff. Just get in there and blast 'em!
You take a little damage and I'll heal you up in no time flat."

"Yeah, I'm counting on you." Haruyuki smiled back and
stared up at their route. The bus had already gone from the old
Yamate-dori onto Komazawa-dori and was heading east. All he
could see through the front windshield was clusters of buildings
on both sides of the road, but in the distance, overlaid on the
image of the city, he glimpsed a chalky palace shimmering like
a mirage—the Acceleration Research Society headquarters he'd
seen once in the Unlimited Neutral Field. He'd gotten caught
then in the shadow-slipping ability of the self-professed vice
president of the Society, Black Vise, and charged into the place
without any idea of anything, but this time was different. He was
prepared, he was with his comrades, and he was attacking of his
own will.

According to the map on the ceiling, there were about two
kilometers left. A little over four minutes, then.

Looking at the display brought a question back to his mind,

so Haruyuki hurriedly turned around once more. "O-oh, right! Master, I forgot to ask something important."

"What's that, Corvus?"

"Um, now that Shibuya's Nega Nebulus territory, our names won't show up on the matching list if we connect to the global net, right?"

"Well, basically, yes." Fuko nodded.

He heaved a sigh of relief. "Then can I just contact CobaManga for a sec? I want to tell them what time to expect us."

"That's fine. But once you're done, please cut the connection again just in case."

"Roger!" He faced forward again and hurried to connect globally before launching his mailer. When he sent the Takanouchi sisters the anticipated time of the start of the Territories fight, he immediately got a ROGER from Koto and a GOOD LUCK! from Yuki.

The reason Burst Linkers didn't use messenger apps or any other SNS services to contact members of other Legions was to protect their privacy. Registering a person on SNS meant running the risk of unintentionally giving out information, and if you wanted to cut all contact later on, the person's SNS ID itself would have to be deleted. But if you simply exchanged so-called "burner mail" addresses, you could simply delete the address.

But the twin blade sisters had already revealed their faces and real names to him, so it was impossible for them to cut all connections with him. As he considered this, he sent a mail to Trilead as well. And then he figured he might as well report on the current situation in a voice call to Kuroyukihime while he was at it. Instead of her voice, however, he got a message on his virtual desktop that the person he was calling was not connected to the global net.

"Huh?" He cocked his head. It was already well past four, and Kuroyukihime and Niko were supposedly on defense standby in Suginami. And obviously, you had to be connected globally for a sortie in the Territories. Maybe their bus back to Suginami had been delayed or something.

"What's up, Haru?" Chiyuri asked.

Haruyuki shook his head. "I'm okay. It's nothing."

Even if Kuroyukihime and Niko were a few minutes late, they could count on the members of the former Prominence to help out with the defense of Suginami, so there was no issue. He got a reply of I UNDERSTAND. IT'S FINALLY HAPPENING, HMM? from Trilead, so he decided to call it all good and disconnected his Neurolinker from the global net.

✳✳✳

"Now look, Kuroyuki," Niko said from the seat beside her, and Kuroyukihime awoke from her reverie.

"What?"

"I was just thinkin'…this bus we're on, it'll never ever catch up with the bus with Haruyuki and them or the one with your pal, yeah?"

"Of course not," Kuroyukihime sniffed. "It's an automatic bus on a circular route. If we did pass the vehicles ahead of us, it would mean the AI was out of control."

"No, not that!" Niko rolled her eyes. "I *mean*, if they start the Territories the instant the bus with Haruyuki and them gets into Minato Three, we won't make it in time!" She pressed a finger into the area around Kuroyukihime's kneecap.

In return, Kuroyukihime jabbed her in the side of her red T-shirt as she replied in the same hushed voice, "I know that much at least, you know! Shibuya area here should already be our territory, so I'd very much like to connect globally and let someone there know the situation. But even if I did tell them you and I are going to take part so they should hold off on starting, do you think they'll simply agree with that?"

"…Definitely not. One hundred percent no way." Niko groaned.

"Exactly. If we do this wrong, the whole mission itself might be canceled. That's why…"

"That's why what?"

"I'm thinking about what we should do."

Fwmp! Niko slumped down in her seat and looked at her, exasperated. "You were talkin' so high and mighty, I figured you had a plan. Hmm. Even if we grab a taxi now, there's no way they'll go fast enough to overtake the buses, either."

In the present year, 2047, when all vehicles had AI controls, no vehicle—driverless or not—could exceed the legal speed limit. In an emergency, a driver in a manual vehicle could temporarily turn off the AI, but doing that without a good reason carried the penalty of no mere fine but an actual arrest. And no matter how they pleaded, there was no way a taxi driver would do something like that for two strange girls, anyway.

But Niko was right—the possibility that Fuko and the others would start the Territories the instant they had crossed the area boundary was definitely nonzero. She assumed that in reality, they would take a few minutes to prepare, but even still, she didn't know whether the bus they were on would catch up in that time.

The worst case would be if Megumi Wakamiya made it in time for the Territories and Kuroyukihime and Niko didn't. In that case, this whole chase would have been pointless, and Kuroyukihime had the feeling that something would be decisively destroyed if they failed to force Megumi's hand here.

"So we have no choice then," she muttered, and she launched her taxi app.

Her Neurolinker wasn't connected globally, so she couldn't choose her preferred taxi company and car make from a wide range, but if there was an empty taxi nearby, she could call it on an ad hoc connection. She checked the driverless option and did a search. She got an immediate hit, fortunately, although it was just the one vehicle. She set the pickup location at the next bus stop and their destination as a random spot in Minato Area No. 3 before whispering to Niko, "We're getting off at the next stop and taking a taxi."

"Sure, sure," Niko agreed. "You got a trick up your sleeve?"

"A trick I don't really want to use."

"I have a very bad feeling about this." Niko looked highly doubtful, so Kuroyukihime jabbed her in the side once more before standing up and heading toward the rear doors. When the bus stopped in the bus bay a minute or so later, they jumped down onto the sidewalk and ran over to the small taxi that pulled up behind the bus.

She pressed the confirmation button on the taxi app and climbed in through the rear door that opened automatically. Since she'd already specified their destination, the taxi pulled out immediately, and the AI's synthetic voice rang out in the cabin. "Thank you for using Smart Cab Tokyo's automatic taxi service. For your safety and comfort, please pay attention to the following important points…"

Ignoring the fixed announcement, Niko clicked her tongue in irritation. "Totally driverless car? Now there's no way we can switch to emergency mode and fly out of here."

"Now, now. You're talking quite dangerously there." Kuroyukihime gave her a wry smile, but Niko was right. The vehicle was completely automatic, with no steering wheel or pedals for human use. Both front and back seats were for passengers, and all that was on the dashboard was a large information panel. They indeed could not use the emergency driving mode, even if they were prepared to be arrested for doing so.

But Kuroyukihime had had a reason for choosing a completely automatic car. She pulled a wound-up XSB cable from the pocket of her school uniform and inserted one end into her Neurolinker. Leaning forward, she pushed the other end into the connector beneath the dashboard. The only change in the display on her virtual desktop was a wired charging mark in the top right. And this was only natural. The connector was there for passengers to charge devices, and it was impossible to use this port to access the car's system. Normally, anyway.

"Whoa, hey there. You're charging *now*?"

Kuroyukihime glanced at Niko's exasperated face before closing her eyes and giving the voice command she had never once used in front of someone else. "Triple S Order! Activate!"

Bwan. As a virtual vibration sounded, a complicated emblem appeared in the center of her field of view. Two types of flowers winding around two swords standing side by side, intersecting diagonally to draw out a circle. The emblem soon vanished, and in its place, a control window for the taxi system popped up.

"System administrator log-in confirmed."

"Wha—?!" Hearing the AI voice, Niko bounced up from her reclining position. "Wh-wh-what's going on?!"

"I'll explain later."

"E-explain now! What the hell's this admin..." The Red King pushed forward. Kuroyukihime put a palm to her forehead to push her back before turning her attention to the control window.

First, she turned off the camera monitoring the cabin and gave the order to arrive in the minimum time at the legal speed limit. Instantly, the taxi switched to the right lane and, with a force that pressed their backs into the seat, accelerated to a speed of eighty kilometers an hour, just barely under the legal limit.

"Whoa! A-are we gonna be okay?!"

"Hang on tight. We're flying!"

Now the car swung into the left lane and sped along Yamate-dori, slipping into and out of the three lanes as though sewing them together.

Niko grabbed the armrest inside the door to stabilize herself and shifted from panic back to exasperation. "Dang! Where exactly did you pick up this kind of hacking tech?!" she shouted over the high-pitched whine of the motor.

"My former master taught me all kinds of things."

"Master?" Niko frowned. "*That* guy? Graphite Edge?"

She nodded. And indeed, the Anomaly had schooled her in

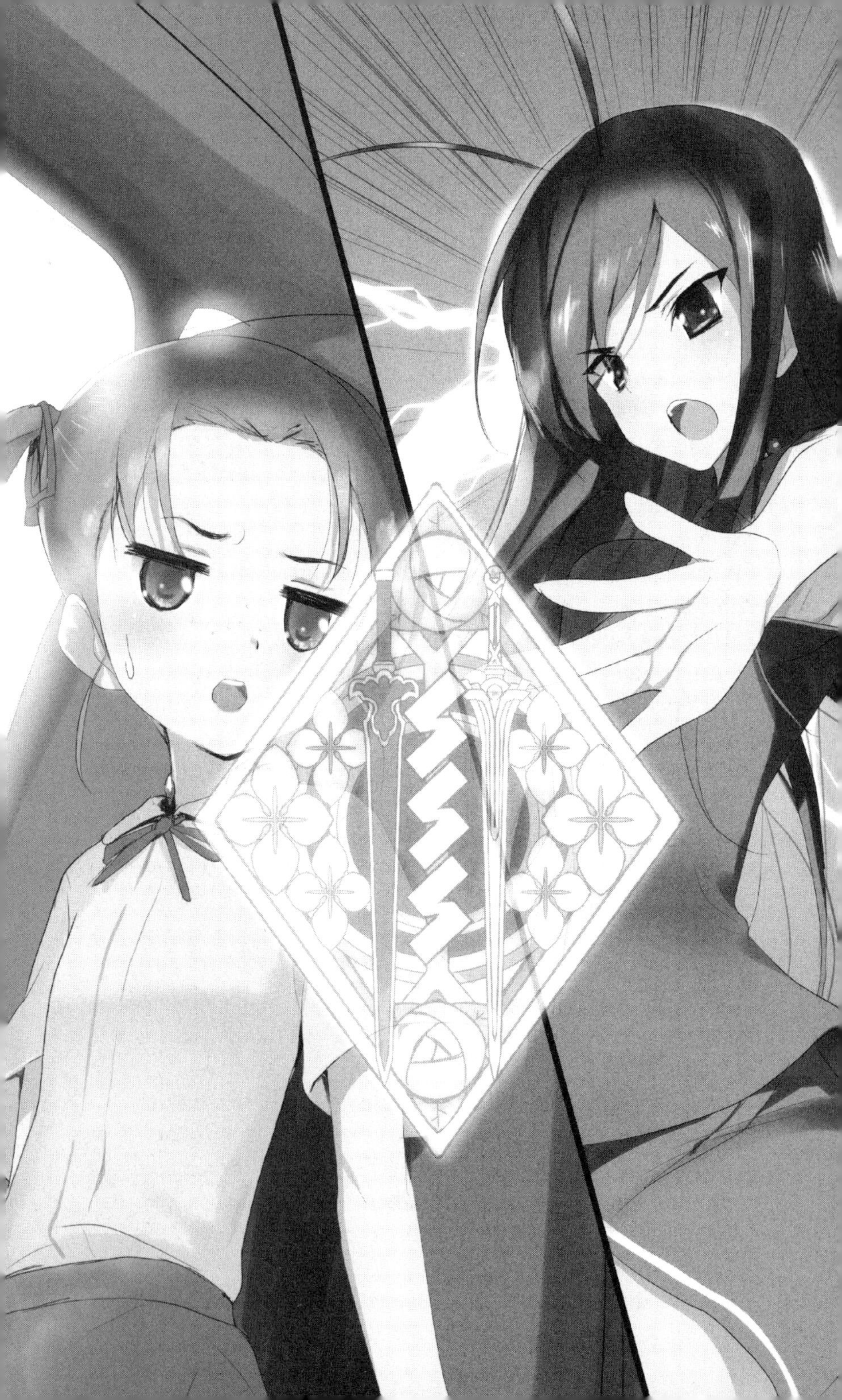

the ways not only of Brain Burst but also of the global net. But immediately before the attack on the Castle that would spell the doom of the first Nega Nebulus, he had also given Kuroyukihime a mysterious program. The emblem of the double swords and flowers—SSS Order.

Using this, Kuroyukihime's Neurolinker could execute administrator privileges for essentially all systems connected to the global net. She could even overwrite name tags verified by the basic residents' register, one of the country's most critical systems. The only places SSS Order couldn't interfere were the social camera network and the Brain Burst central server.

Why had Graphite Edge given Kuroyukihime this incredible power? She hadn't understood at the time. But once the Legion had collapsed, a bounty had been put on her head, and she'd moved from Minato to Suginami, she'd finally thought it made sense.

Anticipating the future, Graphite Edge had given Kuroyukihime a way to survive as a Burst Linker. In fact, it was because of SSS Order that she'd been able to freely manipulate the in-school net at Umesato Junior High and discover the true identity of her random attacker, Cyan Pile. She'd also been able to look up the name of the player who'd gotten that incredible high score in the squash game, as well as set up a remote access gate so Fuko, Utai, and the others could connect to the Umesato Junior High local net.

But she avoided using SSS Order for anything other than her main objective of defending the Umesato space—except for the time when she tested out overwriting name tags. One reason for this was that the power it contained was simply overwhelming, but part of her reluctance to use it stemmed from her frustration with Graph's overprotectiveness.

She could forgive herself for breaking that self-inflicted prohibition now, however. For Megumi's sake. And the sake of her Legion comrades.

"Sheesh. No matter how deep ya dig, you're a woman of many secrets," Niko remarked.

"Well, keep digging. Maybe you'll get to the bottom one day," she replied, looking out ahead of them. She caught a glimpse in the distance of a large green vehicle—the bus that carried Megumi Wakamiya.

***

The Brain Burst area boundaries were naturally invisible in the real world, but the majority of Burst Linkers had customized the navigation functions in their Neurolinkers so that the lines would be displayed in AR. Haruyuki was no exception; he could clearly see the approaching red line through the bus's large front window. The intersection at Tengenjibashi where Meiji-dori and Gaien Nishi-dori crossed…once they went through it, the bus would be in Minato Area No. 3.

His heart kept trying to pick up speed, and Haruyuki did his best to be calm. In the end, he turned to Fuko through the gap in the headrest behind him. "Master, when will we start?"

"Hmm." Fuko tilted her head slightly to one side, and her smooth long hair swung back and forth as she spoke. "Our initial location in the Territories is always somewhere on the edge, regardless of location in the real, so it's not an issue to start the instant we cross the boundary. But it wouldn't be a waste to get a sense of the area for a little bit on this side. Since we've come all this way, how about we start once we've reached the intersection at Furukawabashi, the start of Meiji-dori?"

"Understood." Nodding, he looked forward again.

A minute or two later, the bus crossed the bright red line that only Haruyuki and his friends could see and entered Minato Area No. 3. He wasn't actually expecting anything to happen right away since their connections to the global net were still off. Nevertheless, he felt as if the color and temperature of the air had changed somehow, and he grabbed hold of his seat tightly.

The group of three elderly women got off at the next stop, Korinjimae, leaving only the fourteen on the attack team inside the automatic bus. Takumu and Rui were sitting in the seat in front of Haruyuki and Chiyuri, with the three former members of Petit Paquet across the aisle with Rin. Fuko and Utai were in the seat behind him, and Akira was across from them. And then, on the bench seat in the very back of the bus, was the former Prominence's Triplex—Pard, Cassis Moose, and Thistle Porcupine.

Meeting these last two in the real for the first time, he'd found that they matched their images in the Accelerated World fairly well. Cassis was a large and artless ninth grader, while Thistle was a small, seemingly clever seventh grader. Haruyuki's usual shy-person mode had immediately been activated, so he hadn't really talked to them, but Akira, Utai, and the others had been exchanging information with them during their trip. Once the mission was over, they were supposed to return to Suginami and have a meeting—the venue being, naturally, the Arita home—so he would have the chance to talk to them then.

The fight that was about to start was the biggest mission Haruyuki had been on since becoming a Burst Linker, but it definitely wouldn't be the decisive final battle. It was merely the first step in revealing the evil deeds of the Society, taking back Niko's Enhanced Armament, and freeing Wolfram Cerberus.

Hang on, Cerberus. I will *free you from the Catastrophe that's tormenting you. So many people helped me when I ended up Chrome Disaster, and now it's my turn to help you.*

"Next stop, Furukawabashi," a synthetic voice announced. "Furukawabashi. Passengers traveling to Shirokanetakanawa Station, please change here."

The speaker had no sooner gone silent than Fuko stood up in the seat behind him and shouted resolutely, "Everyone, get ready to connect globally!"

All present touched their Neurolinkers.

"Once the connection's complete, I'll accelerate immediately and challenge Oscillatory Universe to a territory fight. Now that we've come all this way, there's only one thing I can say to you... We're going to win!"

""""Yeah!!""""

The whole team responded at a shout, and Fuko lowered herself into her seat. Haruyuki pressed his back firmly against his own seat and readied himself to accelerate.

The bus made a gentle left turn and approached Furukawabashi. The sunlight, starting to incline, reflected off the countless windows of the skyscraper condo rising up in front of them and made them glitter.

"I'm starting the count!" came her voice. "Five, four, three, two, one...connect!"

Haruyuki pushed down on the physical switch on his Neurolinker, and an icon flashed in his field of view to inform him that he was connected to the global net.

"Burst Link!!" Fuko called.

Skreeeeee!! The cold, dry sound of acceleration chased Haruyuki from behind and sent him flying to the fateful battleground.

5

The instant Silver Crow's feet touched the ground of the stage, Haruyuki spun himself around to check the situation.

It was night. He couldn't see a single star in the inky sky, but several pale blue dots rose up through it like searchlights, illuminating thick clouds. The source of the light was a group of buildings that sported a blue-black metallic luster and ornamentation that looked like massive blades encircling their walls. The ground was covered with tightly packed tiles in complicated shapes, and there wasn't a single plant to be found.

"...De..." He opened his mouth, but the intense roar of an engine cut him off—and then was itself drowned out by an even louder shout.

"Hey, hey, heeeeeey!! Demon City stage, seriously noice choice! Giga-greatastic compared with a Desert or an Ocean, anywayyyyyy!!"

"I totally feel you, but what's 'greatastic,' bro?"

"You gotta be kidding! Even I know that one! Just means 'great,' right, bro-man?"

"Ah, gotcha. Just like it sounds then, sweet!"

"......"

Haruyuki's brain shut down completely for few seconds, until he shook his head to reboot and recommence his espionage.

The stage attribute was a Demon stage, just as the "bro" on the motorcycle had noted. In normal duels and the Territories, it was always night, and the buildings were so hard they were basically indestructible, but there were no annoying gimmicks like poison or insects or pitfalls.

They were currently smack in the middle of an intersection where two large streets crossed, and skyscrapers rose up in front of him as if to pierce the night sky; behind him, a steel circuit ran parallel to the ground in midair, likely an overhead expressway in the real world, be it for cars or trains.

The only human figures in the area were the group of three putting on their little show a ways off. There should have been a total of eighteen people on the Nega Nebulus territory attacking team, but there was no one else as far as he could see.

Was it possible that the Oscillatory Universe defense team was a mere four people, and so the attack team had been whittled down to that number to match? The thought crossed his mind, but he quickly rejected it. If that were the case, the rule was that the members with the highest levels were selected in order, so there was no way level eighters Fuko and Pard would be skipped in favor of himself, a level six. The health gauges displayed in the upper part of his view, too—only Haruyuki and the three others were displayed in the top left, while the top right was completely blank.

Haruyuki walked over to the little group, thinking to discuss the incomprehensible situation. "Um, Ash…"

Ash Roller snapped his index fingers out at him, straddling his extremely over-the-top American motorcycle, and shouted, "Hey! Finally, the radical epoch, ya damned bird!!"

"R-radical epoch?" Haruyuki frowned. "What's that?"

"Whoa, whoa, catch my drift already! You've known me too long to be confused now! 'Radical' is 'big' and 'epoch' is 'day.' Put it together and you got the big day, obviosoroso!"

Haruyuki suppressed the sigh that rose up within him. "Totally obviosoroso…but, like, this isn't the time for that! For some reason, there's only the four of us here. I can't see the gauges of any of our comrades or the enemy. What's going on here?"

In the normal way of things, this would be the time when Ash finally noticed the abnormality and started freaking out with his "Realiousy?!" But this time was different. He whirled his index fingers around, and a grin crept onto his skull face.

"So then, Crow, this's your first time in a large-scale territory fight, huh?"

"Th-that's obvious, isn't it? Nega Nebulus's been a single-digit Legion this whole time."

"Okaykaykay. U, Oli. Explain the sitch to our newbie bird here."

"Roger that, boss man!" Bush Utan responded enthusiastically and slammed his gorilla-like arm up against his gorilla-like chest before stepping out in front of Haruyuki. "Um, so Crow—the rules are just a little different for large-scale territory fights with a total of twelve or more people involved, you feel me? For the initial placement, okay, you're distributed in teams of four, and only the health gauges of allies and enemies that are right near you are displayed."

When Utan closed his mouth, Olive Grab stepped up, the light of the buildings reflecting off his rich green armor almost wetly, and added, "But there's no need to panic. Both teams are split up and placed either east-west or north-south, so everyone else should appear somewhere near here. You and Oli and them'll meet up with them as we move toward the center."

"I—I get it…Giga-thanks for the explanation…" After he dipped his head in appreciation, Haruyuki asked the question that wouldn't stop nagging him. "So like, Olive, the last time I saw you, you referred to yourself as 'I,' right? When did this 'Oli' start?"

"Olio, oh, you noticed, huh?" A grin spread across his simple elliptical face mask. "It's just like, compared with Bro and U, Oli's character's kinda weak, yeah? Oli thinks maybe that's the reason the ISS kit ate way deeper into Oli, so from now on, Oli's gonna really set up a real character to connect with! Third person it is!"

"……"

"I—I get it...I can understand that..." Nodding once more, Haruyuki looked around. Now that they mentioned it, he remembered being told at the pre-mission briefing to head for the center while occupying any visible bases if team members appeared in separate locations. He'd just assumed that wouldn't happen, but it did seem now that they would have to move at first as a small group.

"So then, let's hurry up and get moving, Ash," Haruyuki stated as he started to walk.

Ash crossed his arms in front of his chest and shook his index finger back and forth in a tut-tut-tut motion. "Don't be in such a rush, Crow. First, you gotta take a *deeeep breath.*"

"Huh? O-okay..." Thus ordered in unusually correct English, he couldn't exactly say no. He stopped, stood up straight, and spread his arms out together with Utan and Olive as he breathed iiiiin and oooooout.

Ash continued calmly, "Me and U and Oli, we ran into a giga-terrible time being parasitized by the ISS kits. But we're not part of the mission just 'cos we want to get our revenge on those Acceleration Research Society jerks."

Haruyuki continued to breathe deeply, in and out.

The skull rider stared at him as he continued his monologue. "I just really like duels. O'course, I got all kinds of plans...But more than anything else, I'm happy if I can get that red heat while I'm fighting. How! Ev! Er! We just go letting the Society do whatever they want, we won't be able to have any real good duels soon. If Negabu are gonna fight to protect what I love, then I can't exactly sit back and watch, y'know? That's why I'm here. But, like..."

At some point, Haruyuki had forgotten to breathe deeply, and the words Ash spoke next penetrated deep into his heart.

"I ain't inclined to bend now. Whatever happens, I'm not bringing any grudges or hatred into the duel, get it? I'm just gonna burn red and fight...Are you understanding?"

"……Yep, I completely understand." Haruyuki bobbed his head. "The important thing is to burn with everything you've got on the battlefield, and not be bound by the Society. We can't forget that."

"Nail hit with that answer, Crow." Instead of Ash's finger guns, he got a solid thumbs-up, and Utan and Olive also clenched their hands into tight fists.

This might have been a critical mission, but it was also the Brain Burst Territories. So he would have fun with the fight like Ash. And even if he couldn't get to that point, he could just plant his feet firmly on the ground, look around carefully, and fight the way he always did.

Now that he was thinking about it, he didn't actually know where in Minato Area No. 3 they'd appeared. "First, let's check on our current location!" Haruyuki ran over to the nearest skyscraper. The building itself was too hard to smash easily, but maybe the lance-like railing that encircled the site could be broken.

"Hng…aaaah!"

He mowed down over ten meters of the black iron railing with three roundhouse kicks in succession to build up his special-attack gauge to around 30 percent. A moment later, he deployed the wings on his back and jumped with everything he had. The metal fins shook and ascended to an altitude of around thirty meters in an instant.

Hovering, he spun around to look at his surroundings and saw a large waterway on the other side of the overhead line and a dark body of water beyond that that was probably the ocean. Even farther in the distance was the reclaimed land, complete with a demon king's castle and a large Ferris wheel, plus a bridge that was now a network of large lances. That would be Odaiba and its Rainbow Bridge. Which meant they were currently on the southeastern edge of Minato Area No. 3.

Here his special-attack gauge started to run out, so he began to glide down. Right before he hit the ground, Haruyuki spent the last of his thrust to come down softly. "I figured it out! We're a little to the north of Tennozu Isle!"

As he opened the map he'd memorized in the back of his mind, he pointed to the west. "Shinagawa Station's this way, and on the other side of that is the center of the area!"

"Awriiiight! Team Rough Valley Rollers Plus One, mission start!"

Ash made his engine roar with panache.

""Roger!"" Utan and Olive cried out together.

Huh? That's the team name you picked? Haruyuki thought in dismay, but in the end, all he could say was "Roger."

✼ ✼ ✼

Rui Odagiri/Magenta Scissor had never fought in the Territories. Given that she had just become a part of a Legion for the first time that very day, this was only natural. But she'd gone over the rules and basic knowledge of the whole thing very carefully so that she wouldn't drag the rest of the team down just because she was new to this.

The Territories were essentially a tug-of-war for footholds. These footholds, metallic rings floating in the air, would charge the special-attack gauge of any duel avatar who stood inside one. But to turn on the charging function, you first needed to "occupy" the foothold, and for that you had to be on standby beneath the metal ring for thirty seconds.

These thirty seconds seemed short and yet were incredibly long, Sky Raker had told Rui and the Chocolat Puppeter team in their Territories lecture. Indeed, in a place where there were no surrounding obstacles, it was painful just to imagine standing there for a full thirty seconds while enduring fierce enemy attacks. Given Magenta Scissor's thin armor, she probably wouldn't be assigned the role of occupying.

In which case Rui's role had to be that of thoroughly protecting the avatar who did. To that end she would need to go ahead and use the ability she normally did her utmost to avoid using, and she would have to do it without any reservation right from the initial stages of the battle.

Do me right today, she murmured in her heart as she stroked the pair of large knives equipped on her hips.

"I knew it. Looks like there's no one in the immediate vicinity, huh?" A large close-range avatar—Cyan Pile—trotted over to her.

The small, defensive avatar whirling her head around next to Rui—Lime Bell—tilted her triangular witch hat. "I think we got distributed over a pretty wide range. So should we move toward the center like in the strategy?"

"Yeah, that'd make sense." Pile nodded.

"Roger," Rui replied.

They had appeared right beside Shibaura-futo Station on the Yurikamome line, in the northeastern part of Minato Area No. 3. If they proceeded west on the road in front of them, they would run into the JR line in a kilometer or so, and the central area was on the other side of that. The enemy was probably also starting to move, so they had to reach the center first before the critical stronghold was taken from them.

They started to run along the deserted main thoroughfare in a triangle formation, with Cyan Pile in the lead. The Demon City was dark, quiet, and immaculate, so it was one of Rui's favorite stages, but she was forced to admit that its one major failing was that the sound of their footsteps carried far on the hard-tiled earth.

Listening to the *kashk-kashk* of Pile's heavy feet and Bell's rhythmic *tuk-tok-tuk-tok*, a question—or rather a curiosity she'd felt any number of times—abruptly popped up in her mind, and Rui opened her mouth. "You mind if I ask you one thing, maybe?"

"Ask away!" the Watch Witch replied cheerfully.

Rui looked at her out of the corner of her eye and casually asked, "Are you and Pile dating in the real?"

"Gaaaah!" Cyan Pile slipped ahead of them. He threw his arms out wildly and just barely managed to regain his balance.

Bell, however, kept both feet moving calmly—or so it seemed—as she groaned. "And herrrre it is!" She glanced at Pile's back with her catlike eye lenses, and then replied with another question: "Why do you think that, Magenta?"

"Um..." *Why* do *I think that, actually?* She traced her own thoughts backward. "Seeing you in the real together, I just thought that...I guess. That and the form of your duel avatars."

"Our avatars?" Lime Bell seemed to frown. "But they have absolutely nothing in common."

"Oh my, they do, though." Rui giggled a little and pointed at the handbell equipped on Bell's left hand. "You and Pile both have a large Enhanced Armament equipped on one hand, and your silhouettes are asymmetrical, y'know? You look pretty compatible."

"Sh-she said it..." Groaning once again, Bell raised her left arm and lightly rang the clapper inside the bell that had apparently been fixed in place until then. *Rinnng...*She turned her ear to the faint trail of the sound and murmured, "Hrm...Are Taku and I dating...? To be honest, I wonder about that myself...I haven't really been able to see him much."

Pile's large back shook just a little. But he kept silent.

"You two and Crow've known one another since you were little?" Rui asked.

"Yup. We have." Bell nodded right away. "Since right after we were born, actually."

"So then, longer than me and Avo, huh...? I wonder if there's anything you can't see when you're this close for that long."

"It's not about how long you've known someone or the physical distance or anything...or, like, that's what I've been thinking lately anyway." Bell looked up at Rui, and a smile that had a somehow plaintive air to it rose up on her face.

"In fact, if you're always right next to each other, then that gradually becomes 'just the way things are'...Like maybe you stop understanding how fleeting and precious what you have really is. So I'm really grateful to Brain Burst, because it connected me and Taku and Haru again when we were on the verge of breaking apart. Of course, the Accelerated World might not continue forever either...If Kuroyukihime clears the game, it might disappear, and maybe the day will come when we're all adults and we stop accelerating. But that's exactly why I want to protect everything here now—Nega Nebulus, all our friends, and the Accelerated World itself. That's what I think, anyway."

This was the most Lime Bell, the girl named Chiyuri Kurashima, had ever said in a conversation with her, and Rui felt the emotion of what she was saying deep in her own heart.

Rui had actually tried to destroy the existing order of the Accelerated World using the ISS kits. But that was also because her initial desire had been to protect. She'd wanted to save weaker Burst Linkers like Avocado Avoider who were simply exploited for their points before they disappeared. She wanted to make a world where even those players who were born without a cool look or powerful abilities and who lacked Enhanced Armaments could stand up tall and live proudly. And because she wanted this, Rui had sought strength.

But her mistake there was twofold.

The ISS kit was not just an object to redress the ability gap among duel avatars. It was an evil parasite that tried to corrupt the minds of users, including Rui, and breed endless self-hatred. And her other, even bigger mistake was that for a long time, she hadn't even questioned whether the disparity and unfairness she was blindly attempting to correct really existed in the Accelerated World. She realized this in the fight with Black Lotus and Silver Crow in the Unlimited Neutral Field, and again in the duel she watched between Chocolat Puppeter and Avocado Avoider.

Avocado's fighting style went far beyond Rui's expectations; he was brave, persistent, wonderful. The duel itself had ended in a TKO loss for Avocado, a decision from Rui based on everything she'd seen up to that point, but if she'd let them keep going, he might have even been able to turn things around in a one-in-a-million chance for the win.

It was Rui herself who had arbitrarily decided that Avocado Avoider was a weak person only there to be exploited. Avocado could boast of his own particular strength, and he had potential. She wasn't so naïve that she believed in the whole "same level, same potential" spiel at this stage in the game, but if Avocado Avoider wanted to get stronger…and if he had comrades besides Rui who would train him, guide him, laugh with him, and fight with him, then maybe he would someday beat Chocolat or Silver Crow or even Rui. No one, especially not Rui, could deny this possibility, and as long as that possibility existed, she had to protect this world she had once tried to destroy.

"…Right…I have a dream. No, I *found* my dream," she murmured, and Lime Bell turned her large eye lenses on her quizzically. "I want to go and apologize to each and every one of the Burst Linkers in the Setagaya area who suffered so much because of me—Melon Splitter, Terracotta Bowl, Mud Halibut, Hay Saikidai, Honey Bee, Butter Bar, Almond Urchin, Taupe Mole, Pimento Ant, Pewter Guppy, Corn Corn, Meadow Sheep, and Avocado Avoider—and if I can be forgiven, I want to fight together to find fun things this time."

"Sounds great!" Lime Bell responded immediately, with a huge, bright smile. "So you can just invite them all to join the Legion, right? And boom! We announce our ownership of Setagaya Areas Two to Four. GW might come and attack, but we'll all help out for a solid defense!"

"I appreciate that." Rui nodded with a dry smile at this future that Bell had put forth so casually. Her original question had disappeared into the ether at some point, but it would be uncouth to pry any further, so she decided to just let it go for now.

Amusingly, an air of relief wafted up around Cyan Pile as he ran ahead of them, and so Rui found herself grinning again. Before she knew it, the steel railways cutting north-south across the stage appeared up ahead.

✳ ✳ ✳

"So, like, Cassis? I thought the groups were random with the distributed start in a large-scale Territories fight?"

At this question from the Triplex's Thistle Porcupine, Cassis Moose shook his massive horns from side to side. "No. I remember it being not completely random. The groups are split up based on duel and tag team histories, with the addition of your location in the real…I believe. It should be."

"Aah, I get it. So then it totally makes sense we'd get lumped together." Thistle nodded, the fur on her back fluttering in the breeze, and Mihaya looked away from her and up at the dark sky of the Demon City stage.

For Mihaya as well, it had been a long time since a large-scale Territories battle with a grand total of more than twenty people. Now that she was thinking about it, it might have been since back in the days when Prominence was still led by the first Red King. She'd expected them to be split up, but she hadn't thought that they would be so far apart that she couldn't see any of their comrades even with Blood Leopard's enhanced vision.

"So what're we doing, Pard?" Thistle asked. "Find our comrades or head for the center?"

After a second's thought, she made her decision. "The center. I want to pin down the stronghold before the enemy."

"Awright! Doing it!"

"Roger that."

Thistle and Cassis replied at the same time, and the triad started running to the west, slipping under the overhead expressway.

It was said that there were few objects in the Demon City stage that could be destroyed, but that wasn't necessarily the case for high rankers. They systematically smashed the stone pillars and iron fencing along either side of the wide road, Mihaya with the sharp claws of her hands, Cassis with his horns like a bulldozer blade, and Thistle with high-speed tumbling body slams.

Once their special-attack gauges were charged to a certain degree, she shouted, "Shape Change!!"

The three avatars were enveloped in light, and Mihaya became a sleek leopard, Cassis a burly moose, and Thistle a nimble porcupine. Then the three beasts charged down the midnight road, 30 percent faster than before.

In this Territories fight, Mihaya and her comrades were positioned as helpers, but they were definitely not sidelined observers. She had her own tie to the White Legion—the Acceleration Research Society—that rivaled that of the Black King.

In the attack on Midtown Tower twenty days earlier, she had been deeply humiliated when Niko, as the Red King, had been kidnapped by Black Vise before her very eyes, given that she had sworn to protect the girl for all time. Although she chased after them and made it into the Society's headquarters, Mihaya had been unable to break through Vise's long-distance Incarnate technique Octahedral Isolation and had been forced to watch as four parts of the Red King's Enhanced Armament were stolen from her.

Silver Crow had done everything he could, too, and they'd gotten three of the parts back, but the rear thrusters remained in the thief's possession. On top of that, the massive amount of negative Incarnate accumulated through the ISS kits was poured into those thrusters to transform them into the Armor of Catastrophe, Mark II, and the White King had described this as none other than a "precious hope."

Today, for sure, she would get them back. And then she would smash to pieces this scheme of the Acceleration Research Society and the White King.

"Grar!" Unconsciously, the roar of a wild beast slipped from her throat, and Mihaya kicked at the road beneath her even harder.

✳ ✳ ✳

"Pwaaah, it's daaaark. It's haaaard. I'm scaaaared," Yume—Plum Flipper—whined as she punched half-heartedly at the dark iron fence.

"Now loooook!" Satomi—Mint Mitten—called out to her in exasperation from behind. "There's plenty of other dark stages. Like, there's no way we're gonna be able to break these pillars. They look haaaard."

"But, liiiiike, I feel all anxious when my special-attack gauge isn't charged."

"That's why I'm always telling you, Yume—I mean Plum—that you should practice fighting with us. It's all well and good to be able to knock a plum pit flying, but for a duel, you actually need to know the basics of punching and kicking—"

"It's not a plum pit! It's a plum seeeeed!"

"Same thing!"

"Look, both of you," Shihoko interjected with a sigh, since she didn't know how long they'd keep this up if she stayed silent, "it's about time we got moving."

"Huh?" Satomi wondered. "Aren't we going to wait for Crow and the others, Choco?"

"We're not." She nodded hard enough to push away the uncertainty and fear in her chest. "The location we appeared in is most likely the closest to the center of the stage. In which case, this is our chance to lock down the stronghold before the enemy!"

"Th-that might be true, but we might encounter the enemy—just us," Yume pointed out uneasily.

"We'll think about that when it happens!" Shihoko barked. "If we get freaked out before we fight, we won't be able to win a winnable fight!"

"Guuurl. You're just getting carried away because you won in that solo duel yesterday," Satomi grumbled, but then brought her hands, ensconced in their large mittens, together. "But, yeah, if you're talking about chances, this is a chance. Yume, the dead center of Minato Three's right up ahead, yeah?"

"Prob'ly. I think it's on the other side of the station building there." Yume pointed with her slender hand at the skyscraper rising up nefariously on the southern side.

They were standing on the platform of the Yamanote Line's Takanawa Station, which had opened for the 2020 Tokyo Olympics. Naturally, in line with the design of the Demon City stage, it had been given a sort of sci-fi noir look, but the silver tracks below the platform shone with a pale light.

Nodding at each other, they jumped down from the platform and came out onto the Dai-ichi Keihin highway, straddling the tracks, which were sharp like knives, and started to run alongside each other. Large buildings stood on the other side of the wide six-lane highway, but beyond them, she could see the hazy shimmer of a blue light. It was probably…

"The stronghold…maybe. It's close," Satomi murmured, and Shihoko and Yume nodded wordlessly.

At the moment, there was no sign of any other Burst Linkers in the area. No enemy health gauges were displayed in the upper right of her field of view, either.

"All right, we'll occupy the fort first and protect it until Crow and the others catch up!" Shihoko instructed in a hushed cheer before running again.

Chocolat Puppeter was level five, while Mint and Plum were both four, meaning they were likely the bottom-ranked team on the battlefield in terms of strength. But they could put up a solid fight as long as they could just occupy the stronghold. She could create Chocopets, chocolate AI fighting puppets, without limit if the stronghold kept charging her special-attack gauge. That together with Satomi's close-range skills and Yume's long-range attacks should be enough for a defense the enemy wouldn't be able to break through so easily as all that.

But conversely, if the fort was occupied before they got there, approaching it alone would be a suicide mission. If that happened, they would have no choice but to quietly retreat and await the arrival of their allies. In other words, they needed to approach the stronghold as quickly and quietly as possible.

Minimizing the echo of their feet on the hard ground as they crossed the highway, the three Burst Linkers moved through the gaps in the buildings farther west.

Soon a dense forest came into view ahead of them. The trees were tinged with a metallic luster, the branches and leaves pointed like weapons. In the center of this forest, an ostentatious building rose up like a pagan temple. The walls and roof were made up of enormous swords layered over each other, and blue watch fires shimmered ominously along the sides of the building. Countless sharply pointed iron pillars formed lines to threaten potential intruders. This would undoubtedly be the lair of the boss monster in any other stage.

"What would that building be in the real world?" Satomi asked.

"Probably Sengakuji Temple," Yume replied, plucking from her vast stores of knowledge. "The place with the graves of the forty-seven *ronin*."

"Whoa." Satomi looked impressed. "What'll we do if we see the ghost of Kira Yoshinaka?!"

"Look, that's the guy who got *hit* by the forty-seven *ronin*."

If she let them start, they'd never stop, so Shihoko cleared her throat to interrupt them. "Right now, the enemy's scarier than any ghosts. Do you sense them in the area?"

"Not at the mo."

"Seems okay."

She nodded firmly. "Then we're going in." Stepping from the road into the forest, she cast a glance at the timer in the upper part of her field of view and found that nearly three minutes had already passed.

Minato Area No. 3 was about three kilometers wide east to west, which meant it was about a kilometer and a half from the edge to Sengakuji. Even hurrying, it would take at least four or five minutes to get there while occupying the footholds along the way. As long as no other team had been placed near the center like Shihoko and her friends in some kind of coincidence, they would have the time to occupy the fort.

They trotted forward beneath metal trees until the grove finally ended and her field of view opened up.

In front of the ostentatious temple was a square plaza about thirty meters on each side with a square altar in the middle. A metallic ring with a complicated design carved into it floated above the center of the altar, a mere fifty centimeters off the ground. Humming quietly and emitting blue light as it rotated slowly, the ring was a lone stronghold, the center of the Territories stage. And it was still empty.

"Yassss! We're first!" Satomi cried out in a small voice, and she leapt forward.

Shihoko reflexively moved to pull her back, but then thought it over and stepped out of the forest herself. She couldn't imagine an enemy ambush in this situation. If anyone had arrived earlier, they would have been trying to occupy the fort themselves.

She chased after Satomi, cutting across the plaza to reach the altar. The three players quickly exchanged nods and then jumped onto the altar at the same time to set foot in the magic circle pattern drawn directly beneath the ring.

Instantly the ring grew brighter, and it started to rotate faster. Three digital displays of 30 popped up around them and started to drop with a beep each second. Once the counter reached zero, their occupation of the base would be complete.

"Hurry! Hurry!" Satomi stared impatiently at the numbers.

Shihoko grabbed her head without hesitation and yanked it forward. "It feels slow because you're counting down! You should be keeping an eye out for danger!"

"Fiiiiine." Satomi turned her gaze to the western side of the plaza.

Yume was already checking the east, so Shihoko set her attention on the south. There was an indestructible temple immediately to the north, so there was no fear of being attacked from that direction.

Even as she kept watch over the field, she couldn't stop counting down silently with the *beep-beep*. Twenty-three...twenty-two...twenty-one...

Just as Sky Raker had told them in the lecture beforehand, a mere thirty seconds was unbelievably long. She was seized with dread that an enemy group would appear at any moment at the southern entrance or from the forest to the east and west, and her breathing became shallower. Fifteen...fourteen...thirteen...

*Maybe we should have charged our special-attack gauges at the station like Yume said. But if we had, we would have been two minutes later getting here...*As her thoughts turned this way, the time remaining was finally dropping into the single digits.

And then Shihoko noticed her feet were being swallowed up by a white mist. Satomi and Yume also looked down at the ground at the same time.

"What the heck?!"

"Fog...?"

But the Demon City stage wasn't supposed to have any terrain effects. The mist was coming in from behind them and rolling off to the south. After exchanging a look with each other, the three girls turned slowly to the north.

Originally the main hall of Sengakuji, the jet-black temple had been enveloped in snow-white frost at some point while they weren't looking. It flowed down from the entire building and crawled along the ground—meaning it was no simple frost but a cold front. The steel temple was completely frozen.

The countdown hit zero, and the ring above her head flashed brilliantly. At basically the same time, the ground of the stage shook violently and delicate stitch-like cracks raced across the surface of the steel temple.

And then the building she'd thought was indestructible shattered into a million pieces. A thunderous roar shook the ground of the stage again, causing the dumbfounded girls to stagger and grab each other's hands to narrowly avoid falling over.

Shihoko squeezed her friends' hands hard when she saw it.

Someone—no, *something*—was standing on the other side of the ruined temple. She couldn't imagine it was a duel avatar. It was just too big.

Its height—altitude?—was nearly three meters, and its overall span was twice that. Bent as far forward as it could go, the creature was closer to a beast than a person, and the two thick, rounded arms touched the ground. The shape of its head was completely that of a carnivore, and a total of four long horns—from shoulders and forehead—pierced the sky. A long tail stretched out from its backside. The heavy armor encasing its body was pale like ice, and cold air from the fanged mouth spilled out in the form of a frosty mist. Most likely, this beast had completely frozen the temple and then smashed it with a body blow.

"I-is that...an Enemy...?" Yume croaked.

"Can't be." Satomi shook her head slightly. "I mean, this is the Territories battles."

"But there's no way any duel avatar's that huge..."

Satomi didn't rebut Yume again. And Shihoko also thought it was impossible, but she couldn't get her mouth to open.

As far as she knew, the largest avatar was Avocado Avoider, whom she'd fought the previous day—but he was only two and a half meters tall. In contrast, this white beast would be five meters tall if it stood up on its hind legs. That was closing in on the Wild class—or even Beast class—of Enemy. And if it really was Beast class, then it would rout the three girls of levels four and five with a single blow.

But then the eyes of the white beast shone a pale blue, and a new health gauge was displayed in the top right of Shihoko's view. Not only was this fully charged, of course, but the special-attack gauge was also full. Below that, a simple font shone in pearlescent white: GLACIER BEHEMOTH. Beside this: Lv 8.

"That's an enemy Burst Linker!" Shihoko shouted. "Plum! Mint! Get ready to fight!!"

Satomi and Yume quickly dropped into position. But their legs were shaking. And no wonder—level eight was for all practical purposes the highest rank in the Accelerated World. For the three junior players, this opponent was not all that different from a large Enemy. Actually, given the fact that they couldn't leave the stronghold to flee, its threat level might have been even higher.

But if they were going to helplessly vacate the base they'd only just occupied, then she didn't know why they'd volunteered for the Territories team—or why they'd even joined Nega Nebulus in the first place. If they couldn't win, they had to at least buy time until one of their allies caught up.

She glanced up to check their own gauges. Although their special-attack gauges were steadily charging thanks to the base ring, they were still far from full. Meanwhile, the enemy's gauge was practically bursting thanks to the fact that it had smashed an entire temple. They had to attack now rather than wait for their gauges to charge and risk getting slammed with a special attack. Shihoko took a deep breath to call up her Chocopets.

But before she could shout the technique name, the enormous white beast jumped. With a movement so nimble it belied its girth, it bounded over the mountain of rubble and landed immediately to the north of the stronghold Shihoko and her friends were occupying. And then its dragon mouth moved.

"My, my…I haven't seen you girls before."

""I-it spoke!!"" Satomi and Yume shouted at the same time.

The knife-like fangs of the beast avatar's mouth arranged themselves in something akin to a wry smile. "Oh yes, well, I do talk, you know. I apologize for not introducing myself sooner. I'm a member of Oscillatory Universe, Glacier Behemoth of the Seven Dwarves. My nicknames are Sneezy or Habakkuk. It is a pleasure to make your acquaintance."

""Sev—,"" Satomi and Yume started to shout, but Shihoko

silenced them by jabbing a finger up to the second knuckle into each of their backs as she returned the greeting.

"Th-thank you for the kind introduction. My name is Chocolat Puppeter. This is Mint Mitten, and this is Plum Flipper. We're pleased to meet you." She somehow managed to sound normal, if slightly awkward, but in her mind, Shihoko wanted so badly to shriek like her friends that she could hardly stand it.

Glacier Behemoth. The name had definitely been on the list of Oscillatory Universe members that Kuroyukihime handed out. And this was no ordinary Legion member, either, but one of the Seven Dwarves, the executive group. Given that he was one of the White Legion's top players, she would be wise to assume that even among the very few level eighters, he belonged to a more powerful class.

The three girls stayed where they were in the base ring with their frantic thoughts while the Burst Linker Glacier Behemoth looked down on them, eye lenses shining with pale light.

"Mm-hmm, mm-hmm. I have heard those names before. If I'm not mistaken, you belong to a small Legion in Setagaya? The Legion name…It was something like Pettit Pocket…"

"It's Petit Paquet!" Shihoko corrected unconsciously.

"Yes, yes. That's what it was." The beast nodded several times. "So, members of Pattit Piquant, what do you find yourselves here for?"

"It's obvious!" Satomi yelled, and Shihoko jabbed her in the side to shut her up.

He might know the name Petit Paquet, but he doesn't know we transferred to Nega Nebulus!

In which case, their best move here would be to drag out the misunderstanding. She inhaled deeply and called out boldly, "Yes, it's quite obvious! We cannot stay a rootless Legion forever, so we came to test our strength against the most powerful Legion to make the challenge of the Territories a little more exciting!"

Behemoth narrowed his eyes doubtfully, but nodded once more nonetheless. "Oh, oh, that is quite the laudable spirit, but to be quite honest, it comes at not entirely the best of times. We're actually in the middle of an important mission…Well, I suppose that's all right. In that case…" Muttering and mumbling, he looked up at the night sky. "Congeal Ray."

Following the sudden calling of the technique name, the left of the two horns growing from Behemoth's forehead glittered bright blue, so Shihoko and her friends stiffened defensively. But the pale ray of light shot straight up into the clouds in the distant sky above and did nothing more than make them shine blue for a few seconds before disappearing.

"What was that?" Satomi murmured.

"Probably a signal to his allies," Yume replied. "Calling them here or…"

If it *was* a signal to come together, Shihoko and her friends were in a precarious situation. But when Behemoth turned back to them, he shook his head in a kindly exasperated way. "Now then, I shall be your opponent for a brief period," he said, his tone completely out of sync with his menacing appearance. "The Seven Dwarves do not usually participate in the defense, so if I do say so myself, you are blessed with a precious experience here. Please do take it as a seed for your future growth."

"We deeply appreciate your kindness!!" Shihoko thrust both hands behind her. During the conversation, her special-attack gauge had finished charging. "Cocoa Fountain!!"

It wasn't visible to Shihoko, but behind the stronghold, a large chocolate pond should have appeared. With the darkness of the stage, it should have blended in with the ground and not really have been visible from Behemoth's position, either. That said, however, the chocolate pond was at best a prerequisite. Until her now-empty special-attack gauge was fully charged once again, she would need Satomi and Yume to fight and cover her as best they could.

Taking Shihoko's call as her cue, Yume thrust a hand out, and two more small balls flew out from the ball-shaped armor of her wrist. Connected to her wrist with a Y-shaft, this was

Plum Flipper's main weapon, a slingshot. When she drew the rubber band connecting the small balls with her other hand, a reddish-purple light grew in the holder area.

"Cyanide Shot!!" Yume launched the light bullet. There was no way it could miss the massive Enemy-level form standing still a mere ten meters away, and just so, the ball made a direct hit with the armor of his left shoulder. She launched one bullet after another, shouting the technique name each time.

Next to her, Satomi clenched her gloved right hand into a tight fist, and a minty light started to shine. "Menthol Blow!!"

She threw her fist forward with all her weight behind it, and a transparent mint-colored, fist-shaped aura shot out to slam into Behemoth and envelop his enormous body in a light of the same color.

Glacier Behemoth merely welcomed their special attacks, neither defending against nor evading them, and yet his health gauge didn't decrease at all. But that was to be expected—the girls hadn't used physical attacks intended to do damage, but rather de-buff techniques to exploit weak points.

Pale-blue smoke started to waft out of the five scars Yume's light bullets had carved in the icy armor. Cyanide Shot produced hydrocyanic gas from the bullets buried in the enemy's armor—Yume's so-called plum seeds—that caused continuous poison damage. And although it was just an illusion, Satomi's Menthol Blow made recipients feel a chill so powerful, it prevented movement.

As Behemoth was enveloped in the poisonous gas, his health gauge started to decrease slowly. But the massive beast seemed utterly unperturbed. "Hoh-hoh, coming in with a de-buff instead of a simple damage technique shows fairly good judgment, hmm? And the poison gas attack doesn't need to pierce the armor to be effective. Even better. But…"

He turned his head, long horns swinging through the air, and stared at Satomi.

"Your cold front—or is it a cool sensation attack? At any rate, it's honestly unacceptable. It's clear from both my name and appearance that I am an ice-type duel avatar, yes? A chill like this is a gentle breeze to me." As he spoke, he raised a sturdy front leg and took a ponderous step forward. Eight meters separated them now.

Satomi didn't lose heart at the criticism. "Weird. That was just a little test! Try seeing if you can move after taking a hit of this!" This time, she clenched her left hand and got into position. "Icilin Strike!"

The remaining 70 percent in her special-attack gauge was completely drained, and in exchange, a bright light enveloped her fist, much more intense than with the Menthol Blow.

Menthol, a compound found in mint leaves, causes a sensation of sudden coolness when applied to the skin, not because skin temperature is actually being lowered, but because the cold receptors in the skin are being stimulated. Over a thousand other similarly chilling compounds have been discovered, but the strongest among them is a compound called icilin, which has a chilling effect two hundred times greater than that of menthol. When Shihoko had been hit with this level-four special attack of Satomi's, a powerful cold had made her whole body shiver so fiercely she couldn't move from the spot.

The phantom fist looked quite chilly indeed as it hit Behemoth squarely on the thick armor of his chest. The instant he was wrapped in the fine diamond dust of light microparticles, the massive body shuddered. "H-hoh-hoh, this is rather...cold, hmm?" he said haltingly. Even he apparently couldn't treat Icilin Strike as a light breeze.

The issue, however, was that Satomi's chill techniques had no actual attack power. She could stop enemies in their tracks, but it was pointless unless that was followed up with an actual attack. Yume's poison gas was doing damage, but perhaps because Behemoth's defensive abilities and health value were high to start with, his gauge hadn't even gone down 5 percent yet.

"Wohkay...Here we go!" Satomi shouted as if to encourage herself and jumped out of the stronghold ring.

Yume fired her slingshot repeatedly to cover Satomi as she boldly sallied forth to engage in hand-to-hand combat with a level-eight opponent. Meanwhile, Shihoko used her half-recharged special-attack gauge and played her next trick.

"Puppet Maker!!"

Brble, brble, brble! The eagerly awaited Chocopets sprang forth one after another from the chocolate pond behind the altar. The chocolate automatic fighting dolls, which appeared four at a time, slipped past Shihoko and Yume on either side and flew at Behemoth.

"Chocopets! Support Mint!" Shihoko ordered, and the chocolate dolls split into two groups to attack Behemoth's bulk from the sides. Satomi took up the front and launched a series of punches and kicks straight from her dojo training.

The level eighter was apparently not going to sit down and take this layered attack, and he tried to mow Satomi down with his sinister claws, but with the chill of the Icilin and the slingshots to the face, not to mention the continuous motion of the Chocopets on either side, his aim was always slightly off. Dancing nimbly around the giant, Satomi evaded Behemoth's attacks as she got in one clean hit after another.

Since Shihoko was also a close-range fighting type, she deeply wanted to charge in and lend a hand, but she needed to take full advantage of the base for the time being. If she called forth another four Chocopets, they'd start to have a chance at wearing down even this powerful enemy.

Satomi piled on the physical attacks with intense focus and finally got the beast's health gauge down 10 percent.

"Tut-tut-tut, this is…I mustn't underestimate the tiny Legions," Behemoth said as he raised one hand to protect his face from Yume's slingshot. "The balance here with close range, long distance, and intermediate is quite nice."

"Heh! We're only getting started!" Satomi retorted. "Once you get another taste of my icilin, you're not gonna be able to talk so high and mighty!" She leapt back and readied her left fist.

Glacier Behemoth looked down at her, and when he spoke, his voice was distinctly icier. "No, no, that's quite enough data collection. And if I play around any more than this, my comrades are sure to become cross with me. If you don't mind, it's about time to put an end to this." And then the pale beast inhaled deeply enough to make his thick chest swell up. He swiftly exhaled toward the ground in front of him.

The instant Shihoko noticed that his flow of air contained a diamond dust several times denser than Satomi's Icilin Strike, Shihoko shouted, "Mint! Chocopets! Retreat—!"

But she was too late. The ground beneath the plume made several bursting sounds and then froze a snowy white. The frozen area instantly spread, swallowing the feet of the Chocopets and Satomi before racing ever farther outward.

"Choco! Run!" Yume shouted and shoved Shihoko backward. In the next instant, the snowy white of the cold front pushed all the way to the base ring and caught Yume.

"Ngh!" Gritting her teeth, Shihoko did a backflip to escape to the south side of the altar. But her foot got caught in the chocolate pond she'd created and she fell. Although she hurried to stand again, the chill caught up with her, freezing her feet and the chocolate pond around them.

When the freeze finally stopped speeding outward, the area that was frozen white was twenty meters across. Shihoko and Yume only had their feet frozen, but Satomi, who had been right in front of Behemoth, was covered in white frost up to her chest, and the four Chocopets were completely frozen. All this with but a simple breath attack from Glacier Behemoth; he hadn't called the technique name or spent any of his special-attack gauge. Which meant…

"I-Incarnate?!" Shihoko cried hoarsely.

Behemoth shrugged his horned shoulders. "My my, this is unexpected. There's no reason why I, the most gentlemanly of the Seven Dwarves, would use Incarnate in the Territories—and against such weak F-type avatars as yourselves—now, is there? This is merely my normally activated ability. It's called Sigh of Cocytus. Please remember this at least when you leave, all right?" The icy beast smiled, revealing his sharp fangs. "Now then, now then… That was a nice fight, Pottit Pecking members."

The massive body bent to the right and then spun in the opposite direction with impressive force. Using every scrap of the power generated, his long tail whined as it mowed down the surrounding area, shattering the four frozen Chocopets into brown fragments before closing in on the motionless avatar of Satomi.

"Min-Min!!" Shihoko cried.

Satomi forced her frozen arms to move into a defensive posture. In the next instant, the tail slammed into her, and she was peeled away from the ground and flung off with terrifying force. She crashed into Yume, still inside the base ring, but this was not enough to stop the momentum, and the tangle of girls came flying toward Shihoko.

With her feet frozen in the chocolate pond, Shihoko couldn't possibly get out of the way, and she had no intention of doing that, anyway. She spread her arms and attempted to catch them, but the impact was nearly enough to knock her consciousness out of her avatar. Her feet were yanked out of the chocolate pond, and she hit the ground hard.

"Unh!" Groaning, she managed to get to her feet and then gasped at the sight of her friends.

Satomi, who appeared to have temporarily lost consciousness, was horribly battered. The armor that had guarded against the tail was completely destroyed, exposing the naked gray avatar body inside, and her chest and head armor were cruelly cracked. The damage to Yume, also unconscious, was not so serious in comparison, but a deep crack ran along the armor of her chest where Satomi had hit her, and the slingshot affixed to her left hand had been broken away at the base. Their health gauges were at 70 percent for Shihoko, 40 percent for Yume, and 10 percent for Satomi.

With a single sweep of his tail—one hit of a normal attack—Glacier Behemoth had completely destroyed four Chocopets and dealt significant damage to three Mid-Level Burst Linkers. But he seemed somehow displeased with this result.

"Dear, dear," he said as he straightened up. "I had intended to bring all three of you down with a combination shot. Your defense is surprisingly good, ladies. I do apologize. This time, I will make sure to end this, so please don't move, all right?" He announced their death sentence in his endlessly courteous way and then lowered his head to turn the large horns on his forehead squarely at them.

He was going to strike the final blow with the laser beam attack he'd used to signal his allies before. Satomi and Yume were still unconscious, so Shihoko was going to have to get them out of there on her own. But she had also been hit with enough force to whisk away 30 percent of her health gauge in one go, and her avatar wasn't listening to what she was telling it to do. She tried to stand with Satomi in her left arm and Yume in her right, but her legs only trembled.

A pale phosphorescence quietly grew around Behemoth's horns. He moved his dragon mouth to casually utter the technique name. "Congeal Ray."

One of the horns on the head of the massive beast flashed, and a pale beam of light shot out toward the girls.

Thwnnk.

Something fell with incredible force from the sky to block the path between Shihoko and Behemoth. The silhouette that popped up in the middle of the intense blue light had widely spread, sharp-edged wings like an array of swords.

"…Crow…" Shihoko muttered, but her voice was drowned out by the sound of impact as Behemoth's beam of light hit the winged silhouette.

The intruder, Silver Crow, was trying to defend against the blue light with both arms crossed in front of his body. But tiny

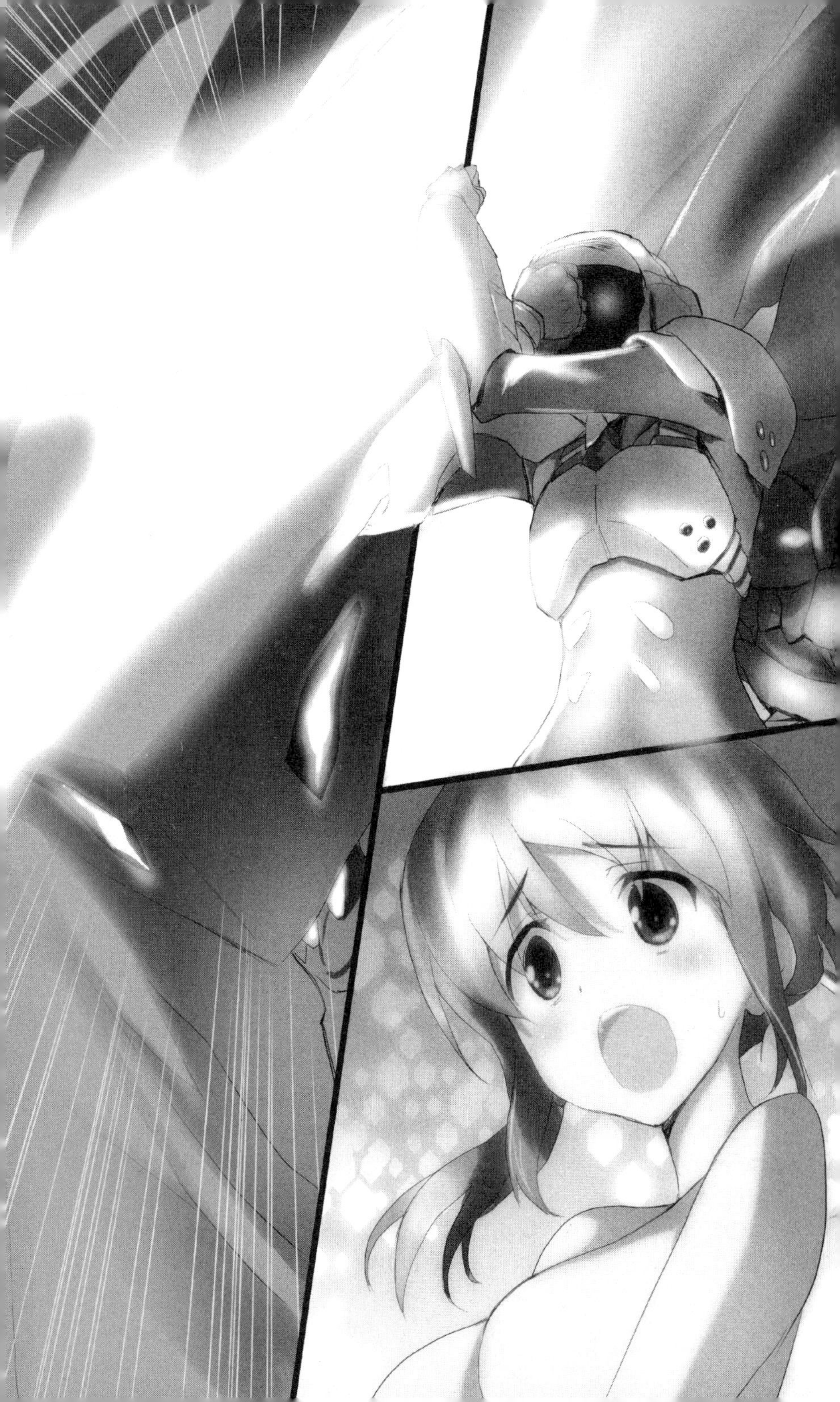

particles of ice danced up around him, and the ground at his feet was frozen white. She remembered that the English word *congeal* actually meant "freeze." In other words, this was a freezing light beam, and it would freeze Crow's avatar whether he guarded with his arms or not.

"Crow, run!! We'll be okay!!" Shihoko shouted, lost in the battle. He was the cornerstone of the attacking team, the sole avatar with the ability to fly in Nega Nebulus—in the entire Accelerated World. He couldn't be retired from the battle when it had only just started, not for the sake of Shihoko and her comrades and the little battle power they had.

But he didn't move. Instead, he braced his feet, silver light scattering from his wings, and resisted the pressure of the freezing light beam.

"Unh…Aaaaah!"

The battle cry was strained, but it did reach Shihoko's ears. His feet were already covered in a thick film of ice, though. And his helmet and shoulders, even his wings, all made a hard snapping sound as they started to freeze from the tips.

Clank! The metal armor covering Silver Crow's forearms split open to the sides.

Shihoko thought his armor had been destroyed—but that wasn't it. From inside the separated armor, a transparent crystal pushed out and absorbed Behemoth's blue beam of light, transforming the energy into a ball of light in Silver Crow's arms.

"Aaaaaah!!" With a fierce cry, he thrust his crossed arms straight upward and then set his sights on Glacier Behemoth in the distance.

Zwwwanshk!

The air shook, and a pale beam of light jetted from Crow's arms to slam into Behemoth.

"What?! …This…!!" Behemoth tried to leap back, but his arms and feet were already frozen to the ground. His reflected beam didn't eat away at his health gauge very much, perhaps because he had a strong resistance to low temperatures, but he apparently wasn't immune to the freezing effect, and his massive body was instantly swallowed up to the shoulders in a mountain of ice.

Reflection of a light technique. Shihoko had seen the exact same phenomenon up close once before; it had been at the end of the previous month, the first time she'd met Silver Crow in the Setagaya area in the Unlimited Neutral Field. Coolu, the lesser-class Lava Carbuncle Shihoko and her comrades had befriended, had fired a heat ray, and Crow had caught this deliberately, reflected it with his arms, and gotten a direct hit on Avocado Avoider, who was still infected with the ISS kit at that time.

That meant that in the month that had passed since he learned it, Crow had refined this Optical Conduction ability to the point where he could even repel the special attack of a high ranker. Having reflected the freezing beam of light and taken essentially no damage, Silver Crow closed his bracer armor again and slowly straightened up.

"This form…" Behemoth opened his eyes wide. "You're Nega Nebulus's Silver Crow! What are *you* doing here?!"

"It's obvious, isn't it?" Crow replied in a low voice and snapped a finger at the frozen Behemoth before starting to shout. "Your—"

But his voice was drowned out by the ferocious roar of an engine to the rear of the plaza.

When she turned around, a spiky motorcycle was charging recklessly in through the south gate of Sengakuji Temple. At the handlebars was a duel avatar in a skull-shaped helmet, with a monkey avatar and an oily avatar crammed onto the seat behind him. Ash Roller, Bush Utan, and Olive Grab…Shihoko and her friends had met them for the first time in the Territories the other day.

"Hey hey heeeeeeeey!!" Ash shouted as he made the tires squeal ostentatiously before coming to a stop next to the three young ladies. "I know ya been waitiiiing!! But! Now that we're on the scene, we're forever never letting you have this base! Biggie over there, we're gonna pay you back a million times over for hurting our pals!!"

"...He's just as loud as ever, huh...?" Satomi murmured, propped up to one side of Shihoko.

"So noisy it makes me dizzy, yah," Yume agreed from the other side.

"A-are you both okay?!" Shihoko hurriedly asked her newly conscious friends.

"Fine, totes fine," Satomi said. "But ugh, I hate that I got totally slammed."

Yume reached out to gently stroke her battered armor. "Nuh-uh. You did great, Min-Min. Nice fight."

"*Both* of you did so great," Shihoko murmured, and she stood up with an assist from her friends.

Ash glanced back at them and signaled with his thumb for them to get back. Nodding, they retreated to the vicinity of the south gate. It was too bad they wouldn't be able to take part in the real fight that was about to start, but what they had to prioritize at that moment was surviving. As long as they were still on the battlefield, they'd find a role to play.

Stopping beneath a large tree rising up in front of the gate, Shihoko stared hard at Silver Crow. The silver avatar had suddenly dropped out of the sky at the critical moment, even though he couldn't be counted on in a pinch in regular life. Here, to her, he looked somehow bigger than usual.

❄ ❄ ❄

Glacier Behemoth. A high ranker, one of the Seven Dwarves, the executive group of the White Legion. Although his massive body was 70 percent frozen thanks to his own freezing light beam turned back on him, there was no sign of his intense winter blizzard aura weakening at all. Haruyuki felt a chill creeping up from the tips of his toes just facing a beast like this.

But he pushed back against the aura and stepped forward to enter the stronghold that Chocolat Puppeter and the others had occupied for them. A hazy, warm light enveloped his body and charged his special-attack gauge. This wasn't all that the efforts of Team Chocolat had won: Behemoth's health gauge was down over 10 percent by the time Haruyuki charged in. Their battered and beaten forms made it painfully clear just how hard they had fought against what was, for all practical purposes, the most powerful member of the defensive team.

Thank you, Choco, Mint, Plum. We'll make sure to take full advantage of the stronghold you snatched away from the enemy.

As he sent this thought to the girls in the rear, Haruyuki looked up at the enormous beast avatar. He was used to seeing Pard's Beast Mode, so the beast form on all fours was not so unusual in and of itself. But he couldn't immediately take in the sheer incredible size of the other avatar, even though it said "Basically huge" in Kuroyukihime's file. This was a size and weight similar to that of Scarlet Rain when she had Invincible fully deployed.

If he tried straightforward hand-to-hand combat against that thick armor and those sinister claws, he'd be soundly defeated. If he was going to attack, it'd have to be from the sides or the rear. And to that end, he'd have to first knock the other avatar off balance with speed.

While Haruyuki considered the best strategy as he waited for his special-attack gauge to charge, the giant beast, still encased in ice, snapped his sharply fanged mouth. The beautifully courteous voice that came out was a complete mismatch with his external appearance.

"I see…I see. Given the situation, I shall omit my greetings. Silver Crow, you didn't transfer from Nega Nebulus to Petit Paquet, now, did you?"

"No," Haruyuki agreed.

"Mm-hmm, mm-hmm." Behemoth nodded slowly, twice. "Meaning the opposite is true…Petit Paquet joined forces with Nega Nebulus, then? Those young ladies pulled the wool right over my eyes." He grinned ruefully and then lowered his voice the slightest bit. "This is a tad sooner than expected…So then you've come, hmm? You've come to challenge Oscillatory Universe with all your fighting power in order to resolve the long-standing issue between the Black King and our White King...Am I correct in my assumption?"

That's exactly right!! Haruyuki had the shout in his open mouth and then abruptly closed it. What Behemoth had said was, in fact, true. But he didn't like the implications the beast brought to that truth. He took a deep breath to cool down before he replied calmly, "'Long-standing issue'? We're not here for such a theatrical reason as that. Your White Legion is sneaking around doing vicious stuff behind the scenes, so we came to stop you. That's all."

"Hoh-hoh." Behemoth's eyes glittered like swords of ice. "'Sneaking around,' 'vicious stuff.' I'm afraid I must take issue with that. When would we have done such terrible deeds?"

"Right from the start. Ever since the start of the Accelerated World." Haruyuki thought back to the unfortunate fate of Chrome Falcon and Saffron Blossom. Losing any inclination to speak politely, he spat out his next words.

"Your White Legion's a front for the Acceleration Research Society. You've put together any number of dark plots and made so many Burst Linkers suffer. The Armor of Catastrophe, the backdoor program, the ISS kits...All of them were your doing. 'Vicious' doesn't even begin to cover what you've done...Not at all."

"......"

Here, finally, the unexpectedly loquacious beast closed his mouth. He nodded deeply once, twice, his head the only part of him that could move, as if trying to understand something. Then he closed his eyes and let out a long sigh.

"......!!"

Abruptly, the mountain of ice encasing Glacier Behemoth's bulk clouded over a snowy white, and Haruyuki realized that countless tiny cracks had instantly sprung up all over the ice. Then the glacier exploded in all directions, with more than a few of the pieces shooting all the way to the inside of the base ring.

Haruyuki instantly dropped into a defensive position and knocked away a large chunk with both hands. But several of the smaller pieces bounced off the surface of his armor and shaved away his health gauge, albeit by the tiniest amount.

Freed from his icy imprisonment, Behemoth took the feet supporting his upper body off of the ground and stood up, tiny bits of ice falling from all over his massive bulk. When he stood up straight, he was more than five meters tall, and his head melted into darkness, leaving only the pale light of his eye lenses visible.

"I suppose...I suppose so." The voice coming down from on high was so bitingly cold, it would freeze a winter's wind. "You casual Burst Linkers know nothing. That is the sum total of your awareness. But at some point, you too will learn just how cruel and merciless Brain Burst 2039 is. In contrast, there is salvation in the Armor of Catastrophe and the ISS kits. Because they are official bargains—pay the price, receive the power."

"Official?" Haruyuki was overwhelmed by Behemoth's mass, but the rage welling up from deep inside him cleared away all his fear. "You don't know!! All you jerks do is steal and mess around!!"

"Even assuming that was true...those with power take what they will. That is the absolute truth that governs the Accelerated World. You, too, you came to take this area by force, yes?" Behemoth took a step forward.

Reflexively, Haruyuki started to take a step back, but he roused his battle spirit and braced himself in the center of the stronghold ring. "We didn't come to steal it! We came to take back all the things that you've stolen!!"

"In that case, I shall steal even that resolve from you. We are done talking. I will first have the four of you depart this stage!!" Behemoth brandished a forelimb high.

"Ash, you guys secure the base and cover me!" Haruyuki turned and called out to his comrades behind him, and then he kicked off the ground.

Hatchet-like claws at the ready, Behemoth brought his hand down ripping, a pale arc out of the sky. If Haruyuki took a direct hit from that, it might spell the end of his battle. But he added the force from his dash to the thrust of his wings and leapt forward.

It was his first time fighting an individual duel avatar boasting such massive size, but he had some experience with an even bigger enemy when it came to avatar/Enhanced Armament combinations. Haruyuki and his friends had fought an intense battle twenty days earlier against the Armor of Catastrophe, Mark II at the Acceleration Research Society's headquarters, not too far from their current location at Sengakuji. That monster had been over six meters tall and had fired incredibly powerful nihilistic Incarnate lasers from guns in both hands. But its very height made it hard for the monster to effectively deal with high-speed attacks. Behemoth should be the same in this. Knock him off balance with speed and find a chance for victory.

"G...o!!" Haruyuki accelerated even further, and the five claws whizzing above his head just barely scraped his left wing, sending tiny sparks flying.

He felt the explosive impact of the claws against the earth behind him as he beat down on Behemoth's leg with a Spiral Kick bearing his full weight. This kick was the most powerful of all Silver Crow's close-range striking techniques—his foot shot out as he spun at high speed like a drill, controlling the thrust of each wing separately. The only person to have been hit with it and come out unscathed was Avocado Avoider with his peculiar soft armor. But no matter how thick Behemoth's armor might be, there was no way this wouldn't be effective on a fellow duel avatar.

The kick landed squarely on the shin that was likely thirty centimeters thick, producing a spiderweb of cracks on the pale armor, and Behemoth's health gauge did drop from its remaining 90 percent, albeit only slightly.

If he kept attacking this same spot, the armor would break completely, and he could do serious damage to the avatar body inside. Then, once Behemoth was somewhat hobbled, he'd get Ash and them to pile on with long-distance attacks.

Drawing up this plan in his mind, he landed and immediately moved to follow up with a punch to the shin, but he sensed something closing in from a blind spot to his right, so he hurriedly leapt back. What passed before his eyes was an enormous tail, and the tip, crowned with ice-pillar thorns, slammed into the ground and smashed the hard-tiled pavement off the floor of the stage.

Haruyuki used his wings to dash backward and get some distance before looking for his chance to dive back into the fray. But.

"What?!" he cried out in surprise when he saw that the cracks in Behemoth's left leg's armor, the spot where he had only seconds earlier gotten a clean hit with his Spiral Kick, were gradually disappearing. "The, the damage to your armor...is repairing itself?!"

"That is indeed the case. My apologies. You worked so hard." Turning around, Behemoth flashed his eye lenses floating in the darkness. "My armor has the ability to recover automatically in low-temperature environments. In other words, it's a synergistic effect with the Sigh of Cocytus."

Behemoth blew on his own feet, and instantly, the temperature in the area dropped and diamond dust twinkled and danced in the air. The cracks started to heal even more rapidly, shrinking before Haruyuki's eyes.

"I can repair damage without limit. You might say I'm the worst possible opponent for a fighting type like you."

"So is that where your nickname, Habakkuk, comes from?" Haruyuki moaned.

"Oh, oh, so you know it, do you?" the massive beast responded, pleased.

Project Habakkuk had been a British plan for an ice-ship aircraft carrier during World War II. The British would make use of a large quantity of cooling devices inside a warship made of a massive block of ice so that if it was damaged, all they had to do was pour water on it and freeze it for the repair. The plan was like a fever dream, however, and naturally it went nowhere.

The ice ship never happened, but Glacier Behemoth had taken its name as his own, and he was accordingly impervious to striking techniques. They would need some sort of flame-type attack to have any real impact—and no half-hearted flame, either, but something he couldn't counter with his extremely low-temperature breath. So they should've gotten the many Prominence fire users to take part in the attack team.

As Haruyuki's thinking fell into this backward-looking rut, he looked up at Behemoth's bulk once again and noticed any number of small indentations in the thick armor of his shoulders and chest. Given that these were arranged randomly, they probably weren't part of his design. Most likely Chocolat and her team…They were probably holes Plum Flipper had made with her long-distance slingshot. So then, while the cracks Haruyuki made had healed and disappeared, the holes hadn't filled in entirely. Which meant that even if Behemoth's armor's recovery ability could heal cuts and scratches, it couldn't recover lost mass?

"Oi! Ya damned bird!" a voice called out from behind.

Ash Roller was champing at the bit, stuck on standby at the base, but their special-attack gauges still weren't fully charged. Haruyuki quickly threw a hand up to say they should stay a little longer, and then spread his legs and lowered his stance.

Seeing this, Behemoth brought forward his left leg—basically fully repaired now—and said quietly, "Hoh-hoh, so you do not seek aid from your comrades but intend to continue to face me one-on-one? That spirit is commendable…but you're aware that it is also important to study?"

Despite the fact that it was four against one, Behemoth's almost despicable leisureliness showed no signs of going anywhere. Which was no surprise, really, since even four against one was basically child's play for a level eighter like him when the four were at levels six and five. If he got even just a little serious, he could easily wipe them out. His relaxed attitude was certainly not the result of arrogance; he was simply that powerful. But that actually gave Haruyuki an opening.

Come now. What are you doing, servant? Give that overgrown creature a taste of its own medicine.

Haruyuki felt like he could hear Metatron speaking, although they weren't yet linked, and he nodded slightly. If he could force an opening, it would be only the one time. He had to blow away his opponent's lackadaisical cool and join up with Team Ash for a linked attack.

"I've studied plenty," Haruyuki replied briefly, and he brought his hand to his left hip.

"Equip. Lucid Blade!!"

A silver light gathered at his hip and materialized, drawing out a perfectly straight line.

A week earlier, when Haruyuki had reached level six at the same time as Takumu, he'd been shown four level-up bonuses: the flight ability enhancement he'd selected four times in a row already; Digit Pursuit, a special attack that turned the fingers of both hands into small homing missiles; Bulletproof, a special attack that greatly increased resistance to physical bullets for a fixed period; and Lucid Blade, a sword-type Enhanced Armament.

Up to that point, Haruyuki had chosen to enhance his flight ability with little to no hesitation, but for some reason, he hadn't been able to decide so easily this time.

The wings on his back were Silver Crow's greatest weapon and also the reason for his existence. The strong desire within him to fly had given birth to both duel avatar and silver wings. He'd single-mindedly enhanced this ability ever since, wanting nothing more than to go even higher, even faster. And he definitely didn't regret that. There were plenty of fights he would have lost if Crow's flight ability had been even the tiniest bit lacking.

But now that he had reached level six—a step before high ranker—he'd started to wonder if just looking out for himself like this was the best way. Wings for himself, speed for himself. Haruyuki had pursued these things, while many people—so many people—had helped him, guided him, fought alongside him. But he wanted to be able to fight for someone else, too. To that end, he wanted to be able to do more. That desire had led him to choose a new power. The Enhanced Armament Lucid Blade—a sword.

Seeing the weapon that materialized on Haruyuki's hip, Glacier Behemoth shook his head as if in fond exasperation. "My my. Silver Crow, I had heard that your weapons were those wings and your hands and feet. That you would have a sword...A level-up bonus, then? Or perhaps you bought it in the shop?"

"......"

Deciding that he would no longer indulge Behemoth's chatty nature, Haruyuki grabbed the hilt of the sword and drew it with a high-pitched sound.

Just as the word *lucid* would imply, the double-sided straight sword was made of the same silver as Silver Crow's armor. It was somewhat slender, but the blade and the hilt were a little longer than those of the standard one-handed sword. Catching the blue light of the base ring, the smooth edges gleamed crisply like mirrors. Haruyuki readied his new partner in front of his chest.

"In Brain Burst, a sword is the simplest of Enhanced Armaments, and that is precisely why it can't be treated as a stopgap, a mere retempering of a dull blade," Behemoth spat out in admonishment. "From time immemorial, Burst Linkers have obtained swords as a bonus solely because it is 'cool.' They have poured great sums of points into the purchasing of them. But the majority of those Burst Linkers disappeared without ever properly mastering their new weapons." He wasn't merely spouting conjecture; Behemoth was a veteran and had seen more than Haruyuki could imagine.

And indeed, the Accelerated World's Silver Crow had never so much as held a sword, much less the real-world Haruyuki. Meanwhile, Glacier Behemoth had fought any number of sword users up to that point and would be well versed in how to dispose of them. Right from the start, the gap between their actual abilities had been clear; Haruyuki didn't begin to compare in terms of knowledge and experience.

But...But. He brandished the sword in his right hand and

shifted his center of gravity forward. The motion was akin to announcing, *I'm coming for you now.*

Behemoth shook his head slightly once more before raising the fingers of his right hand and motioning the smaller avatar to come at him. Haruyuki could practically hear his voice saying, *Come, then. I will finish you in a single blow.* And if he charged in recklessly, then that was no doubt exactly what would happen.

But.

There's no need to fear, servant. I am with you.

Haruyuki felt as if he could hear the phantom voice of Metatron echoing in his mind once again, along with the voice of someone else who'd once been inside him.

The distance between Haruyuki and his enemy was about twelve meters. It was too far to go slicing in, but Haruyuki kicked off the ground and ran one, two, three steps.

A sigh escaped Behemoth's tightly drawn lips as if to say it wasn't even worth the trouble of moving. The ice crystals of frozen air pushed toward Haruyuki. If he touched the cloud, his limbs and wings would instantly freeze and render him unable to move.

But he had experienced a very similar "gas attack" mere hours earlier in the Nakano area, Iodine Sterilizer's iodine spray attack. And he was pretty sure he could handle this one the same way.

Here we go!

Once the freezing cloud was hanging in front of his nose, he tossed his sword to his opposite hand and thrust it into the earth. The ground of the Demon City stage was covered in super-hard tile, and Silver Crow's sword hand wouldn't have pierced it so easily, but Lucid Blade's extremely sharp tip slid ten centimeters into a seam between tiles. Using this as a support, he put all his power into reverse thrusting with the wings on his back.

Fanned backward, the freezing air instantly reversed course and dissipated, enveloping Behemoth in a cloud. Naturally, its creator would have a hard time seeing Haruyuki.

"Hrmph!" The giant groaned, and Haruyuki sensed him drawing breath to attack again.

He yanked his blade back up, kicked off the ground with everything he had, and flew upward on the diagonal. Prepared to expend the remainder of his special-attack gauge, he charged at maximum speed. Breaking through the diffuse frosty air in an instant, he closed in.

"Aaaah!!" He'd been gripping the Lucid Blade in his right hand alone, but now he brandished it with both hands. Focusing all his energy in the sword itself, he roared and launched a slicing attack with all his weight behind it.

Haruyuki and Silver Crow had never fought with a sword before. But the sixth Chrome Disaster had.

When he'd been parasitized by the Armor of Catastrophe, Haruyuki's main weapon had been a greatsword, and he had swung it freely and easily in fights against the Green Legion's "Fists" Iron Pound and "Invulnerable" Green Grandé, and even "World End" Black Lotus. The greatsword itself had been sealed away in a corner of the Unlimited Neutral Field together with the Armor of Catastrophe, but his memories of that time, the sensation of swinging that massive sword, remained within him.

Beast! Lend me your strength…one more time!! Haruyuki called out in the depths of his heart to his erstwhile partner in battle, as he brought his beloved new sword down with everything he had.

"Nwoon!" Glacier Behemoth moved his head as Haruyuki had expected—to catch the blade with one of the large horns on his forehead.

Skreeeenk! The instant the sharp edges collided, the impact shook the stage, feeling more like a clash of massive war machines.

All the thrust generated by Silver Crow's wings and the physical strength of Behemoth's enormous body clashed at a single minuscule point, making the air burn white hot. If he wavered for even an instant, the balance would collapse, and all the energy released would do instant-death-level damage to Crow.

"Unh...Hngh. Aaaah!" Haruyuki mustered up every scrap of power in him and tried to push his sword through.

"Hng. Unh. Unnnh. RRPH!" But Behemoth pushed back against the blade with a seemingly indestructible horn.

In the upper left of his view, Haruyuki's special-attack gauge was dropping dramatically from the full charge of the stronghold ring. Five seconds left...four seconds...

In the back of his mind, he heard a voice that was neither Metatron's nor the Beast's.

You mustn't try to push back power with power. There's no need for power in sword techniques in the Accelerated World. No matter how hard the item, there is a "seam" to sever. Find the seam and align the blade with it...See?

Shf. Haruyuki's hands moved minutely, and the Lucid Blade slid about half of a half of a millimeter along Behemoth's horn.

Kaaank! His sword slid downward, followed by a moment of silence and stillness.

A straight line of light raced from the tip of Behemoth's enormous horn all the way to the base, and then it split in two. Instantly, it transformed into countless fragments and scattered.

Haruyuki used what little remained of his special-attack gauge to dash backward before coming down once again ten meters away from Behemoth. His knees very nearly gave out under him as a reaction to the intense mental focus his attack had required, but he managed to brace himself somehow. Not letting his guard down, he readied his sword and looked up at the motionless beast.

The left of the two horns on the beast's head had vanished from the root. The cracks on the cross section left behind were steadily being repaired, but the part that was lost indeed did not appear to be coming back.

Behemoth raised a hand to touch the empty spot where his horn had been, and then glared at Haruyuki with pale eye lenses. "That swordsmanship," he said, in a low, hoarse voice. "Silver Crow, are you perhaps...?"

"Perhaps…what?" Haruyuki asked in return, and rather than responding right away, the enormous beast brought his hand down next to his other on the ground, returning to his four-legged beast state.

"No, please pay that no mind. And it seems that the time for playing here must come to an end."

"Just what I was hoping for." Haruyuki repositioned his sword, but Behemoth shrugged deftly, hands still on the ground.

"We will have to settle this at the next opportunity. Above all else, this is the Territories, after all. I can't make my comrades put up with my little games forever." He turned his remaining horn up to the dark sky. "Dissolve Ray."

A red light shot out from his horn, and the inky clouds blanketing the sky of the Demon City stage shone bright red for just a few seconds before the color faded.

That was it. Nothing else happened.

Wait. Abruptly, Haruyuki felt a powerful chill crawl up his spine. This was different from Behemoth's freezing air. In a certain sense, it was far colder, with a sharp pressure like a razor.

"Ya damned bird," Ash Roller called out to Haruyuki, unusually subdued, from the base, his special-attack gauge now fully charged.

But Haruyuki had already noticed.

Several figures had appeared on the roof of a large building on the west side of the stronghold plaza that was Sengakuji in the real world. Although they were all much smaller than Behemoth, the strength of the information pressure they were emitting was the same or greater. It was almost as if space itself were warping slightly.

The red beam of light that Behemoth had fired had most likely been a sign to have his comrades join him. In other words, *this* was the main squad of the Oscillatory Universe defense team for Minato Area No. 3.

Glancing back, Behemoth smiled boldly. Once any one of those team members jumped down into the battlefield, Haruyuki's ragtag team would lose any chance at victory.

A foreboding dread overcame him, and Haruyuki stood rooted to the spot.

"Ya damned crow," Ash called him once more.

Haruyuki was about to bark a sharp reply, but then another kind of pressure enveloped him from the opposite side of the plaza.

Whirling around, he saw a smattering of figures on the roofs of the buildings on the east side of Sengakuji Temple. Even though they were only silhouettes, hazy and bleeding into the night shadows, Haruyuki could tell right away who was who. Sky Raker, Ardor Maiden, Cyan Pile, and Blood Leopard and the others had finished occupying the rear footholds and caught up to them.

Time left on the clock: A little over twenty minutes.

Now the main event would finally start. He took a deep breath and held it in his lungs before readying his beloved sword firmly ahead of him once more. Perhaps reflecting Haruyuki's battle spirit, Lucid Blade shone and glittered blindingly bright.

The auras emitted by the two teams squaring off clashed in the center of the plaza. When this clash reached the breaking point, a general melee of unprecedented power would begin.

The timer in the top center of his field of view dropped toward that instant in time—1205, 1204…

Fwssh! The wind blew. A slight breeze to gently blow away the chill emitted by Oscillatory Universe and the heat released by Nega Nebulus.

Sucked in, Haruyuki looked over at the north side of Sengakuji.

A single, slender building stood precisely midway between the two opposing camps. Someone stood on this roof as well.

He'd never seen the slim silhouette. Which meant it had to be an enemy, but Glacier Behemoth was also looking up doubtfully.

Once again the wind came. The breeze carried the faint scent of flowers as it flowed through the plaza, making the leaves of the steel trees clatter.

A vivid pale-peach light gushed from the body of the Burst Linker on top of the slender building and danced up into the sky.

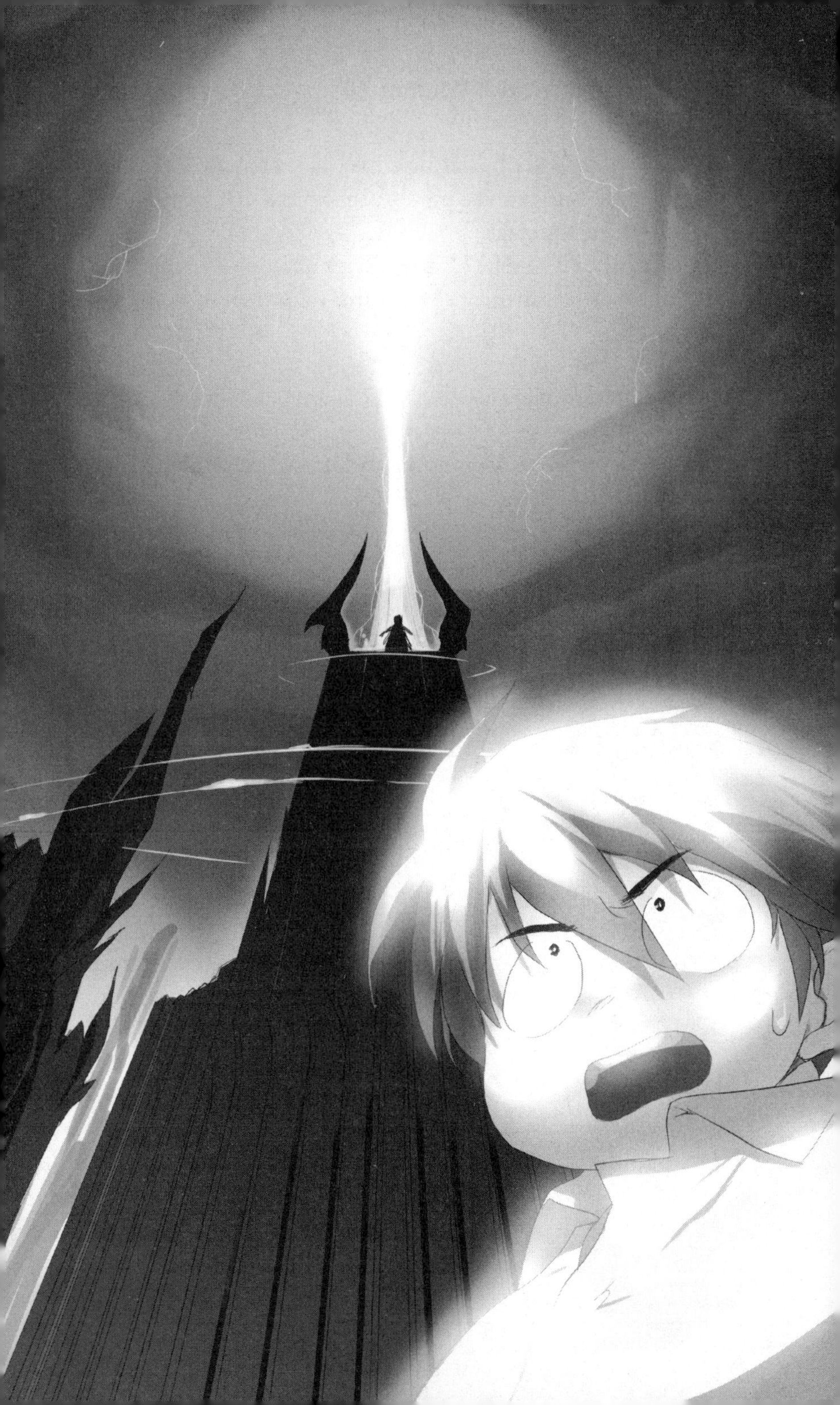

It was not the light effect of a special attack or anything he'd ever seen before. The glow was powerful enough that it seemed to illuminate the entire stage.

"Incarnate…Overlay?" Haruyuki muttered in a warble, and as if to provide an answer, a sweet and yet somehow lonely voice rang out.

"Paradigm Breakdown."

The pale-peach glow blew up and swallowed everything.

6

Light. Tremors. Vibration so powerful, he couldn't stay on his feet.

Desperately long seconds passed, and when he felt all the shaking stop, Haruyuki lifted his face anxiously.

At a glance, nothing had changed. Or so it seemed—but soon he realized that two things were gone. The person on the roof of the building on the north side of Sengakuji. And the large ring of the stronghold that should have been emitting a blue light right beside him.

In the place where the base had been until a few seconds ago, Ash Roller, Bush Utan, and Olive Grab were looking around, dazed. Near the south gate, Chocolat and her friends were looking his way with concern.

The faces of Nega Nebulus lined up on the buildings on the east side, the members of Oscillatory Universe encamped on the west side, and Glacier Behemoth in front of Haruyuki looking up at the night sky appeared to have taken no damage nor had any other changes made to them. In which case, what exactly had the Incarnate released by the mysterious Burst Linker and the vibration that followed it wrought in the Territories stage?

Haruyuki had started to look around once again for some kind of clue when he heard the faint voice of Glacier Behemoth.

"King…does this mean that now is that time?"

Haruyuki didn't understand what this meant. But he realized that Behemoth was staring at the eastern sky as if to burn a hole in it, so he turned around and looked up in the same direction.

Sky Raker and the others were also looking around suspiciously, of course, from their perch on the roofs. But Behemoth wasn't looking at them.

Far, far, far away. In the distant eastern sky, the jet-black darkness receded slightly, changing to an ultramarine color. Dawn was breaking. But there was no way. The night of the Demon City should continue for the full thirty minutes. That dawn would break in this stage…Dawn coming…

Here, finally, Haruyuki noticed the timer was gone. It should have had another 1,200 seconds left on it, and it had vanished from the top of his field of view. The health gauges of Team Ash on the left and Behemoth on the right had also disappeared. All that was left was his own gauge.

An impossible dawn and a simplification of the user interface. There was only one solution to this mystery.

"This is…the Unlimited Neutral Field?"

A cool, dry wind blew up and immediately drowned Haruyuki out.

(To Be Continued)

AFTERWORD

Thank you for reading *Accel World 20: The Rivalry of White and Black*. I wrote this on the inside of the cover, too, but ah, we're finally at Volume 20. Back in 2007, when I was serializing the prototype story *Absolute Acceleration Burst Linker*, I never imagined I would still be telling this tale. But strangely, the story itself is proceeding toward the climax I vaguely envisioned all those years ago, even as it goes off on any number of tangents. Once again, I'm wondering if I have the strength to drive the story where it needs to go.

To begin with, it's incredibly rare for me to feel that I am creating and controlling the story as the author. It's more like I'm simply putting into words a story that already exists. One of my favorite authors, Stephen King, has said something about how an author just digs up the vein of the story that's buried in the earth, and that's really exactly it. There are places where I feel as though I'm just a reader myself, watching over the story and going "Wow" and "Ooh" as it goes along, so I still don't know where *Accel World* will end up, but I'd love it if you would all keep chasing after it with me!

Now, then. On July 23, a month and a half after the release date of this book, the new Accel World animation *Infinite Burst* (IB) will finally be released in theaters.

Naturally, movement started on the IB project quite some time ago, about a year and a half ago, I think. At the time, I wrote the story proposal based on the idea that since they're going to the trouble of making a new anime, rather than go backward into the past of novels, we should do a story about the future. But the story's already very much in the future, so let's set the time axis a little ahead of the novel that will be on sale at the time of the theatrical release. But when I think about it, there's no way that I could arrange something as skillfully as that given how I have no power to control the story, and as I proceeded with Volumes 18 and 19, I was anxious—"Will this really connect with the IB time axis?!" But when I lifted the lid on that pot, the time period for Volume 20 here overlapped perfectly, and I am heaving a huge sigh of relief. The staff from the TV anime were passionate enough to come together once more to pour all their energy into this project to make a giga-wonderful movie, so please do see it on the big screen in the theater! I'd appreciate it very much! And HIMA, Miki, thank you so much for this volume, too! The three Petit Paquet girls on the frontispiece are just amaaaaaazing!!

Reki Kawahara
On a certain day in May 2016

HAVE YOU BEEN TURNED ON TO LIGHT NOVELS YET?

IN STORES NOW!

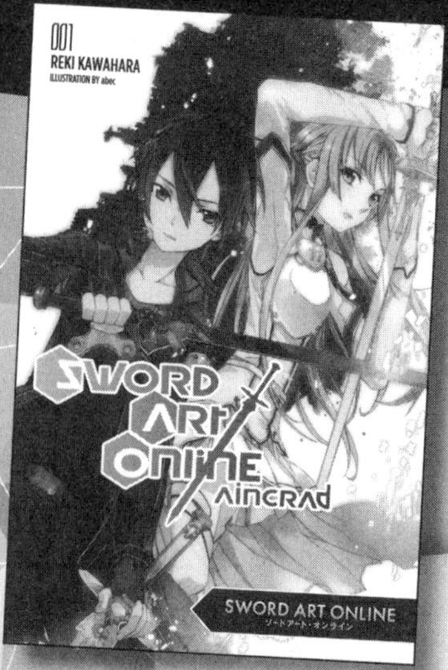

001
REKI KAWAHARA
ILLUSTRATION BY abec
SWORD ART ONLINE
AINCRAD
SWORD ART ONLINE
ソードアート・オンライン

SWORD ART ONLINE, VOL. 1–18
SWORD ART ONLINE, PROGRESSIVE 1–6

The chart-topping light novel series that spawned the explosively popular anime and manga adaptations!

MANGA ADAPTATION AVAILABLE NOW!

ACCEL WORLD, VOL. 1–20

Prepare to accelerate with an action-packed cyber-thriller from the bestselling author of *Sword Art Online*.

MANGA ADAPTATION AVAILABLE NOW!

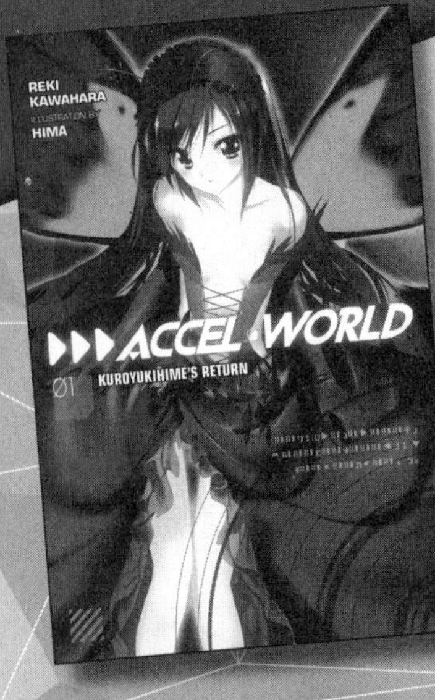

REKI KAWAHARA
ILLUSTRATION BY HIMA
ACCEL WORLD
01
KUROYUKIHIME'S RETURN

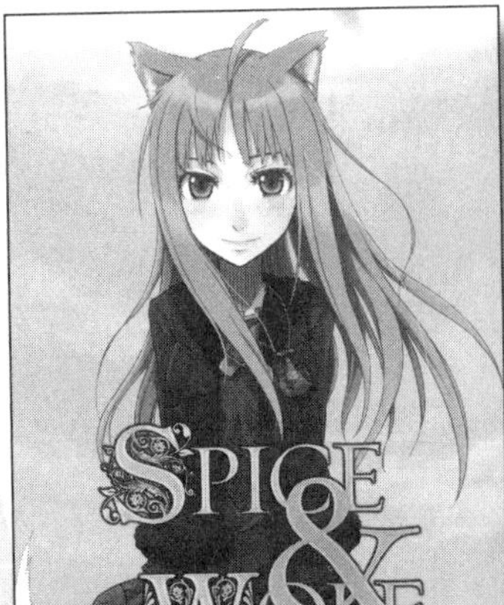

SPICE & WOLF
VOL. 1
ISUNA HASEKURA

SPICE AND WOLF, VOL. 1–21

A disgruntled goddess joins a traveling merchant in this light novel series that inspired the *New York Times* bestselling manga.

MANGA ADAPTATION AVAILABLE NOW!

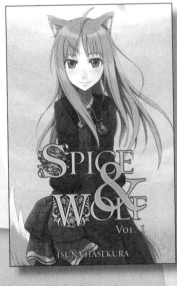

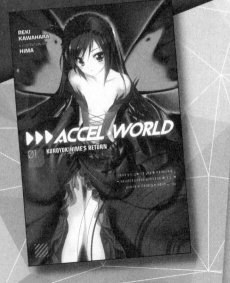

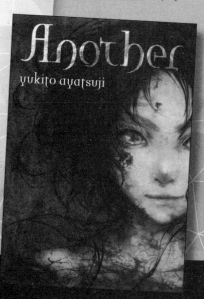

ACCEL WORLD, Volume 20
REKI KAWAHARA

Translation by Jocelyne Allen
Cover art by HIMA

ACCEL WORLD Vol. 20
© REKI KAWAHARA 2016
Edited by Dengeki Bunko
First published in Japan in 2016 by KADOKAWA CORPORATION, Tokyo.
English translation rights arranged with KADOKAWA CORPORATION, Tokyo, through Tuttle-Mori Agency, Inc., Tokyo.

English translation © 2019 by Yen Press, LLC

Yen On
150 West 30th Street, 19th Floor
New York, NY 10001

Visit us at yenpress.com
facebook.com/yenpress
twitter.com/yenpress
yenpress.tumblr.com
instagram.com/yenpress

First Yen On Edition: December 2019

Yen On is an imprint of Yen Press, LLC.
The Yen On name and logo are trademarks of Yen Press, LLC.

Library of Congress Cataloging-in-Publication Data
Names: Kawahara, Reki, author. | HIMA (Comic book artist) illustrator. | bee-pee, designer. | Allen, Jocelyne, 1974– translator.
Title: Accel World / Reki Kawahara ; illustrations, HIMA ; design, bee-pee ; translation by Jocelyne Allen.
Description: First Yen On edition. | New York, NY : Yen On, 2014–
Identifiers: LCCN 2014025099 | ISBN 9780316376730 (v. 1 : pbk.) |
    ISBN 9780316296366 (v. 2 : pbk.) | ISBN 9780316296373 (v. 3 : pbk.) |
    ISBN 9780316296380 (v. 4 : pbk.) | ISBN 9780316296397 (v. 5 : pbk.) |
    ISBN 9780316296403 (v. 6 : pbk.) | ISBN 9780316358194 (v. 7 : pbk.) |
    ISBN 9780316317610 (v. 8 : pbk.) | ISBN 9780316502702 (v. 9 : pbk.) |
    ISBN 9780316466059 (v. 10 : pbk.) | ISBN 9780316466066 (v. 11 : pbk.) |
    ISBN 9780316466073 (v. 12 : pbk.) | ISBN 9781975300067 (v. 13 : pbk.) |
    ISBN 9781975327231 (v. 14 : pbk.) | ISBN 9781975327255 (v. 15 : pbk.) |
    ISBN 9781975327279 (v. 16 : pbk.) | ISBN 9781975327293 (v. 17 : pbk.) |
    ISBN 9781975327316 (v. 18 : pbk.) | ISBN 9781975332181 (v. 19 : pbk.) |
    ISBN 9781975332716 (v. 20 : pbk.)
Subjects: CYAC: Science fiction. | Virtual reality—Fiction. | Fantasy.
Classification: LCC PZ7.K1755Kaw 2014 | DDC [Fic]—dc23
LC record available at https://lccn.loc.gov/2014025099

ISBNs: 978-1-9753-3271-6 (paperback)
        978-1-9753-3272-3 (ebook)

10 9 8 7 6 5 4 3 2 1

LSC-C

Printed in the United States of America